TOXIC CRUISE COCKTAIL

A RACHEL PRINCE MYSTERY
BOOK 13

DAWN BROOKES

Dawn Brookes
Publishing

This novel is entirely a work of fiction. The names, characters and incidents portrayed are the work of the author's imagination, except for those in the public domain. Any resemblance to actual persons, living or dead, is entirely coincidental. Although real-life places are depicted in settings, all situations and people related to those places are fictional.

DAWN BROOKES asserts the moral right to be identified as the author of this work. All rights reserved in all media. No part of this publication may be reproduced, stored in a retrieval system, or transmitted, in any form, or by any means, electronic, mechanical, photocopying, recording or otherwise, without the prior written permission of the author and/or publisher.

Paperback Edition 2024
Kindle Edition 2024
Paperback ISBN: 978-1-916842-08-3
Hardback ISBN: 978-1-916842-09-0
Copyright © DAWN BROOKES 2024
Cover Images: Adobe Stock Images/Creative Fabrica
Cover Design: Dawn Brookes

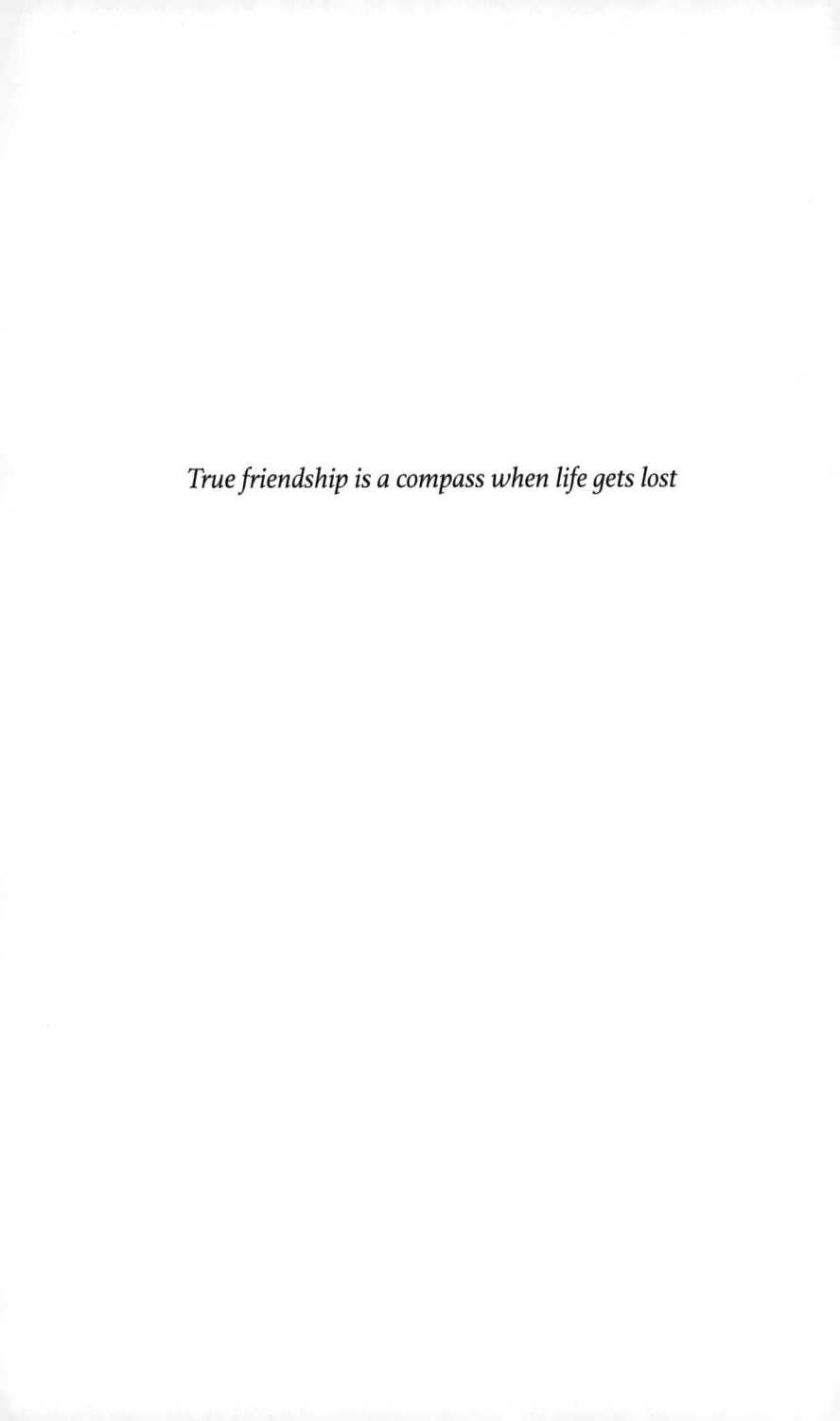

True friendship is a compass when life gets lost

1

Rachel Jacobi-Prince stood in the queue waiting in the cool sanctuary of the famous Raffles Hotel lobby. The air conditioning created a welcome respite from the sweltering Singapore heat outside. With reservations in her hand, she untied and retied her long hair into a loose bun to keep her neck cool.

"Excuse me. Do you come here often?" a man said, nudging her.

Rachel swung around, about to give him an earbashing until she looked down, recognising him. "Bernard! How wonderful to see you! What are you doing here?"

"I've been home for a week and flew in from Manila last night. I'll be back on board the ship tomorrow."

"Are you staying here?"

"Nah, too rich for me, Rachel. I've been on a training

course. We've just finished. They like to keep us updated on the latest medical guidelines. I'd love to stay and chat, but I'm already behind for dinner. A few of the crew are re-boarding tomorrow and we're going out for some proper Chinese food."

Rachel almost wished she could go with him. Bernard was always fun to be around.

"Well, thanks for saying hello, we'll catch up properly during the cruise."

"Looking forward to it. Where's that husband of yours? Sarah told me he's joining you."

"He's gone to retrieve our luggage. My parents brought it from the airport while we went on a whistle-stop tour."

"Let's hope Carlos keeps you out of mischief," Bernard said, tapping his nose. Lowering his voice, he added, "No more murders, please." He hurried away before she quipped back.

Rachel was smiling, happy to have run into Bernard, a nurse from the ship they would be joining. Bernard happened to be a friend and colleague of her best friend Sarah, who also worked in the medical team. The queue cleared ahead of her and she found herself next in line. A shiny marble floor gleamed beneath her feet and a gentle murmur of conversation filled the air behind her. The lobby felt as refreshing as a drink of ice-cold water.

A sharp bump on her right shoulder jolted Rachel from her thoughts. She turned, thinking Bernard might have forgotten something. No Bernard. Instead, a middle-aged man with silver-grey hair barged past her and strutted to the desk.

"Are there any messages for me?" he bellowed at the young receptionist, almost rugby-tackling the people ahead of Rachel, who sidestepped to dodge the angry man. His voice boomed across the lobby, causing people to turn their heads.

The receptionist's eyes betrayed alarm as she tried to maintain her composure. Stammering, she said, "Sir, I apologise, but there's a queue behind you. You must wait your turn."

The side of the man's face contorted into a furious shade of crimson. He leaned menacingly towards the defenceless girl, his anger palpable. "I don't have time for this nonsense. Answer the question."

A manager intervened, preventing the situation escalating out of control.

"My apologies for any delay, Mr Bigham. Please, step this way." The manager's tone came across as deferential and respectful as he gracefully led the man named Bigham to one side. "How may I be of help?" The manager cast a sympathetic glance back at the receptionist as he spoke. "Please continue attending to our other guests, Millie."

Rachel exhaled, thankful she wouldn't be called upon to intervene. She stepped forward to hand over the reservations for herself and Carlos. Mr Bigham's persistent demands for whatever urgent message he was waiting for continued to drown out normal conversation.

Murmurs of disapproval from the guests behind her added to the tense atmosphere he had brought into the lobby.

"Who does he think he is?" a man said to the woman with him.

"I don't know, but he's got a big mouth."

"Another minute and he might have got my fist in it," the man said.

The receptionist named Millie dealt with Rachel's room booking and swiped her credit card before looking up again. "Welcome to Raffles, Mrs Jacobi-Prince. Would you like me to book you a table for dinner?"

"No, thank you. We're here with my parents and my father's handling our dinner reservations. He and my mother checked in earlier."

"In that case, please enjoy your stay at Raffles." The receptionist handed Rachel two room entry cards.

"Thank you. We will." Rachel smiled, but the receptionist's attention soon drifted back to Mr Bigham, who was continuing to make a scene. The next people in line stepped forward, so Rachel moved away from the reception desk to make room for a group of four.

Rachel glared at the odious Mr Bigham, jabbing his

finger in the receptionist's direction, shouting, "You need to train your staff better."

Mr Bigham, evidently not a man to let his deserved humiliation go, glared from one to the other, his face still crimson.

"I'll have your connection soon, Mr Bigham," the manager said, ignoring the man's last remark.

Rachel waited for Carlos to return from the baggage storage area with their suitcases. Her parents, Brendan and Susan Prince, had come straight to the hotel from the airport because her mother was suffering jet lag from the long flight to Singapore. Rachel had asked if her parents minded taking all the luggage with them while she and Carlos saw a little of Singapore.

"Of course. Good idea," her father had said.

After Carlos had helped load the luggage into her parents' taxi, they spent an enjoyable afternoon exploring. First, they visited Tiger Balm Gardens, admiring its sculptures of various buddhas and serene lily ponds.

Afterwards, they took a taxi to a stark contrast, the bustling Change Alley, an area renowned for its vibrant markets and lively street performers.

"Be careful," the taxi driver said when he dropped them off. "It's an interesting place, but I'm sad to say we have a lot of pickpockets. Keep your money safe."

Well warned, they took his advice and kept their valuables close.

Noises around her jogged Rachel back to the present. Still, when she inhaled through her nose she could sense the exotic scents of spices and sizzling street food. She licked her lips, recalling the flavour of chicken satay eaten while strolling hand in hand with Carlos, taking in the sights and sounds of the country.

The aggressive Mr Bigham's voice, yelling into one of the hotel's telephones, pierced through Rachel's reverie again. "It must be there by now... look again! And when you find it, email it to me at this hotel. Stupid woman," he said through gritted teeth while slamming the phone back onto its receiver.

"I wouldn't want to be the person on the other end of the line," a woman next to Rachel said.

"If she's got any sense, she'll hand in her notice," a man replied.

Moments later, the manager reappeared from his office looking relieved as he waved a sheet of paper in his hand. "Here it is, Mr Bigham. The message you've been waiting for."

"About time too." Bigham snatched at it, barely acknowledging the messenger.

His eyes greedily scanned the piece of paper. Whatever it contained appeared to calm him. Without another word, he strode away from the desk and headed towards the lifts. Rachel wasn't the only person staring after him. A few people queueing continued their murmurings, nudging each other and nodding their heads in his direction.

"Rude man."

"He's an entitled American, what can you expect?" said another person.

Rachel didn't agree with the sentiment about Americans, but she concurred with the idea he came across as entitled. Others around her exhaled a collective sigh of relief. Drama over.

As Rachel watched Bigham making his way through the crowd, now calm, she heard the lift ping, announcing its arrival. Pleased when her father stepped into the lobby after the door opened, she waved. Her father didn't see her, but when Bigham, the man who minutes before had created such an unpleasant atmosphere, pulled her father into a bearhug, she stood open-mouthed. On releasing Brendan Prince, Bigham shook his hand vigorously while Rachel stared in disbelief.

"What's going on there?" Rachel muttered to herself.

The interaction between the two men, far from formal or distant, appeared to be infused with a warmth and familiarity that startled her. The men's faces glowed with genuine pleasure as their laughter floated in the air. As she continued to stare in awe, they exchanged animated gestures and lively banter like long-lost friends.

"Is something the matter?" Carlos arrived behind her with their luggage, breaking the spell.

Rachel shook her head, her brow furrowed. "I'm not quite sure. Give me a moment to process it and I'll explain. Let's go to our room, shall we?"

"With pleasure. It's crammed down here. I expect a lot of our soon-to-be cruise companions are spending the night here."

Rachel's eyes scanned the bustling crowds, noting the various travellers checking in, most of them burdened with heavy suitcases. She nodded in agreement, noticing the abundance of *Coral Queen* luggage tags attached to the bags.

"You might be right," she said.

"Excuse me, sir." The porters were working nonstop, expertly manoeuvring their way through the chaos to help guests with their luggage. Carlos stood aside to let the man pass. Rachel and Carlos then wheeled their own suitcases towards the row of lifts, one of which her father had exited moments before.

"Let me buy you a drink?"

The obnoxious Mr Bigham guided Rachel's father towards a café.

"There's Brendan," said Carlos. "It appears he's found a friend already." Before Carlos could call out to him, Rachel grabbed his arm, pulling him inside the lift as it filled up.

"Let's settle in first," she said.

Carlos kept quiet inside the packed lift, but as soon as they arrived at their floor, he looked at her. "What was that all about? Have I missed something?"

Rachel relayed the reception fiasco as they headed towards their room. "And then, having created a nasty atmosphere, the guy strolls off as if nothing's happened. He's lucky someone didn't punch him – one man in the queue threatened to do just that. Minutes later, he's greeting my father like some long-lost buddy."

"Sounds to me like he is. Your dad must know this Bigham chap."

"It appears that way. But the guy's American and dad's never been to America apart from when we went on that Caribbean cruise."

Carlos chuckled. "Just because he's got an American accent doesn't mean he still lives in the States. Maybe he lives near your parents in England."

"May I remind you my parents live in a tiny Hertfordshire village? And I can tell you now, that man doesn't live in Brodthorpe."

"You can't be sure of that, Rachel. It's been years since you lived there. People come and go. Your mum told me on the flight over there have been a lot of newcomers to the village, many of them wealthy types who want a sanctuary in the countryside. He might be one of them."

Carlos swiped his card in the door and held it open for her to pass. She stepped inside with her luggage. He followed with his.

"There might be some new people, Carlos, but I'm sure dad would have mentioned if he planned to meet a friend in Singapore. Besides, any sanctuary that man entered wouldn't remain that way for long. Let's hope he's not invited the horrible Mr Bigham for dinner."

"This isn't like you, Rachel. That guy must have been foul for you to be so unforgiving."

"Sorry. I don't mean to sound judgemental, but I felt so sorry for that poor young receptionist."

"You're not old enough to be calling people young," Carlos said, pulling her into his arms and planting a kiss on her forehead. "Chill."

Rachel relaxed in his arms. "I expect all will be revealed over dinner." Thoughts raced through her head about her father's pleasure at seeing the unpleasant American. How could Brendan Prince be so intimately acquainted with this Bigham man?

Don't dwell on it any further, she thought. *Wait until you speak to your father.*

"I'm going to take a shower before unpacking. I loved our impromptu tour of Singapore's highlights but my clothes are sticking to me. The humidity got to me."

"It was hot out there, wasn't it? You look tired. Go for a shower and I'll get us unpacked."

"Did I ever tell you I'm glad I married you?" Rachel said, opening the bathroom door.

"Not often enough," he said, smirking.

"I'll try to do better," she shot back with a grin.

2

Rachel and Carlos met up with her parents in the lobby before heading into the hotel's Long Bar. They were keen to savour one of the hotel's most famous cocktails: a Singapore Sling. As soon as they stepped inside, Rachel got the feeling of being enveloped in an atmosphere of charm and sophistication.

"The scent from those flowers is gorgeous." Susan pointed to pots planted up with big and bold, exotic, tropical floral arrangements.

Rachel's eyes moved from the plant decor to the long and impressive mahogany counter gleaming from fresh polish. The bar was adorned with shiny brass along the edges. Faux leather high stools lined the counter, and a spiral staircase led to an upper gallery.

People laughing, clinking glasses and enjoying lively conversations injected extra life into the room.

Rachel looped her arm through Carlos's while they waited, watching the bartenders work, filling cocktail shakers and then performing their ritual of shaking the drinks into life.

"What can I get you?" a bartender asked, smiling.

"We'll have four of your famous cocktails please," Brendan said.

"Coming right up, sir."

While the bartender shook their slings, a jazz band started to play.

"I'm so pleased we decided to stay here, Brendan," said Susan, her face flushed with excitement.

Rachel's parents seldom got away from the parish where her father was a vicar, so it hadn't taken too much persuasion to encourage them to celebrate their Coral wedding anniversary on an exotic Southeast Asian cruise. Staying overnight at the Raffles Hotel came as a last-minute decision to tie in with flights and the cruise. Susan initially argued against it, citing the cost. With a little cajoling from the normally frugal Brendan, she eventually agreed, and apart from the earlier conflict in the lobby, which neither of them witnessed, the place was living up to expectations. Rachel got so much happiness just watching her parents winding down and enjoying themselves.

With four Singapore Sling cocktails lined up along the counter, they each took a glass.

A smartly dressed man with shoulder-length blond hair, wearing a beige suit, climbed onto one of the high chairs next to where Brendan stood.

Rachel unlocked her phone and set up the camera to take a selfie of them all when the newcomer held out his hand. "Would you like me to take a photo while Joey gets me one of those?" His head nodded toward their cocktails.

The bartender finished what he was doing, placing a drink in front of a tall man with sandy brown hair who was scowling into his phone while propping up the bar. Next, he picked up his cocktail shaker. "Coming right up, Mr Kearney."

"Thank you," said Rachel, offering the man named Kearney her phone. With drinks in their hands, they posed happily for the camera.

"Smile now," said Kearney.

Rachel's parents drank very little alcohol as a rule but were keen to engage in this once-in-a-lifetime experience. Drinking a Singapore Sling in the place it originated from meant a lot to Brendan and Rachel, both students of history. Before joining the English police force, Rachel thought she would be a teacher, hence a history degree.

Brendan had shared facts about the part Raffles Hotel played during World War II on the flight over.

When Susan had insisted he change the subject, he regaled them with details about Ngiam Tong Boon, the creator of the famous cocktail.

"This drink was primarily intended for ladies, hence the pink colour," he said, holding his glass in the air.

"Yes dear," said Susan, patiently. "You told us during the flight."

"Did I?"

"Are you from England?" Kearney asked when he handed Rachel back her phone.

"We are. I take it you are too?"

The friendly man replied, "I grew up in southeast London but moved to Florida for work and I'm settled there now. My wife's American and my kids were both born there. I wouldn't want to move back now, but the kids have dual nationality if they ever wanted to cross the pond. Not that they are kids anymore. My oldest daughter graduates next year." He held his hand out. "Orlando Kearney. Happy to meet you."

They shook hands, introducing themselves. "Is your family with you?" Brendan asked.

"No. This is a business trip. I've got a bunch of meetings on board a cruise ship starting tomorrow. The cruise line throws in a vacation. The family would have come with me, but the girls have classes and my wife doesn't want to be on her own while I'm in meetings all day."

"Nice work if you can get it," remarked Carlos.

Orlando grinned. "It's not without its pleasures. But I'm a family man at heart. It can be lonesome."

Rachel liked the Anglo-American accent, as she did Carlos's Anglo-Italian.

"It must be hard being away from your family," said Susan.

Rachel noticed the dark lines under Orlando's eyes and a faraway look in his eyes when he replied. "It can be."

"Are you by any chance going to be on board the *Coral Queen*?"

"The very one. You too?"

"Yes. It's our Coral wedding anniversary later this week."

Orlando raised his glass. "Congratulations. That's thirty-five years, right?"

"It seems like yesterday," said Brendan, his eyes sparkling.

"You'll have a wonderful time. She's a fine cruise liner, and this is a beautiful part of the world."

"We've sailed on the ship once before," said Brendan. "Rachel cruises a lot more than we do. Her best friend works as a nurse on board."

Orlando's eyebrow rose. "I haven't met many of the people from the medical team, but I've been introduced to the chief medical officer before – not in his professional capacity, I'm pleased to say. It's the engineering and environmental teams I meet with more often."

"What is it you do?" Susan asked.

"I run an international waste disposal company." Orlando stroked his nose. "In the current climate, as you can imagine, cruise lines are looking at ways to improve on waste disposal and reduce their carbon footprint."

"Don't believe a word he says." A man who looked to be in his early forties appeared behind Orlando Kearney, slapping him on the back. "Great to see you, Orlando."

"You be careful what you say around here, Simon. These good people will be your guests for the next week. This is Simon Peterson. He's your friendly cruise director."

Rachel wondered how Orlando came to be friendly with a cruise director, considering their jobs were so different. Then again, a cruise director's role included being hospitable and welcoming to everyone.

"It will be my pleasure to welcome you aboard," said Simon, shaking everyone's hand.

"When Simon's not looking, people call him Slick," Orlando said, winking.

Rachel understood how Simon had gained the nickname. The man's silky-smooth nature and clothes smacked of overplayed exhibitionism. But he seemed ideal for a job that required a person to be outgoing and able to talk to anybody.

After the second round of introductions, Rachel said. "I didn't think the ship docked until tomorrow?"

"You're right," said Simon. "I hopped on a helicopter during a medical evacuation. It worked out well because I needed to source some new equipment. I left my capable assistant in charge. I'll be back on board tomorrow before anyone realises I'm missing."

"That's his story anyway," said Orlando, a sceptical look in his eyes.

Brendan caught Susan's disapproving eye and made their excuses to move away.

"We'll leave you to enjoy your downtime."

Rachel was happy to move away from the bar, leaving the men to chat. The high chairs were comfortable enough, but not conducive to a group conversation. If Simon AKA Slick wanted to enjoy his time off, he should be allowed space to unwind. They took seats around a nearby table.

"Goodness gracious." Brendan coughed and spluttered after his first full swallow of the cocktail.

"Take it easy, Dad. It might look like pink fruit juice, but considering what's in it, it will be a lot more potent than the communion wine you're familiar with."

"You're telling me." Brendan placed his drink down on the table, wiping his mouth with a handkerchief.

"Your father won't admit to being jet lagged. If he did, he would have sipped the drink at a leisurely pace."

"I won't admit to it because I don't have it. I'm thirsty, that's all, and nothing in that glass is going to help quench my thirst."

"Did you get some sleep, Mum?"

"I slept for two hours solid. As wonderful as it is to arrive in spotless Singapore, I didn't enjoy the exceptionally long flight. It's a shame we won't visit much of it, but I wouldn't have been able to enjoy touring today."

A good point, Rachel mused. The thirteen-hour flight was the worst part about arriving somewhere so beautiful ahead of their cruise. Landing before noon equated to being the middle of the night UK time. Rachel was thankful she and Carlos had driven down from the Midlands a few days earlier to stay with her parents, who lived near the airport.

Brendan glanced at his watch. "As much as I'm enjoying it in here, the alcohol is going to my head. Perhaps we should go to dinner. I've booked us a table at the Butcher's Block."

"Such a peculiar name for a restaurant," remarked Susan.

"But the food will be wonderful. The wood fire cooking will remind Rachel of Hawaii. And she'll be pleased to know they serve plenty of seafood in the restaurant." Carlos placed an arm around Rachel's shoulder.

Brendan left his half-full glass on the table. The rest of them polished off their drinks before getting up to follow. Brendan turned to Carlos. "I haven't asked whether you travelled to Singapore during your army days?"

Rachel's chest tightened remembering her husband's dangerous trip to China just before the pandemic spread worldwide, when he'd stopped off in Singapore fleetingly on the way home.

Carlos didn't need to answer Brendan's question because the dreadful Mr Bigham entered, enveloping Brendan's hand in another vigorous handshake.

Rachel stiffened. If she hadn't witnessed the man's behaviour earlier, she would have been fooled into believing Bigham to be all pleasantness and good humour.

"Darling. Meet my old friend Fabian Bigham," said Brendan. "This is my wife, Susan."

Fabian took Susan's hand, giving her a huge, friendly smile. "Delighted to meet you, Susan. Brendan's told me a lot about you."

If Susan Prince was surprised, she didn't show it.

"And this is my daughter Rachel, who I told you about earlier, and her husband Carlos."

Brendan didn't seem to see it, but a wariness in

Fabian's eyes hinted at a chink in the otherwise exuberant display.

"Hello. Brendan tells me you're in the police force." The smile remained, but it lacked warmth and didn't reach his eyes.

Rachel couldn't work out whether his wary greeting showed disdain for her career choice or whether he had something to hide. Either way, she couldn't take to him. He briefly shook her hand before nodding to Carlos and turning his focus back to Brendan.

It looked as if they might be there for a while, listening to shared reminiscences about old times which Rachel would have been interested to hear, if only to find out how they knew each other. But there was a loud crash as somebody near the bar dropped a glass. Fabian glared over Brendan's shoulder and about turned. His mask slipped again, and he cleared his throat, saying, "Remember what I said, Brendan. We'll meet again when you're on board and we can bore each other with talking about old times."

Rachel turned around, curious to understand what had sent Bigham packing, but saw nothing more unusual than a barman sweeping up the mess and people enjoying themselves. Orlando and Slick were engrossed in conversation at the bar and the tall man who had been served at the same time as Orlando tapped keys on his phone. After Fabian's retreat, Rachel remained curious how he and her father had met, but she didn't want to ruin the only evening they were spending in Singapore talking about the weird stranger. He'd already made enough of an impression, and Rachel wanted to avoid saying something she might regret if they spoke about him.

As they followed her parents out of the Long Bar, Carlos whispered in her ear.

"He can't be all bad. He likes your dad, so he's evidently got great taste."

"If you say so. Did you see the way he scurried away though?"

"I did. Perhaps he forgot something," said Carlos.

"Maybe. Except I think it might have been something else." Rachel looked back inside the crowded bar again. "Let's forget about him for now and eat before I collapse. That cocktail was stronger than I imagined."

Carlos put his arm around her waist. "Well then, madam. Let me escort you to dinner." He lowered his voice a little, "though I'm with your mother on the restaurant's name. With your sleuthing reputation, I hope it's only food we encounter inside the Butcher's Block."

Rachel thumped his arm playfully. "Carlos! I'm surprised at you. Don't even go there."

Chortling, the two of them hurried after Brendan and Susan into the restaurant to be greeted by the aroma of sizzling meats and aromatic herbs.

3

After checking out of Raffles, they left their luggage at the hotel and took Rachel's parents on a quick tour of Singapore. Her grandfather had been a British officer housed at Raffles Hotel during the early days of World War II before Singapore surrendered to the Japanese. After being interned, he had later been released to the same hotel following the liberation of Singapore. Brendan had wanted to visit the sites his father had written about in his war diaries.

After the tour and lunch, they collected their luggage and boarded the ship.

Now they were on board the *Coral Queen,* Rachel's head was buzzing with excitement when the telephone rang. She recognised her parents' stateroom number.

"Hi, Mum."

"Hello Rachel. Did you realise we're invited to a VIP cocktail party this evening?"

Rachel loved hearing the enthusiastic pitch in her mother's voice. Perusing the embossed envelope, she removed the letter as luxurious as the cruise ship itself and printed on fine ivory vellum paper. It had been among a pile waiting for them in the stateroom.

"I'm looking at it now." The welcome letter from the concierge invited her and Carlos to a sailaway party from 7pm. Apparently her parents had received an identical invitation. She grinned, "I take it you want to go?"

"Of course I do. I haven't discussed it with your father yet because he's gone to see that cruise director… Simon, somebody or other."

"Don't you mean Slick? Simon the Slick Peterson." Rachel recalled the outgoing man from the Raffles Long Bar, who appeared to be friendly with Orlando Kearney.

"You have such an excellent memory for names. I do typically, but I'm not quite myself. It must be the jet lag. I can't bring myself to call the cruise director Slick, no matter what Mr Kearney says others might call him."

"As you remember that part of last night's conversation and Orlando's name, you can't be too out of it, so I won't call a doctor yet."

"Stop teasing, Rachel. I didn't say I was out of it, I said I'm jet lagged. There's a difference."

Susan's relaxed tone meant she was open to banter.

"You don't know Simon, do you? I suppose he must have joined after your last cruise."

Rachel had arrived at the same conclusion. "Staff often transfer between ships. Slick wasn't on board for my last sailing, that's for sure."

"Now, back to the topic of your father. I'm not certain, but I think they're going to ask him to take the Sunday service like they did the last time we sailed."

Rachel detected an air of tension in her mother's voice, and no wonder. Visions of a dead nun appeared in Rachel's head like an unwelcome guest. "I doubt that's the reason, Mum."

"Well, I can't think why else the cruise director would want to meet him. Brendan's hardly going to help with the entertainment, is he?"

"Dad can be hilarious when he wants to be."

"Only when he's at home."

"Or in the pulpit," Rachel said, chuckling. One of Brendan Prince's gifts included the ability to put people at ease when taking a service. To do that, he often introduced humour. "Perhaps the meeting's about something else." Rachel, being fully aware of the reason for the meeting, tried to be casual. She and Carlos had planned a thirtieth anniversary treat for her parents and co-opted Brendan into the surprise when they discovered he might be planning something else. So far, they had kept everything a secret from Susan.

"Anyway, I hope that whatever it is Mr Peterson wants, your father turns it down. I couldn't face a repeat of the last cruise when that poor woman died. It took us a long time to recover from that tragedy. And don't think I didn't know you were more involved than you let on."

Her mother had undoubtedly been biding her time before mentioning anything about the nun's demise to Rachel, who foolishly imagined it was all forgotten. The last time Rachel's parents had cruised, it had been to the Caribbean, when her father took the Sunday service to cover for someone. During the service, one of a group of nuns collapsed and died. Rachel and her friend Marjorie Snellthorpe subsequently investigated the death and found the person responsible.

Time to deflect this conversation. "What will you wear?"

"Oh my. I didn't think of that. I only brought two long gowns and one cocktail dress. The rest of my clothes are casual."

"You're not getting away with that one. I know full well you bought a whole new wardrobe before we left England, so I assume one of your *casuals* will do just fine."

"I had difficulty deciding what to bring. I wasn't sure what the weather would be like."

"Hot, Mum. It's Asia... hang on a minute, Carlos is just coming in." She held the phone aloft, miming, 'mother' as a warning. "Mum's asking if we're going to the VIP sailaway function at seven. There's an invitation here."

She handed the letter to Carlos, who glanced at it before checking his watch.

"Sounds perfect," he said.

"Did you hear that, Mum?"

"Yes. Excellent. Your father's coming back now. I'll find out what his session with Simon was about and ask what he thinks about the cocktail event. Ring you back in a little while."

"Okay, Mum."

Rachel put the phone down. Carlos joined her on the sofa, a broad smile on his face.

"How did it go?"

"It's all settled. We'll have dinner with Jason and Sarah and they'll make sure lobster's on the menu and even ask the chef to pop by and say hello during dinner. After dinner, we've got a private booth for the evening show with champagne and chocolates. Halfway through the production, Simon will congratulate them on their anniversary from the stage, then the resident singer and band will sing the first dance song from their wedding day."

"Mum's going to love it," said Rachel.

"I almost forgot. The photographers will take a family photo. It'll be a memorable evening all round. The assistant cruise director was at the meeting, a Spanish woman named Natalie Rodriguez. You won't have met her because both she and Simon joined the ship after your last cruise. I got the impression Natalie does most of the organising – at least I hope she does, because Simon spent most of his time on his phone. A videographer will film the show. Brendan didn't realise we needed special permission for that, but Nat – that's what Natalie likes to be called – sorted it. The videographer will edit the video and later post it online via a private link for family and friends to watch back home."

"Wow! That's a wonderful new addition. I expect Dad will host a film evening at church. All we need to do now is keep it a secret from my mother. And I don't envy Dad trying to evade the interrogation he's about to receive. Mum thought they were going to ask him to take the Sunday service."

Carlos's eyes danced as his face crinkled when he laughed, before becoming solemn.

"I hope that idea hasn't put a dampener on things."

"Mum mentioned the dead nun, but I moved her off the subject. From what she said, it left a scar."

"At least you diverted her. And don't worry about your dad. He makes a living out of keeping parishioners' secrets. I'm sure he'll cope with Susan."

Rachel doubted her father kept many secrets from his wife, but hoped Carlos was right. "If we're going to change for this sailaway bash, we'd better unpack."

"Yes, Ma'am Rachel," he chuckled, mimicking the

stateroom attendant, who, when Rachel asked him to call her Rachel rather than Mrs Jacobi-Prince, called her Ma'am Rachel. Carlos pulled her into his arms. "How about we unpack later?"

She pushed him away, jumping up. "I'm serious, Carlos. Mum will want to eat before we go to this shindig, which means we have little time. Please put those suitcases on the bed."

Carlos got up, sighing. "You only married me for my brawn."

True, his physique had sparked the first attraction, but there was so much more to her husband than his looks. She kissed him on the cheek, teasing, "You're so right. But it's wonderful to have you along for this voyage, darling, even if you have turned it into a working holiday."

He held his palms up. "Not my fault. Let's try not to think about that. We have an event to go to. I guess there'll be officers there?"

"Yes, but I don't think that's where your misper will be, and don't be so obvious. You're already thinking about it."

"You and your police jargon." Carlos deflected. "Why don't you just say missing person?"

Rachel shrugged. "Okay, I don't think your missing person will be at the cocktail party."

"Unless she's working as a bartender or a musician. She used to play a guitar."

"Like thousands of others, Carlos. What else do you know about her?"

Her husband paused from hanging suits and thought for a moment. "Nowhere near enough. Her real name is Emily Graves, but she won't be using that name if her dad's right. She's now twenty-five, but if she's using a false ID that might not be the age recorded. It's going to be like searching for one of your lost earrings on a beach. For all I know, my client's intel that she's hiding on board this cruise ship might be out of date."

"Intel? Now who's using jargon? Which drawer would you like?" Rachel pointed to the drawers.

"You choose."

"And Emily Graves might have a sound reason for not wanting to be found. What are you going to do about that?" She wondered why a wealthy young girl and her mother had run away over a decade before.

"Emily needs to be told about her inheritance, if only to fulfil her grandmother's last wish."

"Are you sure this Graves chap wants a friendly reunion with his daughter? What if he's using it as an excuse to get his hands on the family fortune?"

"The thought has crossed my mind, but he's unlikely to admit that to me. Besides, he's wealthy in his own right. Don't worry; once I find her, I'll present the facts and then it's up to her what she does with the information. I've laid out my conditions, and he agreed to pay me on providing evidence I've found her, not for taking her to him. She's an adult."

Rachel and Carlos unpacked, then sat down to drink coffee. The phone rang again.

"Why doesn't she use my mobile?" Rachel exhaled, getting up and walking across the room to the phone next to their bed.

When Rachel put the receiver down, she looked at Carlos. "What did I tell you? We're meeting for dinner in thirty minutes."

"That would send most women into a complete frenzy, but you're so beautiful, you don't need time to get ready." Carlos embraced her. "As for me, I need much longer. I'm all of a dither." He pretend-shook before heading into the bathroom to shower while Rachel laid out a turquoise cocktail dress suitable for the soirée.

Once dressed for the evening, Rachel and Carlos collected her parents, joining the queue outside the restaurant to wait for the maître d' to select a table for them. He looked up from his screen, handing four menus to one of the line of waiters escorting people to tables.

"Table 57," he said before turning back to them. "Enjoy your meal."

As soon as they sat around the table, they were treated like royalty, which Susan enjoyed. Rachel's mother typically did the hospitality thing, and Rachel once again took pleasure in watching her being pampered.

After the succulent meal, Rachel would have happily sat and chatted, but her mother seemed in a hurry. Her focus was set on the cocktail party and they were running late. It didn't matter as the invitation stated the event would go on for a few hours, but Susan hated being late to anything so they left.

Brendan put his arm around Rachel as they left the restaurant. "Thank you for suggesting this. I didn't think your mother would ever cruise again after what happened last time. But I'm certain this cruise is going to be the best."

"I'm sure it will be, Dad." Rachel hoped Carlos's missing person wouldn't put a dampener on things. Her parents knew nothing about his case.

4

When they arrived at the venue on the lawn of deck fifteen, it couldn't have been lusher. The lawn on a private part of the ship reminded Rachel of a British summer's day in the park, and the invitation-only cocktail gathering made her think of her dear friend, Marjorie, who would be much more likely to receive an invitation than her. The reason for the invitations, Rachel guessed, had to do with her knowing several officers and crew from her onboard sleuthing activities.

By the time they arrived, a crowd filled the roped-off area, congregating in small groups. The ship's officers circulated and exchanged pleasantries with guests. Though she was sociable in general, the meet-and-greet thing was more Rachel's parents' gift than hers.

It would be good to leave the port, always an

exciting part of any cruise. An extra bonus would be that the sea breeze might remove some of the humidity.

"I didn't realise they had a real lawn," Susan remarked.

"It used to be one of those false things, but like that man Orlando said last night, modern cruise ships are doing what they can to offset their carbon footprint," said Brendan. "I wonder if he's here. I'd love to talk to him about his work."

"He's around somewhere," said Susan. "I spotted his blond waves contrasting with a black evening suit. But don't go overwhelming the man with questions, Brendan."

"I'm fascinated by that sort of thing," Brendan said, determined.

Rachel smiled. She and her father shared the same inquisitiveness, and once they got started, they found it hard to stop. The desire to question came in handy in her work as a detective, but it could be hard learning when to rein it in.

The hubbub of conversation stopped when a ship-wide announcement came from the bridge.

"Good evening, ladies and gentlemen. This is Captain Jenson speaking. I'd like to welcome you all aboard the magnificent *Coral Queen*. We are about to release moorings and will be sailing north..." The captain explained there would be two sea days before they arrived in Bangkok after sailing through the Gulf of Thailand. Once the captain finished his announcement, a musical duo set up on the small stage and began playing.

Both women looked and sounded beautiful: a pianist and a violinist. The violinist's long black hair wrapped around her shoulders like a shawl. Her hands skilfully drew her bow across the strings while the pianist's fingers moved effortlessly across the keyboard, keeping time with her partner. The pleasant melody, gentle yet strong, carried through the air above the noise of people chattering, each note they played woven together. The sound soothed something in Rachel's soul, and she found herself mesmerised by the talent of the exceptional violinist.

"This is my kind of music," said Brendan.

Rachel nodded. With the spell broken, her eyes searched in the hope her friend Sarah would be at the function. Waiting staff circulated, offering them champagne and cocktails. Others followed with trays laden with canapés.

"I could get accustomed to this... oh look, Rachel, there's Sarah," Susan called.

"Brilliant. I hoped she'd be here," said Rachel, grinning.

Sarah Bradshaw-Goodridge, dressed in her officer's whites, beamed at them. Like Rachel, she went by her maiden name, Bradshaw, for work after marrying Jason

Goodridge, one of the security guards and a close friend.

Following hugs all round because Rachel's parents had known Sarah most of her life, Sarah beamed, saying, "It's great to see you all. You've joined us for one of the best cruises, and considering some places we visit, that's saying something."

"It's wonderful to see you, Sarah," said Susan. "Your mother sends her love."

Mary Bradshaw also sent a raft of extra diktats to pass on to Sarah. She had visited Rachel and Susan the night before they left England.

"Ask her when she's coming home...

"It's time she gave up gallivanting around the world...

"Doesn't she think it's time to have a baby?

"I'm dying to be a grandmother..." being chief among her demands.

Sarah couldn't suppress an eye roll. "Don't worry. I phoned her last night, so I'll save you the trouble. I've heard the rest."

"We weren't going to say anything," said Brendan, taking a sip of champagne. "Are you on duty?"

"I'm on mingling duty at the moment," Sarah replied, grinning as she swept her arm out to encompass the busy crowd.

Rachel looked around at the colourful array of beautiful evening gowns and cocktail dresses. The colours ranged from pastel pinks and blues to glimmering metallics and sparkling sequins. Most male guests had donned suits rather than tuxedos. Carlos looked irresistible in a tux. Rachel's face heated at the thought. To distract herself, she continued to look around. The musicians wore black and gold evening dresses, their movements graceful and precise as they played. "She's a wonderful violinist."

"That's Brandi Chang. Simon Peterson tells me she's hoping for something big in America after this contract."

"Just rewards if you ask me," said Brendan.

"We met Simon last night at Raffles. Why a new cruise director?" Rachel asked.

"Carla left at the end of her last contract to get married, and Tatum, her assistant, transferred to a new ship based mainly in America. It's a tough gig having to be happy twenty-four-seven. But Simon's well suited to it."

"We also spoke with a waste disposal businessman, Orlando Kearney, who knew him. He joked about people calling Simon, Slick."

"They usually do that behind his back, so if he didn't know before, he obviously does now. Simon's been with us for five months, but he's experienced, having joined us from another cruise line. He's made quite an impression."

"A man not to be ignored, I imagine. He's over there."

Sarah turned around, tracking Rachel's gaze. The animated, dark-haired cruise director raised a glass while surrounded by a group of laughing passengers, enthralled by whatever he was saying. He wore an open-collared short-sleeved shirt and white trousers.

"He's a popular guy from the looks of things," said Brendan.

"A little too flirty for my liking," said Susan. "You still haven't told me what he wanted you for earlier."

"I guess he has to be friendly in his job," said Rachel, intervening. "Sarah's just said you can't have a miserable cruise director."

"Mm." Susan frowned.

Slick Peterson handed around cocktails from a nearby tray to another group of passengers. One of the waiters silently circulating through the crowd took the empty tray back to a bar. There, a man wearing a white-collared shirt and black bow tie was mixing cocktails. While most of the waiting staff attempted to be friendly, he didn't try. With a stern expression, he glared into the crowd.

Rachel noticed Orlando Kearney taking a cocktail from a tray and perching himself on a stool near the bar. Her eyes were drawn back to the mixologist who had resumed shaking cocktails and filling a row of glasses. Job done, the unhappy man crossed his arms, his mouth drawn into a thin line. One of the waiting staff took the freshly loaded tray, saying something to the mixologist. He muttered a reply before mixing another lot of drinks. *If it weren't for such a dour expression, you'd be attractive,* thought Rachel, admiring his slicked-back dark hair.

"Can I take your glass, ma'am?" A waitress pulled her attention away from the scowling man.

"Thank you."

Sarah continued catching up with Susan and Brendan while Carlos scanned the room, no doubt in search of his misper. More people arrived, enjoying the atmosphere on the very first night of the cruise.

"I'd better go back to mingling," said Sarah.

"Catch you later," said Rachel.

Sarah left them to speak to a couple hovering nearby.

The musicians continued to play soothing melodies in the background. Slick strolled across to Rachel and her family. "Hello again. I believe we met last night." He shook Susan's hand. "If there's anything I can do to improve your cruise, please don't hesitate to find me."

Simon gave nothing away regarding his meeting with Brendan and Carlos earlier, but Susan opened her mouth, about to ask something, when Brendan took her arm to point to a blue silk gown a woman was wearing. Susan loved silk.

"It's a pleasure to meet you again," continued

Simon, taking Rachel's hand and attempting to bring it to his lips. Fortunately, someone tugged his arm before she pulled her hand away.

"You're wanted," the woman hissed in his ear.

Simon winked at Rachel before moving on to the next group.

Rachel couldn't deny being inwardly pleased to see the back of him.

"Slick's living up to his name, but I don't think he means any harm," said Brendan, happy to distract Susan from more questions about their earlier meeting. "He appears to be a pleasant enough chap."

Rachel thought it a shame Slick Peterson was involved in her mother's surprise, but she'd leave Carlos to manage him. "The woman who dragged him away is Nat, the assistant I told you about," Carlos whispered.

Moments later, the music stopped, and a microphone crackled into life. Slick took a place in front of the musicians with a huge grin pasted on his face, looking like an advert for toothpaste. "Good evening, ladies and gentlemen. My name is Simon Peterson, your cruise director. We would like to welcome you all on board the *Coral Queen*. I hope you're enjoying the cocktails and canapés – the first of many parties, I hope." He winked – evidently his signature move – at an elderly woman dressed in a turquoise cocktail dress, decorated with sequins. She held her glass up in salutation while he carried on smooth talking before finishing with, "If I, or my team, can help make your cruise stand out, please let us know."

Nat cleared her throat loudly.

"Oh yes, I almost forgot. This is Natalie Rodriguez, your assistant cruise director. Natalie and I intend to make your voyage the best experience ever."

A round of applause rippled through the air before the musicians resumed their playing.

Nat Rodriguez forced a smile when Simon handed her the microphone before heading for the woman he had winked at. Nat puffed out her cheeks, handing the microphone to a technician standing by. She then turned around and marched toward the open-air café.

"He's charming, but I wouldn't want to work with him," said Susan.

In a few words, Susan Prince summed up Rachel's feelings about the charismatic Simon Peterson. Rachel's mother had a talent for being an excellent judge of character. Rachel credited her mother with her own intuition.

With people resuming conversations and returning to their drinks, nobody other than Rachel noticed a woman at the side of the room doubling over. Rachel hurried over.

"Excuse me. Are you unwell? Can I fetch someone to help?"

"It's just a spasm. If you could help me to a seat, I'd be most grateful."

Carlos joined Rachel and assisted her in guiding the frail-looking woman to a chair.

"You really don't look well. I can call for one of the medical team to have a look at you." Rachel tried looking for Sarah, but crowds standing in clusters made it impossible to see her.

"There's no need for any of that. Perhaps a glass of water, please."

Carlos disappeared, returning seconds later with a bottle of water and a glass. He poured it before handing it over.

"My name's Rachel and this is my husband, Carlos." Rachel sat down, not wanting to leave the woman who Rachel guessed at being in her mid-to-late sixties.

"Evelyn Mitchell, but please call me Evie – everyone does." Evie released her side after a few sips of water. "There you are, you see. I'm better already."

"That's a relief," said Rachel. "Are you travelling with anyone? Shall I fetch them?"

"Alas, no. I'm travelling alone. I have a few people I know on board, but I wouldn't want to bother them. We play bridge... I seem to be keeping you. I think those people might be looking for you."

Rachel swivelled her neck and found her parents hovering in the background. "My parents," she explained.

"How wonderful to cruise with family." Evie's eyes

drifted into a world of her own before she patted Rachel's hand.

"I'll be fine now, Rachel. Thank you. And you Carlos. Go and enjoy yourselves."

"Are you sure?"

"Quite sure." Rachel recognised the similar determined air that Marjorie would put on in a situation like this, and accepted the dismissal.

"It was nice to meet you, Evie."

After rejoining her parents, Carlos explained what had happened.

"Should we call for a doctor?" Susan asked.

"I offered, Mum."

"She insists she's better now," said Carlos.

Rachel turned around to watch Evie crossing the lawn to stand at the ship's rail, gazing into the glorious sunset.

Not long afterwards, more groans reached her ears. Several people appeared to be doubling over. Officers sprang into action, ordering the drinks and canapés to be removed. One of them spoke to Slick, who silenced the musicians and took the microphone once more.

"Thank you all for attending our sailaway cocktail bash. There are plenty more activities going on throughout the evening and into the night. Please be careful about descending the stairs. Explore the ship. I look forward to seeing you around."

Once they realised the event was over, most people made their way down the steps.

"Why don't you go on? I'll finish my drink and catch a word with Sarah before I leave," said Rachel.

Susan Prince glanced over at someone retching and muttered something about people drinking too much free booze.

"Shall we call it a night?" Brendan said. "I'd like to rest my legs, although I'm wide awake from the jet lag."

"I thought you didn't have jet lag?" Susan said with a smirk.

"Touché. Goodnight, Rachel. We'll see you in the morning." Brendan kissed her on the cheek and her mother followed suit.

"I'll walk with you part of the way," said Carlos. "I'll meet you and Sarah in the Jazz Bar, darling."

Rachel suspected he wanted to do some side digging into his missing person.

Half a dozen people remained, all clutching at their abdomens. Could something have been wrong with the canapés? *Maybe the dreaded norovirus is putting in an appearance.* Sarah set about examining one of the worst affected women. Bernard, her friend and colleague, appeared and saw to the assistant cruise director. Then Rachel's heart sank when she saw a man slumped in a chair.

5
———

Rachel's heart hammered against her ribs as she took in the unsettling sight of the unconscious man she recognised as Fabian Bigham slumped back in the chair. The angry red face from her observations the day before was now drained of colour and resembled that of a porcelain doll. His starched white shirt was marred by a crimson stain, where the remains of his cocktail spread across his chest. Without hesitation, she reached out and plucked the glass from his knee, setting it down on the nearby table. Leaning in, she gripped his shoulder and gave it a firm shake.

"Mr Bigham... Fabian? Can you hear me?" Her voice sounded calm but insistent as she tried to rouse him.

He remained still and unresponsive, his arms dropped by his side. Rachel swallowed hard, moving her attention to his pulse. As her fingers rested over the carotid artery, she noted his clammy and chilled skin. With no sign of any rhythmic throb beneath her fingertips, adrenaline surged through her veins as she scanned the room for the medics.

Sarah was in the throes of sending the woman she had been examining to the infirmary via a stretcher when she looked up and Rachel caught her gaze. With a sense of urgency, Rachel conveyed the seriousness of the situation through her eyes. Summoning her through her head and gesture, she mouthed, "Help!"

By now a few of the confused-looking waiting staff were staring wide-eyed at Fabian. They moved to make room for Sarah, who bent over and double-checked the man's pulse. "Put him on the floor," she instructed.

Rachel and a waiter manoeuvred Fabian from the chair, gently lowering him to the ground. Rachel removed his already loosened tie while her friend unbuttoned his shirt. Sarah assessed his airway before looking at Rachel. "Start chest compressions while I radio for more help."

Rachel wasted no time starting resuscitation. She positioned her hands over Fabian's sternum and began. She had been in this situation many times as a police officer and knew what to do. "One, two, three, four..." she counted out loud, staying laser-focussed, trying to stimulate the heart to beat again.

Sarah got on her radio, "Code Blue, top lawn. I need medics, stat."

Toxic Cruise Cocktail 47

As Rachel and Sarah worked together in their resuscitation efforts, Bernard sprinted to join them, armed with a medical bag. He hurriedly set up a defibrillator, applying pads to Fabian's bare chest and connecting the leads.

"Clear!" he shouted.

Rachel stepped back as the machine discharged its thunderbolt, causing Fabian's body to jerk.

With the medics now on scene and doing everything within their power, Rachel retreated to Fabian's abandoned table and sat down. Now it was time to use her own skills. She analysed the scene, scrutinising the empty cocktail glass.

A waiter, dressed in a crisp white uniform, approached the table with a nervous smile on his lips. "Excuse me, ma'am, would you like me to take that away for you?"

"Not until we understand what's happened," Rachel replied, her tone making it clear this was non-negotiable. She eyed the staff clearing tables. "I insist you leave everything as it is and inform your manager we need the security team up here. Make sure no-one throws anything away."

The waiter gulped and scurried off towards the bar, speaking to the miserable mixologist. They engaged in a hurried conversation before the waiter picked up a telephone.

After making the call, the two men huddled into a

group with a few other startled waiters, whispering and gesturing in confusion. Rachel sat too far away to make out what they were saying. She leaned back in her seat, trying to piece together what just happened.

"Why is it always me?" she muttered under her breath with a shake of her head.

The remaining staff made sure nobody entered the lush lawn area while encouraging a few stragglers to leave. Within minutes, Dr Graham Bentley, the ship's senior medical officer, arrived on scene, accompanied by Jack Waverley, the chief security officer. A crew member hurried after them carrying an oxygen cylinder.

Rachel knew both senior officers from previous cruises. They each cast a curious glance towards her before joining Sarah and Bernard at the side of the lifeless body of Fabian Bigham. Bernard had shocked him at least three times with no response.

"Put it there," Bernard instructed the crewman, who placed the cylinder on the ground. Bernard quickly connected tubing to the mask and fired up the oxygen. "We've shocked three times. Nothing," Bernard told Dr Bentley.

"How long?" Dr Bentley asked.

"Around ten minutes so far," said Sarah. "But we don't know how long he'd been unconscious before Rachel found him."

"Right then. Continue with chest compressions and increase the oxygen. Hand me the adrenaline."

Once given a loaded syringe, Dr Bentley asked them to pause while he injected the drug directly into the man's heart.

"No response," said Sarah, looking at the monitor.

The team continued shocking with the defibrillator and working for another half an hour before Dr Bentley made the call.

"Cease resuscitation. Time of death 21:33." Their heads drooped as they accepted the unwelcome outcome.

With the decision made, Waverley pounced on Sarah with no preamble. "Did anyone witness what happened to him?" His gruff voice echoed in the now subdued air.

Sarah shrugged her shoulders, exhausted. "We were busy with passengers getting sick. He hadn't made a sound as far as I'm aware. It looked like some kind of outbreak."

"I'd appreciate it, Jack, if you didn't shout at my team," said Dr Bentley.

Waverley apologised, lowering his voice, and a mumbled conversation continued. Satisfied he'd got all he could from Sarah and Bernard about the events, he strode over to join Rachel.

His jaw clenched with tension as he stared at her,

disbelief in his eyes. "You found Mr Bigham," he snapped.

"Hello to you too," Rachel retorted.

"My apologies. It's just that every time you..."

He didn't need to finish the sentence, instead rubbing a hand over his haggard face.

"I know. Trouble follows me around. I can't help that." Whenever Rachel cruised, something happened. She wondered if there would ever be a day when Queen Cruises banned her from cruising, but now wasn't the time to contemplate such things. It really wasn't her fault, and her presence was coincidental.

"Sarah said..." his tone softened. "Sarah mentioned there's been some sort of sickness outbreak this evening. Passengers complaining of stomach cramps and nausea. Did you observe anything out of the ordinary?"

"Other than it happening suddenly? As you've been told, people started clutching their stomachs, and a few were retching. I thought at first it could be a norovirus outbreak."

"Quite." Waverley hesitated, grasping the implication from her phrasing. "At first, you say. That suggests you've changed your mind." His brow furrowed.

"Look at this." Rachel handed over the cocktail glass.

Waverley inspected the empty glass, bringing it to

his nose, sniffing. His brow furrowed. "I can't see or smell anything unusual."

"Neither could I. But he drank from that glass before he collapsed, and the remains spilt onto his shirt. What if it's a case of poisoning?"

"Food poisoning, you mean?"

"That's one option," said Rachel.

Waverley's frown deepened. "What are you suggesting here, Rachel?" His eyes made it clear he already knew the answer.

"I think we need to consider it's possible that someone poisoned Fabian Bigham."

Waverley recoiled, a vein pulsating in his temple. "Look Rachel. As much as I appreciate your knowledge and enthusiasm for catching criminals, let's not jump to conclusions. The symptoms observed by the medical team are consistent with a gastrointestinal virus – norovirus being one – or food poisoning. One of those is what Dr Bentley suspects caused the outbreak."

"I'd agree if nobody had died. But the dead man, what about him?" Rachel pressed.

"Who knows? An unfortunate, but purely coincidental, heart attack," Waverley replied matter-of-factly.

Rachel shook her head, frustrated. "I'm not one for coincidences. You're suggesting that on the same night a number of people suffer stomach cramps, an unpleasant man coincidentally dies of a heart attack."

"These things happen. You have to remember that our ship is like a small village and medical emergencies occur from time to time, just as they do on land." Waverley ran his hand through his thinning hair, face flushing from the neck up. "Just because you're here doesn't mean a man's been murdered."

"Before dismissing the possibility, at least have the glass examined and pass my suspicions on to Dr Bentley. It would be negligent not to carry out toxicology tests given the circumstances."

Waverley let out a deep breath. "If I consent, will you leave us to do our jobs and concentrate on your holiday?"

"Of course. I don't want this to be a murder any more than you do."

"Okay. It's a deal," he said, conceding.

"Thank you."

"I'll do my part, but please don't turn this into one of your crusades."

Rachel glared at him before getting up. "I'll try to keep a low profile, but if I stumble upon evidence that suggests motive, I'll do whatever it takes." With that, she turned and headed across the lawn.

"Why doesn't that surprise me?" Waverley shot his response after her.

Passing the scene where they were loading the body onto a stretcher, Rachel put a hand on Sarah's arm. "Will we see you in the Jazz Bar?"

"I doubt it. There are still several people who are going to need a follow up after this outbreak, and now we have a body and a couple of infirmary admissions. I reckon we'll be on duty for hours yet. Graham's asking the catering manager and health and safety officer to take samples from food and drinks to see if we can track down the cause. It's not looking like norovirus because nobody's actually been sick. At least not as far as we know."

"Thank heavens for Dr Bentley," Rachel said with relief. "We'll catch you tomorrow." Rachel hugged her friend and left, continuing towards the stairs.

"Rachel?" Waverley stopped her in her tracks. She turned back to face him.

"What made you say you thought Fabian Bigham an unpleasant man? Did you know him?"

"Not at all. Our paths crossed yesterday, that's all. It's just the impression he gave."

"Your encounter yesterday. Is that why you suspect foul play?"

Rachel studied Waverley. He wasn't a man who liked hunches any more than she like coincidences. "I suppose it is. That, and the strange outbreak this evening. By the look on your face, you're well aware of what kind of man he was. People like him make enemies."

"But if there is anything malevolent going on here, he can't have been a target. Any of the people who took ill could have died." Waverley held his arms out in desperation. "You're wrong, Rachel, because what you suggest isn't possible. And if he was poisoned, it would be by a callous and dangerous individual who didn't care how many people got hurt."

"That's a possibility too," said Rachel, recognising the implications of what that would mean. "Maybe I'm wrong and you're right."

"Good." Waverley turned on his heels and marched towards the bar. A man on a mission. She wouldn't like to be a member of the bar or waiting staff right now, but Rachel had other concerns on her mind. She hadn't mentioned her father's friendship with Fabian Bigham to Waverley because if Brendan needed to be told, she would be the one to do it. How would her father react to the news of his friend's death after their joyful reunion?

As the night grew darker, the tension in her chest grew. Rachel didn't like to think there was a poisoner at large. If there was, it could have been anyone at the function, most likely a member of staff. Or was her imagination running away with her? She'd been under a lot of stress recently.

Sarah didn't know about Evie, so she wouldn't be on her list of people to follow up. It was imperative Rachel find her.

6

Confused and disturbed by what happened at the cocktail party, Rachel made her way to the ship's central atrium. Her heels clacked on the polished marble floors. She bypassed a queue of people waiting to speak to a member of the guest services team and picked up a copy of the *Coral Daily* from a magazine rack. Scanning the list of events going on all around the ship, her gaze focussed on one listing – a Bridge Bonanza taking place in the casino. Evie's words echoed in her mind, a casual reference to her fondness for the strategic card game.

Rachel pivoted on the spot. Her hair swayed as she made for the casino, determined to do her own follow-up on the woman she'd met earlier. The broad-shouldered silhouette of Jason Goodridge cut through the bustling crowd, his security uniform crisp and authoritative in contrast to the dressy or leisurely attire of passengers. They locked eyes and beamed at each other before hugging.

"No sooner are you on the ship than pandemonium breaks out." Jason pecked her on the cheek.

"You've heard then?"

"Yep. Just come from the top lawn. I'm on my way to tell the boss's wife, Brenda, he's going to be delayed for dinner, then I'll be heading back to help him with more interviews."

"At least he's taking the situation seriously." Rachel recalled her conversation with Jack Waverley and hadn't been convinced he would pay it due diligence.

"He always takes passenger safety seriously, Rachel. You know that. The situation presented like a medical or health and safety issue at the outset. That's not changed."

Rachel respected Jason's loyalty and internally acknowledged he was right. Jack Waverley cared about passengers and crew even if his reaction could sometimes be slower than she would like in acting on her intuition. "Sorry," she said.

"We've got someone in the brig as a precaution. But nothing's confirmed yet."

"Oh? Who?"

"A guy called Manfred Heinrich. He's a new and

talented mixologist. Maybe too talented if he's been experimenting with poisons."

"Is he the miserable-looking guy I saw shaking cocktails behind the bar?"

"That's the one. Anyway, I'd better find Brenda. Hope to see you later, Rachel." Jason's often cheery demeanour was another thing Rachel liked about him. He put people at ease and rarely appeared ruffled. Jason also had hidden depths where his inner demons used to torment him. He and Carlos shared such demons. Thinking of Carlos, her hand went to her mouth.

"I don't suppose you're going anywhere near the Jazz Bar on your travels, are you?"

"I'll be passing near that way. Why?"

"Carlos is probably waiting for me in there, but I need to see Evie. Would you tell him I've gone to look for her?"

"Sure but—"

"Thanks Jason." Rachel left him and picked up the pace as she hurried towards the casino.

On entering the busy casino, Rachel passed the blackjack tables where most hopeful faces quickly switched to disappointed as the dealer laid her cards down. Another croupier set the roulette wheel spinning in a blur, the clinking of chips punctuating the air. Rachel wove her way through the mixed chimes and melodies created by passengers trying their luck at the slot machines. Finally, she reached the quieter enclave where the bridge players were convened. Three tables set apart from the hustle of the casino floor provided an oasis of strategic thought amid the clamour of gaming.

Evie sat poised at one of the tables, her concentration etched into the delicate lines around her eyes. Rachel hung back, unsure whether to interrupt, but the game was concluding.

"Three no trump," declared a player at Evie's table. Rachel didn't know what it meant, but the other players reacted.

The hands unfolded; each layer revealed more than just cards. It was a game of strategy. Evie appeared to be in her element, her face betraying nothing but the faintest glimmer of satisfaction as she played her hand. As the last card hit the green baize and the scores were tallied, Evie's grin widened. She and her younger partner shared a pile of chips.

Rachel's heart lightened to see Evie looking none the worse for wear. The woman looked up, her expression shifting from focussed competitor to warm recognition. "Hello again, Rachel."

"Hello. How are you?"

"I'm fine," Evie responded, gathering her chips and placing them inside her small evening bag. "Fully recovered, as you see."

"That's excellent."

"Have you come to check up on me?"

Rachel nodded, slightly embarrassed, although Evie's eyes expressed amusement and she appeared flattered by her concern.

"That's very kind of you, but quite unnecessary. I'm stronger than I look."

"I don't doubt it," said Rachel, laughing.

"May I introduce you to Danny? Danny Martinez," Evie gestured toward her bridge partner, who looked vaguely familiar. "Danny, this is Rachel, the young woman who took care of me when I took ill with a funny turn earlier this evening."

"Really? You didn't mention feeling unwell."

"It was nothing." Evie dismissed any concern.

"Well, it's a pleasure to meet you, Rachel." Danny's words were more assured than his handshake. Shy, she presumed. About her height, but skinny, she guessed Danny would be early thirties, with sandy-brown hair and dark green eyes. His pale skin suggested he spent more time indoors than out, and she detected a Devonshire accent.

"Likewise," Rachel replied, noting a hint of intelligence in Danny's eyes when they finally met hers. Maybe a geeky type. "Are you two related?"

"No." Danny's intense eyes fleetingly held hers. "We partnered for a game of bridge. I wanted to learn the skill of the game."

"And a quick learner he is too," said Evie.

"Thanks to an excellent teacher. Video games are more my thing. Much better than real life."

An escapist. No surprise there, thought Rachel.

Swatting away the praise and definitely the topic of video games, Evie took Rachel's arm. "Danny informs me a few more folks got sick up on the top lawn after I left."

"A bartender told me the medics reckon there's a stomach bug going round," Danny added.

"Were you at the cocktail party?" Rachel furrowed her brow. She didn't recall registering the geeky-looking man, but it explained why he looked familiar.

"Yes, and obviously you were, too." Danny's face flushed red.

"Shall we continue our conversation over a mug of hot chocolate?" Evie suggested. "I like a hot drink before going to bed."

"Sounds good to me," Rachel agreed, and the three of them made their way toward Creams patisserie. Rachel found it a welcome surprise, it being open so late.

Once they were settled with hot drinks on the table, Evie broke the silence. "I got off lightly, by all accounts. What I experienced was unpleasant, but I feel sorry for those people who suffered more severely. It's not a great start to their cruise, is it? Danny heard mention someone might have spiked the drinks."

Danny mused over his coffee. "Wouldn't put it past one of the staff."

Rachel halted, bringing her hot chocolate to her lips, facing them. "Why do you think anyone would do that?"

"Dunno really. There's a video game where an overlooked vagrant takes his revenge by going on a murder spree."

Evie raised an eyebrow. "I'm not sure video games are a basis for tonight's scenario."

"You're right but it must grate on them sometimes, being surrounded by wealth. I guess it could make some individuals bitter," Danny replied, his voice dropping to a whisper. "Envy makes people do crazy things."

"I'm sure it's just gossip," said Evie.

"Perhaps," Rachel said thoughtfully.

She shook her head, a strand of hair falling across her face. "I've always found the staff helpful." She tucked the errant lock behind her ear. "Although the mixologist didn't look happy."

"Manfred?" Evie queried. "He seemed harmless enough to me. Mixed me his own wonderful twist on a Poisoned Paradise." Realising what she'd said, her jaw dropped open.

"Is there such a drink?" Rachel asked, recalling how pale Evie looked when she took ill.

"Yes, there is, but he adds his own special ingredients."

"He mixed me one of those too," added Danny. "A white rum base, cranberry and some other stuff. But if you're thinking he might have been spiking the cocktails, I wasn't ill. Although now I think about it, I had a bit of gut rot afterwards, but I put that down to its strength."

Before Rachel could process this new information, or give any sort of reply, another woman, who appeared to be of a similar age to Evie, approached their table, her eyes sparkling and her greeting warm.

"Hello Evie! How nice to see you again."

Evie didn't look as pleased to see the woman as she had been to see Rachel. "Oh, hello Linda. I didn't realise you were on board. It's a small world."

Not to be rebuffed, the woman named Linda took a seat at their table. Nodding to Rachel and Danny, she nudged Evie's arm. "Did you hear, darling? A hideous man died tonight! I, for one, am celebrating." She certainly appeared to be celebrating. Linda's slurred speech and dishevelled hair suggested she had imbibed more than a few drinks at the cocktail function. She'd spilled tomato or something similar on her white jacket. Another person who'd been present and one who sounded as if she'd known Fabian Bigham.

"I hardly think such news is a cause for celebration." Evie's eyes shot a disapproving look at the woman.

"Hello. Linda, is it? I'm Danny and this is Rachel.

Can I ask who died?" He leaned forward. Perhaps he wasn't as shy as Rachel had assumed.

"A dreadful man named Fabian Bigham," Linda announced, unperturbed by Evie's discomfort.

Rachel remained silent, observing their reactions.

"And dreadful is putting it mildly," Linda continued. "He didn't have a decent bone in his body."

"Did you know this person?" Rachel ventured cautiously.

"Only by reputation. And let me tell you, it wasn't a positive one," Linda replied.

"Terrible to think someone died though," Danny added. His tone lacked genuine concern; his face tightened into a scowl. Evie's eyes darted away momentarily. A shadow had settled over their jovial gathering.

"Did either of you know him?" Rachel probed gently.

"No," Evie responded quickly; too quickly, perhaps.

"Me neither." Rachel detected an edge to Danny's voice. His earlier insecurities were even more apparent in his guarded tone.

Rachel noted the subtle nuances – the tension in Danny's jaw, the way Evie avoided eye contact, and Linda's delight at reporting the information. Something didn't add up. She thought of the unfortunate mixologist locked away, a man seemingly bitter enough to spike drinks. But could the poisoning be more personal? Had she been right about Bigham and his enemies?

"If what you say is right," Rachel said to Linda, "it doesn't sound as if many people will miss him?"

"They won't. Good riddance, I say."

Rachel suspected Linda knew Fabian more than by reputation.

"That's harsh," Evie murmured, her gaze fixed on the swirling pattern of her hot chocolate.

A moment of silence hung between them. Rachel could sense the cogs rotating as each person wrestled with their own thoughts.

"Well, I'd say..." Danny finally broke the silence, "...a death on a cruise ship. That's got to be bad for business, right?"

"A plus for me though," said Linda.

"How can it be in any way positive?" said Rachel, shocked.

"She's a blogger," said Evie, "or used to be."

"I still dabble, and Queen Cruises continues to provide me with enough ammunition to keep going."

"You don't have to be so horrid," said Evie.

Rachel's mind raced. She felt pleased none of the trio were aware of her past exploits on board the *Coral Queen*.

"It's laughable, really." Linda's eyes narrowed. "The man who threatened to silence me has now been silenced."

"You should be careful what you say," warned Evie. "If rumours swirling around are true, and the man's death turns out to be suspicious, you might be the prime suspect."

"You've heard then? Well, the rumours are right. The death is being treated as suspicious and the security officers have already nabbed someone..." Linda paused to allow her words to sink in. "...the mixologist did it."

Evie's mouth opened, but no words came out. Her hand shook as she put down her drink.

"Anyway, I thought you'd want to know," she winked at Evie. "Now, I need to leave. I have a story to write." Linda staggered away as quickly as she'd arrived.

"Don't pay too much attention to that Linda Parker. She's not one to let the truth get in the way of a story, as the saying goes." Evie still looked shaken.

"From what we've just witnessed, this poor mixologist is judged and found guilty," said Danny. "As the spreader of bad vibes, your friend is hardly the sort of person you'd want to bring to a party."

"She's not so bad when sober."

"If you'll excuse me, I think I'm going to take a stroll around the decks," Danny said.

"And I'd better go in search of my husband," said Rachel. "Goodnight."

"See you around," said Danny, marching away. Evie remained silent, so Rachel paused before leaving.

"Are you okay?" Rachel asked.

Evie's head jerked up, blinking away tears. "Yes, I'm quite all right. It's the realisation that I may have been poisoned tonight. Thank you for taking care of me, but you go on now, dear. Enjoy your cruise."

"If you're sure."

Evie didn't reply, instead, looking into the distance. As Rachel strolled out of the patisserie she got the impression that Fabian Bigham's negative reach stretched further than she had imagined.

7
———

The soulful crooning of a band playing the trumpet, saxophone and piano echoed into the brightly lit corridor as Carlos approached the Jazz Bar.

Once inside, he climbed onto a barstool and asked for a pint of lager. As he scanned the room he spotted a man who looked familiar. The man didn't make eye contact and vanished into the crowd before Carlos could get a better look. They had mingled with crowds of people since arriving in Singapore and on boarding the ship, so he shook an unwelcome thought from his head and turned his attention back to the ebb and flow of passengers and staff. While sipping his beer, he discreetly studied the women's faces for any signs of familiarity.

Calos retrieved the faded photograph from his

breast pocket and held it up to the dim light coming from above the bar, examining it in detail. In the image, a fourteen-year-old girl with thick brown hair hanging over her face was forcing a smile as if coerced to do so for the camera's sake. Emily Graves had a shiny metal brace attached to her top teeth. Carlos rubbed his forehead, scrunched his eyes and tried to imagine what she would look like today. He wished he had access to age progression technology which would give him a better idea. Allen Graves, his client, had told him that not long after the photo was taken, the girl and her mother vanished without trace, leaving no explanation. Even if he could use technology, the young woman might have changed her appearance so as not to be recognised easily. But why?

Allen Graves assured Carlos that Emily was still alive because she'd kept in sporadic contact with her paternal grandmother, Graves's mother. Graves also said he had no idea where the maternal grandparents were, or whether they were still alive.

Emily's grandmother had decreed in her will that Emily was the sole beneficiary of her estate. Allen already headed up his mother's multi-million-pound logistics business, which reassured Carlos that jealousy couldn't be the driving force behind finding his daughter. Unless – Carlos stared into his beer glass – unless some sort of codicil prevented him from doing what he needed to do. If so, Graves hadn't mentioned it.

Carlos scrutinised the photo again, his mind filled with questions.

Why did your mother take you away from a life of privilege and go into hiding?

Graves insisted there had been no misdemeanour on his part and blamed his wife, citing a lifelong struggle with bipolar disorder and alcoholism. Instinct whispered there could be more to the split than that, particularly as his employer refused to reveal anything other than the contents of a solitary letter, discovered among his late mother's belongings. Instinct told Carlos that Graves was hiding something, or that he couldn't cope with his marriage breakdown. Maybe he was embarrassed, even ashamed about it. The few times they met Carlos got the impression Allen Graves was a wealthy man used to getting what he wanted.

Sometimes Carlos's private investigator jobs didn't sit right, and his gut suggested this might be one of those occasions. Carlos had corroborated Graves's version of events by contacting a handful of people who remembered the couple from the time they were together.

Before leaving for the cruise, Carlos conducted thorough background checks into the Graves family, uncovering a drink-driving charge leading to a two-year driving ban in Charlotte Graves' past, which added credence to Allen's story.

Despite exhaustive efforts, Carlos couldn't trace

Charlotte Graves or her daughter Emily. His searches employed both her married name and the maiden name of Maddison. Still he found nothing. According to Allen Graves, he hardly knew the maternal grandparents before his wife and daughter's disappearance. Graves reckoned they lived in Austria after leaving the UK in the 1990s. They, too, remained untraceable. His client had assumed Charlotte and Emily lived in Austria until he had heard otherwise. Carlos frowned, shaking his head. He'd utilised all the contacts and resources available to him but he couldn't find any record of the Maddisons settling in Austria.

It was eleven years since Charlotte and Emily disappeared, leaving few breadcrumbs for anyone to follow. After eleven years missing, one could reasonably assume the mother and daughter were deceased or in a witness protection programme. But neither explanation fitted the facts in this case. Carlos found it frustrating and a challenge. He wanted to get to grips with it now. The single letter Graves showed Carlos omitted any address, a clear sign Emily didn't want to be found. Melissa Graves, Allen's mother, destroyed the envelopes, concealing the whereabouts of her granddaughter. Why would she do that? Allen suggested it could be a condition of staying in touch with her grandmother and that his wife had polluted his daughter's mind. Legally, the couple remained wed, as no decree nisi, the provisional decree for divorce, had been issued.

Carlos was determined not to be taken for a fool, but he would stick to his side of the well-paying case. He suspected there was more to this story than he'd been told, and the only person to ask about that would be Emily herself.

"Hiya mate. Rachel told me I'd find you in here."

Carlos looked up from the photograph, slipping it back into his pocket. "Jason! Great to see you." Carlos shook the security guard's hand. Jason looked healthy and happy. Marrying Rachel's best friend, Sarah, had healed a multitude of Jason's old wounds, not least that of his previous fiancée breaking off their engagement.

"You were miles away."

"Just cogitating over something. Will my wife be joining me soon?"

"There's been an incident at the VIP cocktail event. She said to tell you she was going to see Evie. Does that make any sense?"

"Yes. We assisted a woman named Evie who took ill at the party. Trust Rachel to want to check she's all right. Is the incident related to the sickness bug?"

Jason gestured to a secluded booth. "Let's talk over there."

Carlos's heart sank as he followed Jason. "What's happened?"

"A man died. Not just any man, he's our director of operations, a bigwig in the company. The boss assumed a stomach outbreak coincided with the guy having a heart attack. But Rachel thinks otherwise."

Carlos groaned. "You've got to be kidding me?"

"Experience has taught us that Rachel's instincts are often right. So now the boss is questioning the bar staff and waiters. Some cocktails might have been laced with a toxin. Rachel suggested the dead man could have been poisoned."

"Why?"

Jason shrugged. "Beats me, but she suggested the man could have enemies. What we don't know is whether the random outbreak and his death are linked. The medical team will take blood samples from those who took ill. We should have more information soon."

"Do you think the guests were poisoned as well? Who would want to do something like that?"

Jason shook his head. "We're not certain, but it's not looking terrific for the mixologist. The chief ordered he be put in the brig just to be on the safe side."

"That's something, at least. If you've caught the culprit, Rachel can relax. She desperately needs a break. Did you know the man?"

"No. A bit too high and mighty to mix with the likes of me, but the boss had some dealings with him."

"Anything that would suggest someone deliberately poisoning him?"

"If there was, I'm not in the loop yet, but you know

what the boss is like. He's hoping Rachel's wrong. Besides, with so many people taking ill, we don't believe he could have been a target. Mercifully, no-one else has died."

"It could be a case of smoke and mirrors, but that would be a dangerous game. Let's hope Waverley's right, or that you've got your man, and your nefarious employee confesses to the crime and gives his reasons."

Jason cleared his throat. "If only our job was that simple. Anyway, I'd better go back to work. I've got some more interviews to conduct. We're going to need solid evidence, and a witness would be helpful. It could still turn out to be what the medical team suspects – a stomach bug caused by a virus or dodgy seafood canapés. But with Rachel suggesting the guy could have been targeted, the boss isn't taking any chances."

Carlos imagined how persuasive Rachel would be if she suspected something was amiss.

"Did Rachel know the guy?"

"I don't think so, but according to the boss, she'd come across him."

Carlos grimaced. "Do you have a name?"

"Fabian Bigham. Did you meet him?"

"We were introduced." Carlos didn't mention the incident in the Raffles lobby or about her dad being an old friend, because Jason seemed in a hurry. "Thanks for dropping by, Jason." Carlos felt a nasty suspicion his wife might be onto something. "Did Rachel say where she was going to meet Evie?"

"Sorry mate. She didn't, appeared to be in a rush."

After Jason left, Carlos resumed staring into his drink, pondering whether to go to bed, find his wife, or continue the search for the elusive Emily Graves. Rachel had suggested he confide in Jason, but he didn't want to compromise the security guard by giving him information he would need to hide from his boss. Chief Waverley demanded loyalty, and Jason was about as loyal as they came. Besides, it sounded like the security team would have its hands full with a fresh investigation in addition to their already busy schedule. He would see where his own enquiries got to first.

A shame his client's intel hadn't given him a better lead. The snippet of information he had came via the late Melissa Graves' nurse, who told Allen how proud the old lady was of her granddaughter for travelling the world at such a young age. The nurse showed his client a *Coral Queen* postcard, most likely not knowing Emily was out of touch with her father. With a Jamaica postmark, Graves had investigated and found the *Coral Queen* had been in Jamaica at the latter end of the previous year.

Now Carlos was on her trail to inform her she could be a multi-millionaire if she wanted to be.

His thoughts drifted back to the cocktail function and the handful of individuals he'd witnessed clutching their stomachs. He didn't remember seeing Bigham, and Brendan can't have or he would have spoken to him. Like the medics, Carlos attributed the illness to seafood or something people had consumed before boarding. Susan suggested people were too quick to drink copious amounts of free alcohol on empty stomachs. Other than the dead man being someone Rachel didn't like, what made her suspect he – and other passengers – had been poisoned?

Carlos was worried that working in the Special Operations Department stretched his wife to her limits. He'd suffered from PTSD for years from his days in the army and working for the secret services, and still grappled with symptoms that occasionally clouded his judgement. Rachel encountered the depths of human darkness daily, and for that reason, he feared her health would eventually suffer. Her unwavering faith in God strengthened her more than most, but she would be the first to admit that it didn't make her immune to the effects of human suffering.

This depressing train of thought would get him nowhere. Carlos slid off the bar stool, drained his glass, and headed into the ship's bustling atrium. When he arrived at the three-storey centrepiece, he paused to listen to the soothing melodies from the musical duo he'd heard performing at the cocktail gathering. An idea stirred in his head.

The one piece of information he had about Emily

was her proficiency on the guitar. Despite what Rachel said earlier about how many people did the same, it was something to go on. If he pursued that avenue to begin with, it might offer a breakthrough in his quest to find his missing person.

8

Sarah had begun the day filled with excitement, looking forward to catching up with her best friends Rachel and Carlos, along with Rachel's parents. Jason had also been full of beans. He and Carlos were close friends who confided in each other. Their shared military history, coupled with their reluctance to discuss their experiences with mere civilians, bonded them. In a way, Sarah was grateful for not knowing all of Jason's past. She hated talk of war, being a pacifist to the core, and never understood why people deliberately set out to kill each other.

Now another person had died and his death was being treated as suspicious. Sarah took swabs from the damp drink stain on Fabian Bigham's shirt before placing it inside a plastic bag. Graham drew blood samples along with swabs from various parts of the dead man's body. Once they'd finished, Graham left while Gwen helped Sarah remove and bag the rest of his clothes.

"Apparently he works, or rather worked, for Queen Cruises. Did you ever meet him, Gwen?" Sarah asked. Being the senior nurse, Gwen would have been likely to cross paths with the late Fabian Bigham.

"We were introduced once or twice. Although an operations manager at the head office, he was not a popular one at all." Gwen lowered her voice. "Graham knew him professionally, but I wouldn't say they were friends."

"Poor man. I hate it when people die during a cruise."

Gwen and Sarah worked together to move the body into the ship's morgue. Sarah shivered when they entered the cool room. As an American citizen, Fabian Bigham's body would be transferred to the US for a detailed postmortem unless one was requested before they got there.

Raggie, the medical centre's indispensable steward, joined them and helped move the body into one of the refrigerated drawers.

"Thank you, Raggie," said Sarah.

"No problem. I've ordered a tray of hot drinks for the patients in the infirmary and snacks for you because I know you won't have eaten properly with all that's gone on."

"You're a gem, Raggie," said Gwen.

The tall Indian man's beaming smile was always a boon when they were busy. He anticipated their needs and made sure they took care of themselves. Leaving, he closed the door behind him.

"I don't like to believe a member of our staff is a poisoner," said Gwen as they pushed the drawer closed.

"Me neither. We can always hope for Rachel's instincts to be proved wrong for once." Sarah sealed the bag of belongings, ready to be stored with the purser until the time came to remove them from the ship. They would keep the shirt separate in case it was needed for evidence.

Gwen lowered her voice, although the only other person in the room was inside a refrigerated drawer. "Graham is gutted about Manfred Heinrich being in the brig. He's been treating him for depression."

Jason had popped into the infirmary earlier to speak to the two patients admitted. He told them the mixologist had been moved to the brig as a precaution. Bernard and the ship's junior doctor, Janet Plover, were collecting samples from the cocktail shakers and opened bottles to send away for analysis when they reached Bangkok.

"I can't believe anyone would do such a thing. It

could still turn out to be dodgy prawns and Manfred will be exonerated," said Sarah.

"We'll find out soon enough. If you take blood from the two in the infirmary, Brigitte and I will visit the other passengers who took ill and returned to their staterooms. While we're at it, we'll request some random stool samples from four of them to test for bacteria and viruses. The passengers can drop them down here whenever they're done."

Sarah didn't normally wish for a viral or bacterial outbreak on board ship, but it would be preferable to the alternative.

When she got to the infirmary, the two patients no longer complained of pain and neither of them felt sick. Sarah went to see Nat, the assistant cruise director, first. It was the first time Sarah had seen Nat with her hair down. She tended to tie it up in a tight bun, but now loose waves of black hair hung around her shoulders. The thirty-four-year-old originally joined them from Spain. Sarah envied her smooth olive skin. Nat's dark brown eyes were staring into space. The woman, renowned for being a bundle of energy, at the moment appeared drained.

"How are you?"

Nat jerked to sit up straight. "Back to normal. I don't know why I was admitted in the first place."

"Sorry, Nat, but Dr Bentley doesn't want to take any

risks. And that applies to staff and passengers. Do you mind if I take a blood sample? We need to run some tests."

"That's fine. But then can you let me out of here? I've got loads of work to do." Sarah glanced at the thick notebook as Nat grabbed it from the bedside table. Another of Nat's skills had to be her meticulous planning and attention to detail. As far as events were concerned, she left nothing to chance, ensuring everything ran flawlessly. Sarah wondered if the rumour that Nat knew the ship's itinerary by heart was true.

"I expect Simon's got it under control for now," said Sarah, applying a tourniquet to Nat's upper arm.

Wrong thing to say. Her patient huffed. "And I'm sure he hasn't. Don't let that man fool you. He's incapable of running any entertainment without me being two steps ahead of him."

Sarah drew blood from Nat's vein into the sample bottles before loosening the tourniquet, removing the needle and applying pressure over the site. "He appears perfectly capable to me." In contrast to Nat's dedication, Sarah knew there were rumours that Simon took credit for his assistant's work, but she hated backbiting, especially among those who were supposed to be working on the same team.

"He's capable all right. Capable of looking attractive,

that's what he is. His only job tonight was to ensure the cocktail event ran smoothly and to give a little spiel. Well, we know how that went, don't we?"

"We can't hold the cruise director responsible for a sickness outbreak," said Sarah. "That's beyond anyone's control."

"If that's what it was, but it wasn't, was it?"

Sarah hesitated. "We're not sure yet."

Ignoring her, Nat went on, "I tried to tell Simon how much Manfred Heinrich's strange behaviour bothered me, but as usual he ignored me. Too busy flirting with rich passengers. I would have gone to the hospitality manager myself, but I was too busy doing Simon's job." Nat's words were running into each other with anger. "As usual," she added for good measure.

Sarah lowered her voice, not wanting to alarm the passenger in the bed opposite. "What concerned you about Manfred's behaviour?"

"Shifty... angry... I don't know... you witnessed what happened... work it out!" Nat, riled, was getting louder. Sarah had only ever come across the approachable and efficient side of the assistant cruise director. The person in the bed was unrecognisable compared to her usual self.

"Keep your voice down; we don't want to alarm passengers," said Sarah, firmly, lowering her own voice. "If Manfred did anything, and we don't know he did, nobody could have imagined he would do anything to harm the passengers and crew."

"Maybe not. But Simon should have sent Manfred off duty, or at least spoken to his manager," Nat mumbled.

"Did you eat anything at the party?" Sarah asked, picking up her clipboard. Having bagged the blood samples, she made a few notes and noted recordings from the monitors.

Nat shook her head. "No. You know what it's like on changeover days. I didn't have the chance to eat much today at all, a few prawns from one platter that returned with food still on." Gone was the angry version of the assistant cruise director, who was speaking more like her usual self.

Changeover days were challenging for most of the crew as one set of passengers disembarked in the morning and a new lot boarded from lunchtime onwards. The medical team was always busy collecting and scrutinising health questionnaires from those joining the ship, as well as topping up supplies. For the entertainment staff like Nat and Simon, their duties included saying goodbye to one lot of passengers and greeting the next group. Although Simon had abandoned ship, boarding a helicopter two days before. His excuse about having work to do ashore could have been a ruse. Sarah wondered whether he was just skiving while Nat did the hard work.

Changeover days were also horrendous for stateroom attendants, as well as kitchen, bar and waiting staff, who bore the brunt of the work. Still, it was something they were all used to and, on the whole, handled with military precision. "What about drinks? Did you have anything to drink?"

"I managed a slurp of water whenever I got the chance. It's important to stay hydrated."

"And you didn't drink any cocktails?"

Nat's eyes almost popped. "Oh, I see what you mean. Now you mention it, I inadvertently sampled Manfred's supposedly famous version of a Poisoned Paradise. Everyone raves about it but in view of tonight's events, I think that might be better renamed. I thought it was cranberry juice because I found the glass next to the soft drinks. To be honest with you, it tasted disgusting, but then I don't drink alcohol. I spat it out in the sink when I realised it contained alcohol. A lot of good that did me." Nat folded her arms across her chest.

Staff weren't allowed to drink on duty, so Sarah would have to take Nat at her word. She'd never seen Nat drink alcohol, but in this case, she'd suffered a disproportionate reaction if she only drank a mouthful of a poisoned drink and spat most of it out. Her heart leapt with optimism. "Perhaps it was the prawns, after all."

"Let's hope so. As much as I don't like Simon's

laziness, I'd hate to see him getting into trouble over what happened tonight."

Nat's tone lacked sincerity. Sarah suspected the other woman would be delighted if Simon got into trouble and she got recognition for all the hard work she put in. Sarah didn't take to Simon herself. She felt him far too familiar with passengers, focussing on the wealthy as Nat had pointed out, but it made him popular. This was the first time Nat herself mentioned he took credit for her hard work. The assistant cruise director usually raced around like a chicken on steroids and seldom stopped, other than to exchange a pleasant hello. Her usually outgoing and friendly air must have recently taken a beating.

Sarah didn't know the assistant cruise director well, but what she knew she'd been impressed by. Gwen carried out the senior staff health checks because Sarah, Bernard and Brigitte were kept busy enough tending the rest of the crew. The doctors carried out officers' checks, including hers along with the other nurses. Staff health was one of the cruise line's priorities and it took its responsibility seriously.

"I'm glad you're feeling better. Dr Bentley will be back soon. I'm sure he'll be happy to discharge you so you can return to work. Although it wouldn't do you any harm to take advantage of the rest."

"If only that were possible, but the night has only just started for us."

Sarah left Nat scribbling in her notebook and went into the back room, where she placed the blood samples in the test-tube rack before going back to the infirmary.

"How are you, Miss Platt?" Georgina Platt insisted on being called Miss, despite her records stating she was married.

"I'm much better now, thanks. Do you think I'll be allowed to leave soon?"

"I don't see why not. Would you mind if I take a blood sample from you?"

"Go ahead." The patient held out her arm, lowering her voice and gesturing with her head to the bed opposite. "I wouldn't want to work with her boss. He sounds horrible."

Sarah hid her irritation at Nat for being so loud. "People sometimes say things when they are not well. They don't always mean them."

"If you say so." The patient looked sceptical but said no more.

Sarah hurried on with her task before saying, "Dr Bentley will be here soon to check on you. You'll be able to ask him if you can be discharged."

"Good, because I didn't take out insurance. Mind you, if it's the cruise line's fault, I won't be charged, will I?"

Sarah suspected Miss Platt's assumption was correct. However this went down, the passengers were unlikely to be charged medical fees. She returned to the lab to put the two sets of blood through their specialist testing machine. The ship's medical centre boasted equipment that tested blood and urine for routine discrepancies, but not for toxicology. Sarah would have to keep some blood back for when they arrived in Bangkok. Staff and crew underwent regular drugs screenings, and those samples weren't tested on board ship. At this rate, they might need additional equipment.

9

Rachel left the Jazz Bar, her mind still preoccupied with thoughts of Fabian Bigham's suspicious death. She strolled through the ship's atrium looking for Carlos. The grand space was quieter, with most passengers either enjoying the nightly entertainment, or settling into their rooms.

Rachel noticed Danny Martinez hunched in an armchair, engrossed in a handheld device, his face twitched as his thumbs moved in rapid succession, participating in whatever scenario was playing out on the screen. *So much for taking a walk,* she mused. But she had more pressing matters on her mind.

She finally gave up searching the ship for Carlos and headed back to their stateroom, her mind still reeling from the events of the evening. Could it be possible another murder had occurred on the ship while she was sailing? Dark blue, plush carpet muffled her footsteps as she made her way along the well-lit corridor. The gentle rocking of the ship created a soothing contrast to her tumultuous thoughts.

She slipped her keycard into the lock and entered their stateroom, only to find Carlos hunched over his laptop, deep in concentration with an AirPod in his left ear. The glow from the screen illuminated his face, casting shadows that stressed the furrow of his dark, concentrated brow. Rachel tiptoed behind him, a small smile playing on her lips as she began massaging his shoulders, working out the knots of tension.

Carlos froze for a millisecond before relaxing. "I hope that's my wife behind me," he quipped, his voice warm with affection.

"You should remember I'm a karate black belt," Rachel teased, leaning down to place a soft kiss on his head, "so if you're expecting anyone else, you'll both be sorry."

As she lifted her head, her gaze fell on the image displayed on Carlos's screen – an attractive woman with long, raven hair and striking features.

"Who's that?" Rachel asked, curiosity piqued.

Carlos stood, stretching his arms high above his head as he worked out the kinks from sitting too long. "One of the many candidates for my missing person," he explained, excitement creeping into his tone. "The idea came to me when the musical duo we'd heard earlier were playing in the atrium. What if Emily Graves is a musician on board?"

Rachel raised an eyebrow, replying sceptically. "Because she played the guitar when she was a child."

"Exactly!" Carlos grinned, his enthusiasm contagious. "So far I've traced around a dozen women of the right age who are among the regular musicians. If I kick off by eliminating each one of them, I can move on to singers, dancers or any others in artistic roles where she might be employed."

"Sounds like a plan," Rachel agreed, "but don't forget, she could work in any number of other jobs – she might even be an officer or engineer."

"I know, I know," Carlos sighed, running a hand through his hair. "But I have to begin somewhere. Call it a hunch."

Rachel wasn't convinced someone in hiding would take on such a public-facing role, but if she'd changed her appearance, Emily might feel confident enough to hide in plain sight. "Okay, absolutely. Start with what you know. Tell me if you need any help." Rachel stifled a yawn, the exhaustion of the day finally catching up with her. "But, in the morning. Right now I need some sleep."

Carlos's expression sobered. "Jason kindly passed on your message. He told me what happened after we left. At least your parents are blissfully unaware for now."

At the reminder of the incident, the weight of the evening settled heavily on her shoulders once more.

She sank onto the edge of the bed, her earlier smile fading. "I'm afraid we might have to tell them," Rachel admitted quietly. "Fabian Bigham is dead."

Carlos raised a concerned eyebrow. "Yes, Jason told me. Are you suggesting that because you think someone murdered him, you'll be interrogating your father in the morning?"

She detected a hint of amusement in his voice, but his eyes were filled with worry as he sat beside her and pulled her gently into his arms. "Are you sure you want to become embroiled in another investigation? Jason says Waverley's already got someone in custody. Nobody else needs to be involved. Especially not––"

Rachel didn't let him finish. "Me... I know." Frowning, she pulled away from his embrace and walked into the bathroom to start her nightly routine. As she began removing her makeup, she called over her shoulder, "Jason mentioned Waverley's put Manfred Heinrich in the brig as a precaution, but that suggests a random killing with no motive. The more I think about it, the less convinced I am. Several people disliked Bigham, and any of them might have wanted him dead. Not to mention these people were also at the cocktail party."

Carlos appeared in the doorway, leaning against the frame, his eyes examine her. "Such as?"

"Evie for one," Rachel muttered, facing his gaze in the mirror as he moved behind her. "Although she took ill herself, and I doubt she'd poison her own drink. But I got the impression his death bothered her more than she admitted."

"Did you break the news?"

"No."

"But it's an understandable reaction. Not everyone comes across death as often as you, or even I, do."

"I met another couple of people tonight who, despite denying it, gave the impression they were lying about not knowing him."

"Oh?" Carlos stroked his chin thoughtfully. "Jason said Fabian Bigham was a bigwig who worked for Queen Cruises. An operational manager or something like that, from head office."

"It makes sense with the way people kowtowed to him. But let's face it, anyone who came across him might want to kill him."

"Now, now. Don't be so harsh. Remember how well he got on with Brendan?"

Rachel paused, shaking that reminder from her head. Instead, she recalled her evening conversations. "A retired blogger, a woman about Evie's age named Linda Parker, joined us while we sat in Creams. Evie fancied a hot drink, so I joined her and her bridge partner, Danny, in Creams. He's a nerdy-looking guy who came across as a little awkward and is obsessed with video games. Linda broke the news about Fabian Bigham's death and openly admitted the man wanted to shut her up because she writes negative blogs about Queen Cruises. What if she shut him up instead?" Not waiting for a reply, Rachel continued, "The woman didn't even try to hide her pleasure at hearing about his demise. Positively celebratory, in fact."

Carlos frowned. "Which makes it unlikely she's the one who killed him."

"Maybe, but some people can't seem to help themselves when it comes to gloating. She might have been less guarded since she knew about the mixologist's arrest." Rachel shrugged. "That, and the fact she was plastered."

"I see. You mentioned someone else caught your interest?" Carlos prompted.

Rachel dried her face with a towel, having concluded the makeup removal routine. "Before Linda arrived, Evie mentioned rumours swirling about drinks being spiked. Danny thought a member of staff might be responsible. He denied knowing Bigham, but something in his eyes and manner after Linda Parker broke the news to Evie suggested he might have. Or maybe he's another person who has an aversion to people dying. I'm convinced Bigham didn't die of a heart attack. He can't have been any older than my father."

"People of his age, and younger, die of heart attacks, Rachel. And bearing in mind how much of a stress-head he was, he's a prime candidate. Granted, what went on this evening was unusual."

"Thanks for entertaining the idea, at least."

Carlos exhaled heavily, his shoulders sagging. "It appears I'm not the only one who's going to be working during the cruise. I wonder if we shouldn't both back off and just enjoy the holiday. I'd hate us to ruin your parents' anniversary celebration for the sake of our curiosity."

"You mean my curiosity," Rachel corrected, walking past him, back into the bedroom. "You're the one who took on a formal job."

"Believe me, darling, I'm beginning to wish I hadn't. Now I've given it more thought, something about this case worries me." Carlos followed her into the room, pouring himself a glass of water. His voice was low, and his expression troubled.

Not for the first time since Carlos told her about his new client, Rachel felt a flicker of unease. "Are you worried your Mr Graves has an ulterior motive for tracking down his estranged daughter?"

Carlos nodded slowly. "Something doesn't sit right. Why did they run away? Why did Emily keep in touch with her grandmother and not her father? At first, I took him at his word, but now..." He trailed off, shaking his head.

"Has something happened?" Rachel asked, her concern growing.

Carlos grimaced, a look of reluctance crossing his features.

"Don't hide things from me, Carlos," Rachel insisted, her voice soft but firm. "That's not who we are. Not anymore."

He sighed, meeting her gaze. "It's just an inkling, and I have no evidence, but I'm uneasy. I keep thinking someone's following me."

A knot formed in Rachel's stomach. "Are you sure you're not being paranoid? Remember, more often than not, it's you who trails people, not the other way around."

"No, I'm not sure, which is why I'm hesitant to mention it. And yes, I could be paranoid. You understand how it is." Carlos's eyes were haunted, and Rachel's heart ached for him.

She did understand. Some of the high-profile cases she'd been involved with of late exposed traitors in the ranks, leaving her uncertain of who to trust. Carlos had been her rock, a sounding board through it all. They both sat on the bed and she took his hand in hers. "We'll be on high alert. If someone is stalking you, we need to find out who and why."

"I could be wrong," he admitted, offering a weak smile. "Your mum would say my brain's addled from jet lag."

Rachel laughed softly. "Right now, Mum reckons everything results from jet lag." She squeezed his hand.

"If someone is shadowing you, do you think it's related to your client?"

"It's a high probability."

"What are you going to do about it?"

Carlos's jaw tightened with determination. "Carry on looking for Emily for now. I can't refuse a job or give up on it over a hunch any more than you will stop trying to find your poisoner."

"If one exists," Rachel reminded him. "Maybe we're both becoming paranoid. If it weren't for me, Sarah and Dr Bentley would lean more towards the stomach bug option for the culprit."

"Jason reassured me he trusts your instincts, although to my inexpert eye, it looked that way. It makes more sense that a bunch of people got a touch of food poisoning than someone poisoning anyone. Maybe the only poisoners around here are a bunch of dodgy prawns," Carlos chuckled, but doubt clouded his features.

Rachel sighed, troubled by the possibility that the wrong man might have been hastily locked in the brig because of her concerns. "I'd agree with you if Fabian Bigham hadn't died. You didn't witness him at his worst, Carlos. That man could cause enough trouble among strangers to make one of them want to punch him. How much worse could he be to people who crossed him? He spoke to a woman on the phone as if she was dirt.

Honestly, I'd never seen him before, but one encounter created an intense dislike."

Carlos stroked her arm. "Which is so unlike you."

"Let's go to bed and see how we feel about everything in the morning. I might not need to tell Dad his old friend is dead." Even as she said the words, Rachel didn't sound convincing to herself, let alone Carlos.

Once they were settled beneath the covers, the gentle hum of the ship's engines sang a soothing lullaby. Rachel tried to relax as she snuggled down, but her mind continued to churn over the threads of the evening. She tried to make sense of her tangled thoughts – Fabian Bigham's death, the illness that struck people at the cocktail party, her father's connection to the victim, and the potential suspects who appeared to be hiding something. Could it all be a figment of her overly suspicious imagination?

And then Carlos's case of the missing heiress and the shadows that could lurk behind his client's motivation for finding his long-lost daughter. Was someone following Carlos? She hoped not.

10

"Phew! I feel better for that." Rachel paused to catch her breath after jogging thirty laps around deck sixteen.

Carlos drew to a halt next to her, leaning on the rail. They gazed upon the South China Sea. "I love how peaceful it is at this time of the morning wherever you are in the world. It's a good thing we were up early though. It's going to be a hot one."

With her hair tied into a ponytail, the heat already burned into the back of her neck and shoulders. "Captain Jenson said it would be in his announcement last night, and he's always right," she replied.

"And so he should be with some of the best technology at his fingertips."

"Who needs a sauna when you've got weather like this?"

"At least our stateroom and everywhere else indoors is air-conditioned. I hope your parents got a decent night's sleep."

"Me too. Dad wouldn't admit to it, but he looked exhausted when you left."

Rachel felt revitalised, having decided in the early hours of the morning not to bring up Fabian Bigham's unexpected death to her father and to put it all behind her. Whether or not foul play was involved, it wasn't for her to investigate or to interfere in any investigation the security team might carry out. Time to enjoy the holiday of a lifetime with her gorgeous husband. A new determination to enjoy the rare time they got to spend together filled her with relief. Joy swept through her as she inhaled the warm sea air, in deep through her nose, and exhaled again.

They stood in comfortable silence, transfixed by the calm sea view and their thoughts. The only thing they needed to worry about was Carlos's missing-person enquiry. On that, she wouldn't hold him back. That wasn't how they operated, but Rachel hoped to persuade him to enlist Jason's help if he struggled to make progress. She understood his reluctance to do so, but he could work much quicker with a security guard's help.

"It's beautiful," said Carlos, almost mirroring her thoughts.

They were sailing north, cruising past the whole of

the east coast of Malaysia. The ship wouldn't be stopping until they arrived in Bangkok. The cruise included stops at two of Malaysia's west coast ports on the last leg of the journey before returning to Singapore. This morning the sea was as still as a millpond and the enormous ship cut through it with ease. Two days at sea after the long journey to Singapore lay ahead of them. With the events of the previous night being well and truly buried, Rachel looked forward to precious family time.

"I'm going to take a shower and get ready for breakfast. How about you?"

"A quick workout in the gym and then I'll join you."

"Okay, but don't be too long. Mum and Dad like to eat early."

"Be back in thirty minutes." Carlos kissed her before jogging towards the gym.

Rachel watched her husband, tempted to follow, but her parents would be waiting for her to call them. Taking another glance out to sea, her thoughts switched irritatingly back to the death of Fabian Bigham.

"Stop it Rachel," she scolded herself. "Bigham's death has nothing to do with you."

"I'm pleased you feel that way." Sarah's cheerful voice distracted her from the dilemma raging inside her head once more.

"Hey! It's lovely to see you up so early, but don't hug me, I'm all sweaty."

"So I see. I knew you wouldn't be able to resist your morning exercise even in this heat." Sarah had never been one for exercise, but she got more than enough traipsing around the ship attending medical emergencies.

"You know me too well. How was your night?"

"Busy, although we discharged the two patients admitted to the infirmary pretty quickly. Slight stomach upset, that's all. Did you mean what you said just now?"

"I hope so," said Rachel. "Honestly, I'd decided to, but I can't help believing Waverley has got the wrong person in the brig."

"If he has, I'm sure he'll realise soon enough. Not that we're certain anyone needed to be placed in the brig at all," said Sarah. "What makes you so certain someone poisoned the man?"

Rachel shrugged. "I'm not, but..." she hesitated while Sarah put her 'go-on-then' face on, "...it's just that... if you'd witnessed his behaviour like I did."

Sarah looked confused.

"The day before yesterday, while checking in to Raffles, he barged past me and created a right scene. He gave a good impression of being a bully, yelling at people and treating them like filth. If not for that experience, I might agree he died of a heart attack."

Instead of rebuking her and explaining that his behaviour could have caused him to have high blood pressure, Sarah nodded. "Graham hinted at something similar, but he wouldn't elaborate, not being one to speak ill of people, especially not the dead."

The fact that the kind Dr Bentley might agree with her assessment made Rachel more determined. "So you can understand why someone might have wanted him dead. I only saw him for five minutes and he made my blood boil."

"I understand what you're getting at, Rachel, but there are a lot of nasty people in this world, some of whom might be on board this ship, and they don't all end up being murdered. Not to mention that you must know from your line of work that it's not always unrighteous or bad people that are murdered."

Sarah could be right, but Rachel couldn't shake off the feeling someone killed him, despite her earlier resolve not to get involved. "Any updates on the prawns?"

"The illness had nothing to do with the food. It was meticulously prepared to the exacting standards the ship's chefs demand. None of the staff preparing or serving the food were ill, so it's unlikely they spread the illness. Most people who ate the prawns remained well, and a few of the people who got sick had eaten nothing at all. I hate to admit it, but the one common denominator appears to have been a distinctive twist on one cocktail—"

"Poisoned Paradise."

"How did you know?"

"Just an inkling."

"Did I ever tell you how exasperating you are at times?"

"Frequently," Rachel replied, smirking.

"But there could be something else we're not aware of. For example, how these people were when they came on board. Passengers aren't always honest when we ask them to complete health questionnaires before boarding, particularly when it comes to gastric symptoms. Seasoned cruisers know any such declaration means they would be confined to their cabins for a few days."

"Good point, Sarah. I'm sure your team will rule out any such link. With what you've just said about the Poisoned Paradise, it seems like a case of deliberate spiking of drinks. What do you know about the mixologist in the brig? My sources tell me he's the one who gave that cocktail his unique twist?"

Sarah bit her bottom lip, a sure sign she was stressing about something. "Don't let this go any further, and I didn't tell you, but he's being treated for depression."

"I see," said Rachel. "How bad?"

"Quite bad before Graham started him on medication. But his negative thoughts veered towards self-harm, not mass murder!"

Rachel remembered how unhappy the mixologist looked the night before. "Things can change. Has he responded to treatment?" Rachel wondered if a switch had flicked in poor Manfred Heinrich's head prior to the party. Or maybe he'd stopped taking medication. He wouldn't be the first.

"Graham thought he responded well to the medication and counselling – we have a counsellor attached to the team now to help staff through mental illness or stress."

"What a great addition. I'm surprised they didn't employ a counsellor before now."

"It was always left to the medics. You know. The idea being there's a tablet for everything, but modern-day medicine includes recognising that other therapies are just as valid as medication. The crew have rated the counselling service as one of the best new initiatives. However, if this turns out to be an instance of one of our own trying to poison passengers, Graham will take it badly. You know how much he cares."

"You all do, that's why you do the jobs you do," said Rachel. "I don't suppose Waverley would let me talk to the mixologist."

"Am I talking to the person who, minutes ago, said they would mind their own business?" Sarah put her hands on her hips.

"I know, I'm impossible."

"Well, I doubt he would let you anywhere near

Manfred. And you still haven't told me how you know about the cocktail in the first place? Don't say intuition if you want to remain friends." Sarah folded her arms, pouting.

Rachel chuckled. "*Best friends forever*, you know that. I know because another woman took ill last night before the lurgy spread wider. Carlos and I helped her and offered to call for a medic, but she insisted we didn't and flat out refused. After Bigham died, I remembered her and wanted to make sure there were no lingering effects. She'd let slip she liked to play bridge, so I tracked her down in the casino. It turned out to be a false alarm, but she invited me for a hot drink with her and her bridge partner. We went to Creams."

"Excellent choice," said Sarah. They often met in the patisserie themselves for heart-to-hearts when Rachel cruised.

"Her bridge partner, a guy named Danny Martinez, had witnessed more people taking ill. They each told me they drank Poisoned Paradises. Soon afterwards, another woman joined us, a bitter sort named Linda Parker, a retired blogger."

Sarah frowned. "I knew she was on board, although I don't know why she bothers. Her articles have nothing positive to say about the cruise line. If anyone's poison, she is. It's her first trip on the *Coral Queen*."

"I hadn't mentioned Bigham's death, but she informed us of the fact. Although she denied knowing him well, she mentioned him trying to muzzle her. Considering the man was barely cold, she didn't hold back her delight."

Sarah's face fell as she shook her head. "Why are people so cruel?"

"The only thing I can say in her defence was she'd consumed a lot of alcohol – read that as totally wasted. I got the impression Evie – that's the woman who took ill – and possibly Danny knew the dead man."

"Did they say as much?"

"No. They both denied it, but his death affected them."

"Not everybody takes people dying in their stride."

"That's what Carlos said."

"Come on, Rachel, please take your own counsel. This man's death is not your responsibility. Leave Waverley, Jason and the rest of the security team to get on with it."

Rachel struggled to accede now that her suspicions had been all but confirmed. Instead, she smiled. "Jason looked good last night. You've obviously got over the initial marital woes." An early issue with communication had led to misunderstandings, which Sarah used to struggle with. But they had got past it.

"We're happy. Sometimes I have to pinch myself, wondering what I've done to make me so lucky."

"You're both lucky. Not lucky, deserving. I'd better go down to my parents before mum sends out a search party. When will we see you?" Rachel wanted to ask Sarah to sound out the counsellor on their thoughts about Manfred Heinrich, but her friend would be annoyed if she did. And any counsellor worthy of their profession would be unlikely to breach confidentiality. She'd have to find another way.

"This evening. I was supposed to be off duty after the cocktail event last night, but things got out of hand."

"Usual place?" Rachel asked.

"Jazz Bar it is. I'll come up after the evening surgery. Me and Bernard are having dinner and a catch-up in the officer's restaurant. He saved up leave to go home for a week to visit his family. We dropped him in the Philippines and he flew into Singapore the day before yesterday."

Rachel beamed. "I know. We had a quick chat inside Raffles just before the Bigham episode. He was going out for 'proper' Chinese food, so we got little chance to talk. Not then or last night."

"I'm sure you'll get the chance. He loves seeing you, but you'd better expect some teasing with another death on our plate as soon as you join the ship."

"I don't mind, as long as he says nothing in front of my parents."

"I'll warn him. Give Susan and Brendan my love again. I hope to catch them later."

"If mum doesn't want to go to a show, you will. She's

determined to give me and Carlos space while getting the best out of her trip. Catch you later."

Rachel started the journey back to her stateroom. Carlos would be there before her at this rate. A cloud descended as she mulled over the cocktail link. Why couldn't she just let it go?

11

Carlos breathed in deeply as he strode toward the gym, the tension in his shoulders easing with every step. After their morning run, Rachel seemed more at peace than the night before. Her tossing and turning during the night told him she hadn't slept well, but since waking she hadn't mentioned the deceased once. He interpreted her silence on the matter as a positive sign and followed her lead, allowing the subject to rest. By the time he arrived at the gym, his muscles were less tense, optimism flowed through him. The cruise would be the balm they both needed.

"Welcome, sir!" The reception desk attendant welcomed him with a cheery smile. "Are you familiar with our exercise equipment, or would you like a quick tour?"

Carlos returned the smile. "Thanks, but no need for

a tour, I've cruised on the ship before and worked out in here."

"Excellent. If you could just sign in here, then." The attendant slid the guest log across the polished wood countertop and tapped his finger beside the empty line. "And your cabin number please."

Carlos scribbled his signature and cabin number, accepting the fluffy white towel on offer. With a nod of thanks, he walked towards the back, entering the exercise room. Rows of gleaming equipment beckoned, but only one person occupied the space, one he recognised.

"You should be careful. That's too heavy for a lightweight like you," Carlos called out.

Jason dropped the barbell with a clang and a grunt. "I'd like to watch you try, wise guy."

Carlos usually liked a challenge, but Jason's muscles were far more used to weight bearing than his. He preferred cardiovascular exercise to muscle bulking. He held his hand up in mock surrender, grinning. "I wouldn't want to show you up."

Jason's booming laugh echoed off the mirrored walls. "Yeah, right? You just keep telling yourself that."

The two men walked over to a pair of sleek Peloton bikes. They busied themselves, adjusting seats and handlebars, stowing water bottles in the containers and draping their towels over the handlebars before hopping on. As their legs pedalled and the wheels spun,

Carlos glanced sideways at Jason. "Dare I ask how things have been for you, security-wise? I mean, apart from last night's incident."

Beads of sweat formed on Jason's brow as they both picked up the pace. "It's mostly petty crime, wannabe smugglers, drunken bar brawls, that kind of thing. But still, it crops up more often than I'd prefer. How about you? Is PI life keeping you on your toes?"

Carlos nodded, fixing his eyes ahead as he maintained a steady pace now he'd reached his peak speed. "The cases have been routine lately, nothing too taxing. Lots of insurance fraud and scammers, suspicious spouses wanting proof of cheating partners."

"And are they?"

"Sometimes, yes. If I weren't so happily married, I'd give up on the institution of marriage."

Jason breathed out a laugh. "Yeah. We picked the best wives, that's for sure."

"We did." Carlos couldn't agree more. His eyes settled on his wedding band while his legs continued spinning. "I also get to track down drunk-drivers and burglars the police have given up on, plus tracking down stolen goods. A PI's job is never-ending. I'm glad my most dangerous case was history by the time Rachel and I tied the knot. That one could have put her in danger."

"I don't think you told me about it."

Carlos grimaced at the memories. "I worked

alongside a detective. It involved corrupt lawyers, police, a smuggling ring, trafficking humans and dogs, and murder." He frowned. "It took a lot of effort. Unfortunately the ringleader slipped away."

Jason puffed, his face reddening as their peddling gained momentum. "That's the problem with crime. It never stops, but I suppose it keeps the likes of you, me and Rachel in a job."

"And Sarah, to some extent," added Carlos. "I just hope he doesn't set up another network."

"At least Sarah can try to fix people. We just catch them until the next time. We cut off one tentacle and two more grow in its place."

"Blimey," Carlos slowed down, having reached his peak heart rate. "When did you become so cynical? Isn't that what the justice system is supposed to do these days? Rehabilitate people?"

Jason's grin returned as he, too, slowed down. "I'm not really cynical, but sometimes it feels that way. You'd be amazed to know how many thieves we caught last month alone. Some criminals come on cruises to target people while their guards are down. And that's not taking into account the issues with crew and some of those with false identities sneaking on board the ship to..." Jason raised his fingers in air quotes, "'work'. More realistically, to stay out of the way of the law back home."

Carlos's ears pricked up. "Is it easy to sneak on

board under an assumed name? I thought your protocols were rigorous."

Jason's cycling slowed to a steady pace, and he could talk easier. "It's not simple, but not as difficult as it should be. Fake IDs are state-of-the art nowadays, especially since the advances with AI. There are some excellent forgers out there who can manipulate the new technology."

"I don't doubt it. How do you catch them if they get past your checks?" Carlos frowned as he asked the question. Artificial intelligence came with a lot of benefits and could be helpful in many ways, but with every new invention, there were those who would use it as a tool for evil.

"We don't always. When you employ over two thousand staff and many of them move from ship to ship, it's like trying to spot one rotten starfish among thousands. Sometimes they commit a crime on board or are stupid enough to tell someone their true identity when they're blind drunk and later fall out with the person, then we catch them. That's happened twice."

Carlos rubbed down his face with the towel and placed it around his neck. "What sort of jobs do these people do?"

"It can be anything. Some positions require more in-depth background checks, so it's more difficult for anyone to pass those without slipping up, but not impossible. Staff who work with kids, casino staff and stateroom attendants are vetted a lot more closely than someone who works in the laundry, for instance. Almost all our passenger-facing jobs demand extra checks, but they're not foolproof."

"Would musicians and entertainers fall into that category?" Carlos asked, making his interest sound casual.

"To be honest, all the vetting is done by our land agents and head office, but entertainers and guest speakers are taken on and recommended via an agency."

"Do any of your musicians or entertainers have long-term contracts?"

Jason nodded after wiping his face and neck. "Some, yeah, but most of them are only here for a few months, or swap ships at different ports to join other cruises. They get the best of both worlds, travelling the world while getting paid for it. I wouldn't want their accommodation mind you. It's basic."

"So how many would you say have longer contracts?"

Jason raised an eyebrow. "This is starting to sound like an interview, Carlos."

"Sorry. I can't help being inquisitive. It comes with the territory." Carlos deliberated whether he should mention his secret mission, but Jason switched subjects.

"By the way, circling back to last night. It seems Rachel's hunch was on the money as usual. The mixologist has been receiving treatment for issues recently. The boss suspects he put something in one of the cocktails. We're not sure what yet."

"Are you sure you've got the right guy?"

"As much as we can be. He won't talk to us to confirm or deny, just sits in silence, staring at the wall. Dr Bentley or our on-board counsellor might get him to talk, but the chief's leaving him to reflect for now. We know for sure the people who took ill drank his specialist cocktail."

"I see. What about the dead man? Do you think he died as an unlucky consequence of your poisoner's actions?"

"Something like that. Unless he coincidentally died from natural causes. We can't rule that out until he's had a postmortem. The coroner can decide on that one."

"Will your mixologist be arrested when we get to Bangkok?"

"It's unclear. The boss got a late-night call from the head office last night. It seems they got an earful from his mummy back in Germany. They could be sending a couple of detectives and an expensive lawyer to meet the ship if the Thai authorities allow them to. It turns out Manfred Heinrich comes from a stinking rich family. Ironic, apparently, he joined the ship to get away from his mother's influence and now it's her lawyer who might stop him from being banged up in a Bangkok jail."

"Well, I wouldn't wish the latter on anyone. I've heard conditions can be harsh."

"Our crew know the rules when they take a job on board ship. Misdemeanours are not tolerated. If they want to get off lightly, they should choose an appropriate next destination before committing a crime."

Jason was just letting off steam. Sarah had rubbed away many of his rough edges, even getting him to meet – if not reconcile – with his estranged parents before their wedding. "You could have a point, my friend." Carlos brought his Peloton bike to a halt and climbed off. "I think my legs have turned to jelly. I'd better get back. Rachel's parents like an early breakfast."

The two of them left the gym together.

"Sarah's off tonight. I expect she'll join you in the Jazz Bar," Jason said.

"What about you?"

"I'm working, but I'll come over if I can. I won't be imbibing though," he quipped.

"Well, as you're a pillar of sobriety, that won't be a problem, will it?"

Jason wagged a finger at Carlos. "You're not going to tell me, are you?"

"Tell you what?" said Carlos, holding his palms uppermost.

"Why you're so interested in our musicians?" Jason grinned, slapping a sweaty hand on Carlos's equally damp shoulder. "Considering you're a PI, you're not nearly as skilled at subterfuge as your wife."

Carlos laughed. "I'm not sure whether to take that as a compliment or an insult. But as my wife is better at most things than I am, I'm not offended."

"Nicely ducked, Carlos. Catch you later."

Guilt pangs niggled Carlos for not letting Jason in on his secret, but he didn't want to raise any conflict of interest for his friend.

12

The morning flew past after breakfast. Rachel and family had explored the ship before dining in the Coral Restaurant for lunch. One of the chefs circulating paused at their table, much to Susan's delight. Her eyes brightened when he stopped.

A tall man, even without the chef's hat, and drop-dead handsome. He smiled at Susan, who blushed, and asked, "Is the food to your satisfaction?"

"It's delicious. Thank you, Mason." Susan's eyes, as keen as Rachel's, spotted the name badge.

"And you sir?" He asked Brendan.

"We haven't eaten food as good as this in a long time. Although my wife is a marvellous cook."

"I'm sure she is," said Mason.

He smiled at Rachel and Carlos. "My love of cooking

began at home in my grandmother's kitchen. Since then, I haven't looked back."

"Do you have a signature dish?" asked Susan.

"I have many creations, but I'm well known for my lobster symphony."

"Oh, I love lobster," said Susan.

"Me too," he said. "Enjoy the rest of your meal."

As Mason returned to the kitchens, Susan was positively drooling.

"Another five minutes and you would have been eating out of the palm of his hands," said Brendan, a teasing glint in his eye.

"You know how much I appreciate good food. He's a master at his art. I do hope we get to sample his lobster symphony."

"It probably attracts a surcharge," said Rachel, knowing full well they would eat the dish on the eve of her parents' wedding anniversary.

"Oh well. I'll settle for this." Susan tucked in to the rest of her meal.

Carlos and Brendan went for a walk after lunch because Susan wanted to attend a health lecture in the spa before going for a massage. Carlos and Rachel had gifted the massage to Susan as a late Christmas present. No doubt the men would find loungers and enjoy soaking up the sun for a few hours. Susan wasn't a sun worshipper and worried about Brendan's scalp getting burnt as his hair, according to Susan, was thinning, although Rachel disagreed.

Rachel happily sat with her mother through the health-food lecture presented by a lifestyle guru, although she suspected its ultimate aim was to sell supplements to those enthralled by the claims. The sylphlike woman giving the presentation certainly knew her vitamins and minerals.

"Our guru seems to take the weight loss topic to its limits. She's bordering on anorexic," Susan whispered while the rest of the group laughed at something the woman said.

"Shush Mum. Behave."

"Why? I'm on holiday. Besides, a friend told me before we left that cruise calories don't count."

"I'll get you a t-shirt with that slogan if you're not careful."

"I'd like that," she replied, smirking.

With half-an-hour to spare after the lecture, before Susan's massage, they sauntered toward the waiting room.

"Quick," said Rachel, spotting a man with a stash of the large supplements heading their way. "How about a cup of tea?"

"Lovely," said Susan.

Taking her mother's arm, they avoided the man and his horse pills and entered the treatment waiting area. One of the staff brought them a selection of herbal teas to choose from. Rachel would have preferred a strong coffee, as there hadn't been time for one after lunch. Being a fitness fanatic in every other way, she couldn't deny her mother the pleasure of an alternative to caffeine.

Susan flicked through the leaflet provided along with the talk while Rachel sipped an aromatic jasmine and lily tea, enjoying people-watching. Relaxing music oozed from the speakers buried in each corner of the room, adding to the relaxing ambience. After they drank their teas, Rachel strolled over to a water dispenser and poured them both a glass of cool water. On placing the glasses down on the table, she spotted Evie almost falling through the door, unaware it was a self-opener.

Quickly gathering herself together, Evie headed to the reception desk to book in whatever treatment she was having and turned around.

Rachel caught her eye and waved.

Evie smiled warmly. The shock of last night's events no longer registered on her face as she hurried across the room to greet her.

"Rachel! It's such a pleasure to meet a friendly face. I've wandered around all morning and have seen no-one I recognise."

Rachel stood up to give the woman a peck on the cheek. "Well, you have now. This is my mother, Susan. Mum, this is Evie, a lady I met last night."

"I remember," said Susan. "Would you like to join us?"

"If I'm not intruding, I'd love to," said Evie, hastily grabbing a seat as if afraid Susan might change her mind.

One of the reception staff brought Evie a cup of strong coffee.

Rachel stared, envious. "I didn't realise coffee was an option. We were only offered herbal tea."

Evie tapped her nose. "They know me of old."

"From your entrance, I didn't think you'd been here before," said Rachel with a chuckle.

"You mean the thing with the door? I always make that mistake. In my day, every door needed to be given a hard shove. I forget sometimes. Anyway, I don't touch herbal tea and only eat what's bad for me. I spent far too many years worrying about my weight when married. Now it's time to make up for it."

Susan raised an eyebrow but didn't bring up the health lecture they'd just attended, pushing the brochure into her handbag. She said, "You weren't well last night. Are you any better?"

"It was nothing. Your daughter kindly took good care of me. Where's your handsome husband this afternoon?" Evie asked Rachel.

"He's gone for a walk with my dad. Spas aren't his thing, but mum's having a massage soon."

Relieved when a receptionist appeared to take her

mother away lest Evie refer to the unfortunate demise of Fabian Bigham, Rachel relaxed again.

"See you in forty-five minutes," said Susan, following the beautician along a corridor.

"I'll be here."

After she left, Rachel resumed her conversation with Evie. "Are you booked in for a treatment?"

"Not today. I popped in to book a facial for tomorrow. It's good to take advantage of a bit of pampering on sea days. How about you?"

Rachel shook her head. "I'm not much of a one for spas. I'd rather go for a run."

"Good heavens! I can't imagine anything worse."

Rachel laughed. "It helps clear the mind."

"If you say so. Mind you, with your looks, you don't need a facial," Evie said, chuckling. "And from the looks of you, I'm assuming your husband never has to speak of your weight."

Rachel grinned. "He doesn't, and if he ever did, he'd regret it."

"A strong woman. I like that. Far too many of us pander to men's sensibilities and they never pander to ours."

Thankful Carlos didn't have the sort of sensibilities Evie might be referring to, Rachel grinned to herself. He wasn't perfect, but then, neither was she. "Are you sure you've recovered from everything that happened last night?"

A flicker of a frown crossed Evie's brow, and a sadness appeared in her eyes. "Just about," she muttered.

"You knew the man who died, didn't you?" Rachel said.

Evie's head shot up, her lips tightening, but then she sighed. "What's the point? There's nothing he can do to me now. Yes, our paths crossed decades ago. I haven't seen him in years, but I received a letter out of nowhere a few months back. He heard about my divorce. I don't know how, and he knew I took regular cruises. In his letter he informed me he also cruised regularly on business and suggested we take up where we left off." Evie spluttered out a laugh. "As if that was going to happen. I wrote back politely declining his offer and made it clear the first time was a mistake and a second time would be inexcusable." Evie's hands trembled as she clasped her handbag.

"From what you're saying, you were fond of him once," said Rachel.

"With my husband's sole mission in life to undermine me, I met Fabian at a vulnerable time in my life. He worked in London and at first said he missed his family. I was flattered by the attention. He made me feel like a woman again. I reckon he sensed how insecure and gullible I was, so he said all the right things. Until he got what he wanted and then he changed. An abominable man, he showed his true colours. They say some women always fall for the wrong men. Do you believe that's true, Rachel?"

"I've heard the saying, but if you turn it on its head, the truth is that some men are determined to take advantage of women when they're suffering."

"I prefer your version. You and your husband seem very happy."

"We are," said Rachel. It had taken her a long time to trust Carlos after her cheating ex-fiancé broke her heart, but that seemed a lifetime ago.

"Do you have any children?"

"Not yet," said Rachel, guilt pricking her. "It's not been the right time."

"I have two daughters and I would do anything for them. Most people change with time, but I don't think the passing years mellowed Fabian one iota." Evie looked into the distance. "I never should have replied to that letter."

"I take it he refused to accept the rebuff with good grace?"

"He threatened to tell my daughters about our affair. I couldn't let him do that."

"What do you mean?" Rachel's jaw dropped.

Evie caught her eye. "Oh, nothing like that, dear. I pleaded with him not to be so childish and explained how devastated my daughters would be if they imagined for one moment I'd been unfaithful to their doting father."

"What did he say?"

"He wrote back and suggested we talk about it during this cruise. The wretched man must have checked the passenger list. Linda can be acerbic, but her assessment of Fabian is spot on. He's no great loss to the world. I doubt even his wife will miss him, if he still has one."

"You looked upset when Linda told us about his death last night. Did you still care about him?"

"No. You see, when she said he was dead... actually dead... an enormous weight dropped off my shoulders. But the relief didn't last long."

"You felt guilty for reacting that way?"

"How perceptive you are, Rachel. Yes, I did. Watching Linda bitterly crowing over the man's death seemed heartless and inappropriate."

"Your feelings of relief are only natural, considering he was threatening to destroy the bond you have with your daughters."

"They're still daddy's girls, even though they understand why I divorced their father. There wouldn't be any such understanding if they learned I'd been unfaithful to the man they worship. The girls are all I have left in life. Along with cruising and bridge."

Rachel studied Evie closely, trying to penetrate behind the eyes. Could she be a killer?

"You didn't say whether you agreed to meet him."

"Against my better judgement, I sent a note via the cruise line when I arrived in Singapore."

So that was the urgent message Fabian had been demanding, thought Rachel. "What would you have said if you had talked?"

Evie shrugged. "I'm done with being pushed around by men, so I would have told him to do his worst, hoping against all hope that if he thought he didn't have leverage, he would leave it at that."

After revealing her fear of alienating her daughters, doubts flooded Rachel's mind about Evie being so daring. But then she played bridge. "Isn't there a quote about life's mistakes that comes from bridge?"

"You're thinking of, 'It's not the first mistake that gives you a bad board, it's the second.' Having witnessed Fabian's behaviour from a distance at the cocktail function, I doubt he would have accepted the rejection. So yes, I would have needed to play a convincing hand. Fabian looked more bitter than ever, and so angry. Nobody else knows about the affair, Rachel, and I'd like to keep it that way. You've been so kind to me since we met. I felt I owed you an explanation."

"Is that the only reason?" Rachel asked.

"The other is more selfish. Sometimes offloading to a stranger is so much better than speaking to a counsellor... and a lot cheaper." Evie guffawed, but the laugh sounded hollow.

Evie hadn't been high on Rachel's list of suspects

because she took ill, affected by whatever the cocktail contained. Rachel had also warmed to her. But what if Rachel had become an unwitting opponent in a high-stakes game of strategy? She couldn't ignore the gambling side of her new friend's personality. Still, it sounded as if she'd survived a difficult marriage and come out fighting, so she should have been capable of managing the Bigham situation.

"Your secret's safe with me." *For now,* remained unsaid.

"Thank you, Rachel, and thank you for listening. Now I'd better go. I'm joining Linda for an ice cream."

Before any opportunity arose to ask how Evie and Linda had suddenly become best friends when Evie seemed less than pleased to see the other woman the night before, Evie left. A warm burst of air accompanied her departure into the sunlight beyond the privacy glass of the air-conditioned spa. The weather outside was heating up. Rachel returned to her own thoughts, hoping Evie wasn't taking her for a fool.

13

"Look! There's Orlando Kearney," said Brendan. "If you don't mind, Carlos, I'd like to pick his brains while Susan isn't around. She'd tell me not to bother the man."

Orlando sat at a table beneath a parasol with a glass of iced tea on the table in front of him. His shoulder-length blond hair was tucked out of the way behind his ears. His informal knee-length plaid shorts and black vest revealed tanned arms and legs. If they hadn't met before, Carlos would have taken him for a man enjoying a holiday in the sun rather than one on a business trip. As they approached his table, he placed the sun cream he had been applying to his arms on the table next to his tea.

Carlos wondered whether to excuse himself and continue his search for his misper. Rachel's term for his mission made him smile. He wanted to get on with it, but Brendan might need moral support, so Carlos accompanied him, hoping the amicable man wouldn't object to the intrusion. His concern turned out to be unnecessary. Orlando's eyes crinkled in a warm welcome when he saw them.

"Hello again," he said, standing up to shake their hands. "Are you enjoying the weather?"

After shaking hands, Brendan removed his hat and sunglasses. "The temperature's taking some getting used to."

"I know what you mean. I'm acclimatised now, but when I first moved to the States from England, it took a long time to adjust to the weather in Florida."

"Are you working at the moment?" Brendan asked.

"No. A meeting I had's been cancelled. Can't say I'm sorry. The guy I was supposed to meet is a pain in the backside. Please join me."

Brendan didn't need a second invitation, and in no time, he settled into conversation, putting their host at ease with all the skills gleaned over the years as a man of the cloth. Carlos took a seat, but his concentration drifted in and out as the two men moved from small talk to saving the planet and the ambitious role ecology plays in that aim. On a couple of occasions, things Orlando said didn't sound quite right, but Carlos didn't have enough knowledge to challenge him. It made him wonder about Orlando Kearney's expertise. *Maybe*

Kearney's just a shrewd businessman who employs the right people to be the brains behind his operation.

"You have a huge undertaking ahead, I don't envy you," said Brendan. "Trying to transform these huge polluters of the seas to make them greener is no small task."

Orlando swished a hand, waving away the challenge. "My company is paid a lot of money to do just that and if anyone can do it, we can. We're committed to making it work."

Carlos paid more attention to what Orlando said and how he reacted. His voice and posture became more guarded as the conversation went on. The more interest Brendan showed in the micro-details of what he planned, the stiffer Orlando became.

"I'd love to see what you're working on at the moment," said Brendan. "As you might have guessed, I'm genuinely interested. In another life, I might have been a David Attenborough."

Orlando cleared his throat. "I've got a busy schedule, but maybe." He released a breath when a waiter distracted Brendan while clearing away the tea tray, asking him about his holiday and whether he could get him anything else.

Orlando wasted no time draining his glass and stealthily shifting his chair back so as not to disturb Brendan. He looked at Carlos. "It's been good talking to you both again, but it's time I got back to work."

"Thanks for your time," said Carlos. "Hopefully we'll see you around."

"Sure. You too." And then he scurried away like a man pursued by an unknown enemy.

By the time Brendan turned his head back to the empty chair, the nifty man was long gone.

"I went too far, didn't I? Handling my parishioners is easy. They're accustomed to me, but I'm not always good with strangers."

"You did fine. My guess is he didn't want to give away any trade secrets. Or maybe you have more knowledge of clean waste than he does." Something about Orlando Kearney bothered Carlos, but he chose not to mention it to the affable Brendan Prince. "He wouldn't be the first CEO to hide behind a mask of authority. I bet it's his scientists who keep his business afloat. Excuse the pun."

Brendan went quiet. The conversation had dampened his initial excitement at chatting to someone about a subject he followed passionately.

"Perhaps Orlando's not as friendly as he likes to make out," said Carlos.

"Thank you for trying to make me feel better, Carlos, but Susan's right. I ask too many questions. It started at theological college. In fact, I've been like it since childhood. Do you know the first thing I asked Susan when we met was what books she read? Imagine? Any other girl would have told me where to go. As a matter of fact, she said she would have done just that, but..." Brendan paused, his eyes faraway.

"Go on," Carlos encouraged.

"Our eyes met and something clicked. It sounds corny, but I knew from that instant she was the woman for me. She didn't rebuke me about my clumsy approach until a few months later."

"If it's any consolation, your daughter inherited your inquisitive nature and I love her for it."

"We are very similar, Rachel and I. Susan finds us exasperating at times."

"Don't you believe it. Your wife loves the way you're both wired."

"I'm grateful David is more like his mother. They're close. Did I tell you Amy is expecting their first baby? We're going to be grandparents. Although, as far as we're concerned, Samantha's our grandchild."

"She's turning into a great kid," said Carlos. He forgot sometimes that Samantha was David's stepdaughter. Amy's ex abandoned her as soon as she got pregnant.

"And she's so bright. David takes her to his garage during the school holidays. I swear that girl will know how to change an engine before she's ten."

Carlos grinned. Rachel's quieter and more serious brother loved his work and could talk about cars all day long. Carlos's classic Ford Capri gave them common ground to talk about; the glue that bonded them, according to Rachel.

David and Amy hadn't yet married, which could have been a bone of contention between him and Brendan, but Rachel's father was the least judgemental man Carlos had ever met. He and Rachel took their faith seriously, but somehow they lived it out rather than preaching it at people.

"Congratulations to you and to them. Does Rachel know?"

"I think Susan told her. At least I hope she did. I'm hopeless at remembering these things. As you can imagine, Susan's very excited." Brendan hesitated. "I'm sorry, I hope you don't think—"

"It's okay."

"Parenthood isn't for everyone. I, of all people, understand that. You'll never feel under pressure from me on that account."

So why did Carlos feel under pressure? "We both want kids, just not yet," Carlos said.

"Good." Brendan cleared his throat. "Susan should be done at the spa by now. Thank you for the gift. She appreciated it."

"No problem. You go on ahead, I'm going to stay outside for a while. If you see Rachel, would you tell her where to find me?"

"Of course. We'll meet you for dinner later. Thanks for keeping me company."

Carlos suspected Susan had put his father-in-law up to raising the subject of children when the opportunity arose. And he understood. His mother had been forever asking when she would be a grandmother. Italian families liked to be surrounded by kids. Although since his sister gave birth, all nagging seemed to be temporarily suspended. They wouldn't be pressurised from his side of the family for another year or so. He and Rachel discussed having children every so often and opted to wait, although, truth be told, he was ready.

For now, Rachel's job took all her time and energy. He resigned himself to the fact that if they were lucky enough to have children, he would be the stay-at-home dad. Or, as Rachel teased, their child would sit in the back of his car wearing dark glasses during stakeouts and be a private investigator while still in nappies. He chuckled at the thought. At least their dog, Lady, would keep them on the right path. She would remind them if the baby needed feeding or when to change a nappy. The image of Lady's nose raised in disgust when Carlos's sister, Sophie, and his brother-in-law, Gary, along with their six-month-old visited made him grin.

Moving away from the outdoor café, Carlos headed for the poolside entertainment. Time to continue his hunt for Emily Graves. Except he couldn't get started because his mobile phone was missing.

Carlos retraced the steps he and Brendan had taken earlier. He remembered stopping at the bow of the ship on deck sixteen to take photos of a dolphin pod. He must have put the phone down after they checked each other's photos. Or it could have slipped out of his pocket. Carlos walked up the two flights of stairs and arrived at the quiet area at the bow.

"There you are," he said to the phone when he saw it on the floor next to the seats where they'd sat to share and chat before continuing their walk. Carlos slipped the phone inside his cargo shorts pocket, buttoning it in securely. He turned to head back downstairs to the lido deck when a woman yelping stopped him in his tracks.

"You're hurting! Let go of me."

Carlos tracked the sound of the voices and, as he rounded the starboard side, he saw a burly man grabbing hold of a woman's arm, his face contorted in anger. The woman struggled, but he reached for her other arm, pinning her against the railing.

Carlos sprinted towards them, his heart pounding. "Hey! Leave her alone!"

The man glanced over his shoulder, his grip loosening slightly. The woman seized the opportunity, wrenching her arm free and stumbling backwards away from them.

"Mind your own business," the man growled, shoving his face into Carlos's. The smell of engine oil oozed from his blue overalls.

Carlos stood his ground, adrenaline coursing through his veins. "I suggest you leave the lady alone."

The man took another step forward, fists clenched. Carlos tensed, ready to defend himself. But after a moment, the man scoffed and stalked away, disappearing around the corner.

Carlos hurried to the woman's side. "Are you all right?"

She rubbed her arm, her face pale. "Y-yes, I think so. Thank you for your help."

Carlos nodded, recognising her as the gifted violinist from embarkation night. "You're welcome. Why don't we take a seat for a minute? You're in shock." As he helped the shaken woman to a nearby bench, he asked. "Who was that man?"

"Nobody." She blinked tears away from her eyes. "I mean, he is somebody. We saw each other for a while. He's annoyed because I broke up with him."

"You should report him to security. Would you like me to go with you?"

She shook her head forcefully, fear contorting her face. "There's no need for that. He wouldn't hurt me."

"That's not what it looked like to me," said Carlos.

"He just wanted me to listen to him, that's all."

"That's not the way to get a woman's attention, but if you would rather not report the incident, I'll go along with your decision. If it's any consolation, I think you did the right thing breaking up with him. If he rough handles you now, who knows what he might do if you stayed together much longer?"

The violinist forced a smile. "You might be right. Thanks again for your help."

She made to move, but Carlos delayed her. "I'm Carlos. I heard you play the violin last night at the sailaway do. My wife and I enjoyed hearing you play."

When she glanced at his hand for a wedding ring, she relaxed. "My name's Brandi... Brandi Chang."

"You're very talented. How long have you been playing?" Carlos asked.

"I played the violin as a child then took it up seriously in my late teens. My grandfather played, and he taught me at first. My mother's musical as well. I play multiple instruments."

"It's such a gift," said Carlos. "I'm hopeless and tone-deaf, but I know delightful music when I hear it. Have you worked on the cruise ship for long?"

"About eighteen months. It was supposed to be my big break..." a cloud formed over Brandi's face. She clammed up.

"Do you mind if I ask you a question?"

"Sure."

Carlos reached into his shorts pocket for his wallet and took out the old photo. "Have you ever seen this person? She would be around mid-twenties now."

Brandi didn't seem to look at the photo, her eyes glazed over. "Sorry I can't help you. Thanks again for rescuing me, but I need to go or I'll be late for rehearsal."

"Would you like me to walk you there?"

"No, thank you. You've done enough. Temsin won't bother me again. He'll be too scared you'll report him and won't want to lose his job."

"Okay. If you're sure, but if he approaches you again, tell your manager or a member of security." He almost said he knew some of the team, but something made him stop. "I hope to hear you play again."

"Bye." Brandi Chang hurried away into the safety of the internal recesses of the ship.

Carlos suspected Brandi recognised the girl in the photo, but he couldn't be certain. "Great timing, Carlos," he muttered. "The woman's in shock and you ask about a teenager in a faded photograph. She must think you're crazy."

Time to get to the poolside, although he wished he'd been able to explain to Brandi that he thought the girl in the photo might be a musician. Then he could have asked her about other musicians. Should he mention the boyfriend incident to Jason on the quiet? He didn't want to bring more trouble on the frightened Brandi Chang, but would her ex really leave her alone? Somehow, he doubted it, but he had told her he would respect her decision.

14

The poolside was packed when Rachel arrived. Music blared from the makeshift stage set up in the shade. She couldn't find Carlos near the outdoor café where her father thought he'd be, but it wasn't difficult to work out where to find him. She meandered along a narrow path through the crowds of occupied sun loungers until she found him standing by a pillar.

Rachel stepped up to him, wrapping an arm around his waist. "I thought you'd be here."

"Well, hello Mrs Jacobi-Prince." He turned and kissed her on the forehead. "Where have you been all my life?"

"That's so corny, Carlos, even for you."

"I guess I'm like your dad, then."

Rachel raised an eyebrow before saying. "Sounds

like some father-in-law to son-in-law bonding, has been going on."

He grinned. She loved the way his face softened when he looked at her. "He told me a story about when he first met your mother."

"And asked her what books she liked to read," Rachel said, laughing.

"Exactly. Did he mention we had a drink with Orlando Kearney?"

"No. Don't tell me? He grilled him about his work?"

"Says the woman who spends her life grilling people for a living."

"I guess dad does in a way too, but in a gentler fashion."

"I would hope so or his congregation would dwindle fast if he took, erm... a different approach."

Rachel squeezed his side. "What are you implying?"

"Me? Nothing. I wouldn't dare."

Rachel lowered her voice and moved in closer as the musicians paused between songs. "How are you getting on with your missing person case?"

"Nowhere really. I met Brandi, the violinist from last night, but didn't feel I could ask her too many questions."

"Why not?"

"Because I rescued her from an aggressive brute of an ex-boyfriend. A huge guy wearing greasy blue overalls."

Rachel examined his face and hands for grazes. "What happened?"

"The guy was being rough with her. I told him to leave her alone, and he did."

"Just like that?"

"Pretty much. We faced off for a few seconds, but he must have decided he didn't want to go two rounds with a man of my stature," he said, chuckling. "Or more likely he valued his job too highly to hit a passenger. I'm glad, because he was a lot bigger than me and his overalls reeked of engine oil. I wouldn't have wanted a stain on my favourite shorts."

"I'm sure my knight in shining armour would have held his own, but honestly, Carlos. I can't leave you alone for more than an hour without you getting into trouble. Remember the last time we cruised you got shot!" The memories of their honeymoon cruise were both painful and joyful. Which emotion ruled depended on the circumstances and, right now, happiness reigned.

"If we want to get into point scoring about trouble on a cruise, you'll lose. You've had far more mishaps on this ship than me. Besides, I washed away those painful memories when I joined you for the captain's dinner. Plus I don't need to remind you what happened during that cruise."

"Okay. Okay. You win." Her mood soured as she recalled the death of Fabian Bigham.

Carlos pulled her onto a vacant sun lounger, whispering in her ear. "Guess who's back at work?"

"Who?"

"Over there." Carlos motioned with his head.

Manfred Heinrich, the mixologist, circulated through the gaps between sun loungers, carrying a tray of cocktails effortlessly on his shoulder while one hand supported it. She exhaled. "So no poisoning after all. I really am on holiday."

Carlos kissed her neck. "Yep. Unless the guy's parents pulled some strings."

Rachel held her hand up to attract Manfred's attention.

"Cocktail, madam?"

"Yes please. What is it?"

"This one's a Tequila Sunrise, but I can get you something else if you prefer?"

"Do you have any mocktails? It's a little early in the day for me."

"Yes, madam. I'll bring the menu. What about you, sir?"

Carlos sat on the side of the lounger, pretend-pouting. "Just a coke for me, thanks."

As Manfred walked away, Carlos looked into Rachel's eyes. "You're not going to quiz him while he's serving drinks."

"Really? I'll see you in a minute." She leapt up and followed Manfred.

Manfred stopped a few times to dish out cocktails to other passengers, but when he arrived back at the bar, Rachel tapped him on the shoulder. He turned around. Surprised.

"I thought I'd save you two journeys. Could you go through the mocktail menu with me?"

Manfred clearly knew his stuff, able to explain in great detail what each of the cocktails contained, including the herbs used to infuse aromatic flavours. Rachel saw no sign of the dour attitude from the night of the VIP party. Perhaps he was just happy to be free. "Which one would you like to try?" he asked.

"The Little Sunshine please. Excuse me for asking, but aren't you the mixologist from the welcome aboard event last night?"

Manfred stiffened but continued mixing her order. "Yes."

"It's just that I met a lady who recommended the Poisoned Paradise. She said you gave it a unique twist. When will you be at the cocktail bar again? I'd love to try one."

Manfred shook his head. "We won't be mixing that cocktail again during this sailing. And I've been moved to help with serving. We're short-staffed."

"Is that because people took ill after drinking your cocktail?"

This time, Manfred gave her a hard stare. "That had nothing to do with me. Why are you interested?"

"Let's just say I'm an inquisitive bystander who doesn't believe you're to blame for that passenger's death. Can we talk somewhere quieter?"

Indecision crossed the mixologist's face. "I'm not sure... I—"

"I can help you," said Rachel.

"Over there." Manfred motioned his head towards a few empty tables in the shade. "I'll bring your drink over, madam."

Once Manfred arrived, Carlos was by her side. "What can you tell us about last night?" Rachel asked.

"I'm not saying anything until you tell me who you are."

"My name's Rachel and I'm an English detective. This is my husband, Carlos, who is a private investigator. It sounds as though you're still under suspicion and we'd like to help if we can."

Manfred's shoulders relaxed. "All I can tell you is that some people got ill after drinking the Poisoned Paradise. The security team believe I doctored the drinks but can't prove it. I think if someone added something to the cocktails, they set me up to take the blame."

"Why would anyone do that? Do you know who might have something against you?" Carlos asked.

Manfred shook his head. "No-one that I know of. The ship fosters a healthy rivalry, but what happened last night goes well beyond that. If I didn't know better, I'd suspect my mother was behind it."

Rachel's brow furrowed. "Why?"

"Because my parents – especially my mother – want me to follow in their footsteps. I've been brought up to be a direct replica of them. They're rich."

"But you don't want to follow in their footsteps?" Carlos quizzed.

Manfred shook his head. "Maybe one day I'll be happy to settle down and take over the family business, but they wouldn't let me breathe, so I chose a different path for now."

"Okay. So back to last night," said Rachel. "You say the security team believes the cocktails were spiked. Do you concur?"

"They must have been. The security guy said only those who drank my Poisoned Paradise got sick."

"Having ruled out your parents, what do you suspect the drinks were laced with and who might be behind it?"

Manfred looked at Rachel. His deep blue eyes darted from her to Carlos and back again. His hair was dyed black, judging by the light roots. "I think someone spiked it with an emetic. Sometimes people play jokes, especially if someone gets above themselves and starts lording it over others. They will drop a little dose of ipecac in their drink. They soon learn."

"By an emetic, you mean this ipecac makes people throw up?" Rachel asked.

"Or just feel sick. The symptoms last night fit with the effects of ipecac syrup. I looked it up. It comes from the Carapichea ipecacuanha plant and is easy enough to buy. With its syrup consistency, it's also easy to add to drinks. I reckon someone could have added that to my cocktail."

"But not you?" Carlos asked.

"Definitely not me. Making people sick is not my idea of a joke."

Rachel made a mental note to ask Sarah whether the syrup was stored on board and whether it could kill. "Let me get this straight in my head. You believe one of the crew randomly laced your special cocktail with an emetic syrup intending to get you into trouble? You must have made enemies on board for someone to do such a thing."

"I don't know of any. I keep myself to myself because I suffer from depression. It's just about under control with the tablets the doctor's prescribed, and a counsellor has been helping me. Whoever did this is sicker than I am, and they need to be caught."

"On that point, we agree, but it doesn't make sense. Who would stand to gain from making passengers ill and putting you in the brig?" Rachel felt there was more to this incident than they had been told. Either an enemy Manfred didn't know about meant him harm, or something else was going on which led right back to Fabian Bigham.

"As far as I know, nobody would gain. I don't have any rivals waiting in the wings to take over from me. There are many mixologists on board. I'm not important. I guess my boss could get into trouble over it, but that's unlikely. The only other guy who might get it in the neck would be the cruise director."

"Simon Peterson? Why?" Rachel asked.

"Because he went around recommending my cocktail to everybody. If I didn't know him, it might look like he orchestrated it. After all, he's responsible for overseeing guest events and people listen to him. But he wouldn't do something like that."

"Mm," said Rachel, although she didn't get it. Simon Peterson would gain nothing by recommending passengers try a drink that made them unwell. Quite the opposite. *Unless he's a sicko,* she thought, but Rachel had got him down as a narcissist rather than a Jekyll and Hyde character. "Just one more question. Why did they let you out of the brig?"

Manfred looked down at his shoes before looking up, bashfully. "Mother knows people on the Queen Cruises board. Her view on life is, as you English say, 'it's not what, but who you know.'"

"I see," said Rachel, thoughtfully.

"I should get back to work," said Manfred. "I hope

you find who did this because I want to get back to mixing rather than serving drinks. I'm good at it."

"Thanks for the help," said Rachel. "Just one more question. What's the word among the crew on the man who died?"

"Nobody's got a nice thing to say about him. I have met no-one who's mourning his loss. The night of the sailaway event he annoyed many people, including my musician friend. My parents knew him, but I don't think they will be sorry either. I haven't spoken to them yet. Best to let them cool down before I get in touch." Manfred scurried away with his empty tray, returning to the bar and collecting another full one before circulating among the passengers again.

"What do you think now?" Carlos asked Rachel, taking a sip of his coke.

"The situation could have been a practical joke which got out of hand if Manfred's right about this ipecac thing. If so, Fabian Bigham died from natural causes, unless he had a lethal reaction to it. Some things still don't add up. There's still the why?"

"Maybe Manfred's got an ex with a grudge similar to the guy I chased away from Brandi Chang."

"You didn't mention doing any chasing."

"Figuratively speaking." Carlos smirked.

"Hmm. I wonder if Manfred discussed his theory with Waverley. We need to ask Sarah if the ipecac story fits the picture of what happened."

"And if it does? Although it's a horrible thing to do, it's hardly high crime, so you could leave any further investigating to Waverley and his team."

Rachel wasn't ready to let it go. "It's the Fabian thing that bothers me. Now there's a man who had more enemies than friends. Did one of them take advantage of the sickness event, or did they already plan to kill him?"

"Or did he die of a heart attack?" Carlos said, sighing.

Rachel chuckled. "Or that," she conceded.

15

As they entered the Coral Restaurant and took their seats for dinner, Brendan appeared out of sorts. His eyes were distant and pensive. He had been quieter than usual when they met for pre-dinner drinks.

While Susan and Carlos busied themselves studying the menu, Rachel couldn't take her eyes off her father. Generally ebullient, this didn't fit with his normal behaviour. Carlos had told her about her father's conversation with Orlando and his rude dismissal of Brendan's extensive knowledge about waste disposal. But that alone wouldn't dampen Brendan's spirits. He wasn't so precious he would let that sort of thing bring him down. No, something else was bothering him.

I hope he opens up about what's troubling him over dinner, Rachel thought as she shifted her attention back to the attentive waiters and the menu.

The menu's extensive offerings, reflecting their current sailing location, held her concentration for a while. Rachel loved the way menus on the cruise ship adapted to wherever it was sailing to or from, but also included the stalwarts for those with less adventurous palates. The tempting array of dishes made choosing a challenge.

When Michael, their lead waiter, came for their order, Susan started them off.

"I'm going to have the Prawn Mee to start with and Sambal Udang for the main course, please."

Rachel smiled. "I'll have the same noodle soup starter, but the Sambal Stingray looks delicious." Rachel glanced at the dish being delivered to another table, catching the aroma at the same time. "I'll have that, please."

The waiter turned to Carlos. "And for you Mr Carlos?"

"Chicken satay followed by the Beef Rendang, thank you."

Rachel gently nudged her father. "Dad? What would you like?"

Brendan blinked, surfacing from his reverie. "I'm not very hungry. I think I'll pass on the starter and just have the stir-fried prawns, the same as my Susan, please."

Michael shook his head disapprovingly. Brendan took a sip of water. With Brendan in this frame of mind,

Rachel tried to push down fears he might be ill and not have mentioned it.

The wine waiter appeared, proffering a bottle of white wine. Brendan declined while Carlos and Susan accepted a glass each. Rachel opted for sparkling water, mentally earmarking a martini and lemonade for later in the Jazz Bar.

With the starters in front of them, Susan broached Brendan's sombre mood. "What is the matter with you tonight, Brendan?"

"Nothing. Why?"

"Don't give me that. You've hardly said a word since we sat down. Something's wrong. Are you unwell?"

Brendan sighed, settling down his water glass. He shook his head. "Sorry. I didn't mean to put a dampener on the evening, but I received some rather unfortunate news earlier."

"You never said," Susan scolded. "Did something happen to someone back home in Brodthorpe?"

"No, no, nothing like that. It's... Do you recall the man I introduced you to at Raffles? Fabian Bigham?"

Rachel felt herself holding her breath as Carlos reached for her hand, having polished off his satay.

"Your old friend from university?"

"Yes. Well, as I mentioned, he offered to give me a tour and treat us to a meal at a speciality restaurant during the cruise. We had arranged to meet today in the

Cigar Lounge. He told me he smokes a pipe these days," Brendan explained, "But he didn't show up."

"Perhaps it slipped his mind," said Susan.

Brendan shook his head. "No, he didn't forget. I went to reception and asked them to page him. The next thing I know, Sarah appeared. The lady at reception called Dr Bentley, but because Sarah knew me, she wanted to be the one to break it to me."

Susan put her spoon down, her soup finished. "Break what to you?"

"Fabian... he passed away. Seemingly he collapsed and died at the VIP party." Brendan looked at Rachel, his eyes dull. "They suspect he died of a heart attack."

"Oh, that's sad, I don't recall seeing him there," said Susan, reaching for his hand.

"Me neither. It must have happened after we left."

"Just when you had reconnected after all these years."

"I admit it's hit me hard," said Brendan.

A sombre hush fell over the table as the main courses replaced the starters.

As soon as Michael left the table, Rachel asked. "Had you kept in touch with your friend, Dad?"

"Not really. We were good friends at university, but Fabian was always more ambitious than me and not interested in religion. I was the only one with a car back then, and because I didn't drink much, I ferried everyone to and from parties. Fabian rubbed people the wrong way, to be honest. They found him abrasive, so he didn't have many friends. He tended to rein it in around me."

He hadn't changed much then, thought Rachel. "Did he say whether he knew anyone else on board?" Rachel asked.

"He worked for the cruise line, so he planned to meet with many people. He also told me he would see an old flame. Women always seemed to find him attractive, but I don't think he treated them as well as he should. He told me he had several business meetings to attend. He worked as head of operations for Queen Cruises, that's why he offered to treat us."

"Apart from the old flame, did he mention who else?" Carlos asked, prompted by a gentle kick under the table from Rachel. She didn't want her father to sense her eagerness to know more about Fabian Bigham's relationships.

Brendan scrunched his forehead, trying to remember. "It's possible one of the people he was seeing was Orlando."

"What makes you say that?" Rachel blurted out before she could stop herself.

"I put two and two together. Carlos and I had a chat with Orlando today—"

Susan exhaled. "Another thing you neglected to mention."

"Did I?" Brendan fiddled with his fork. "My

apologies. Anyway, Orlando told us a meeting with someone he disliked had been cancelled. I can't say for sure, but I suspect it could have been with Fabian."

"It makes sense their paths would cross," said Rachel.

"When I met Fabian at Raffles, he took me for a drink. I told you about that, didn't I?"

"Yes," said Susan.

"Oh good. Well, Fabian drank a lot of whiskey while I drank tea. He complained about a few people making nuisances of themselves."

"In what way?" Susan asked this time.

Brendan shrugged. "He didn't go into details, and I don't enjoy talking about people, so I didn't pry. A woman interrupted us. Did I tell you about her?"

"No," said Susan.

"You were saying about a woman?" Carlos steered the conversation back.

"Hmm? Ah yes. Well, this woman showed no love for Fabian either. I suppose he still got on the wrong side of people."

You could say that, thought Rachel, saying, "Was she the old flame?"

"I don't think so. He gave her a chilly reception, embarrassing to witness, to be honest. Fabian told me she was some sort of journalist who spent her life running down the cruise line. Later, while on my way back upstairs, she must have collared him again. I saw them having a heated exchange."

The cogs in Rachel's mind spun into overdrive. Her father had unknowingly corroborated some key details, both known and suspected. If the woman in question was Linda Parker, her omission of the argument when they spoke in the patisserie cast doubt on her innocence and could be a motive. Rachel already knew he had enemies beyond the crew. She still couldn't rule Evie out entirely, but knowing others existed made it less likely to be her.

"I think I met the woman you're describing during a conversation with Evie," said Rachel. "Late sixties, wild brunette hair, wears dark red, cat-eye glasses?"

Brendan nodded. "That's the one."

"She's a blogger." Rachel didn't want to add any further details or Susan would want to know how she knew so much.

"That's it! Although Fabian told me she had retired but continued writing negative stories about them. I can't see what she could write about. We've been treated like royalty from the moment we stepped aboard."

Susan patted Brendan's hand. "I'm sorry your friend is dead, Brendan, but from what you've said, I'm not sure spending an evening with him would have been that pleasant."

"You could be right, darling. It was just that seeing him again after all these years brought back memories of happy times... and youth... we always view the past through rose-tinted spectacles, don't we? It's also a shock. As a vicar, I deal with a lot of funerals and many in our parish have died, but he seemed so full of life... and more content than I remembered."

It's a good thing you didn't see him in the lobby, Rachel thought. She wouldn't want to destroy Brendan's fond, if not wholly accurate, recollections of Fabian. Despite his faults, the man had seen Brendan as a genuine friend, both past and present. And from the sound of it, his only friend, apart from the women, of course. Rachel felt proud her father brought out the best in the man, even on the day before his death.

Susan put her knife and fork down, patting her abdomen. "That meal was delicious. Now, Brendan. I think it's time to change the subject. But first we should drink a toast to your old friend before we move on to desserts."

"You're right. Thank you," said Brendan, looking happier now he'd offloaded the burden. He nodded over to the wine waiter to pour him a glass of wine.

Rachel found it difficult drinking a toast, even with water, to the man whose horrible behaviour she had witnessed. Also, knowing what she did about his threatening behaviour to Evie over a past indiscretion, didn't sit well with her. Brendan might not think so highly of his old buddy if he knew, but he always looked for the best in people, and she wouldn't take that away from him.

Brendan raised his glass, his voice thick with emotion. "To Fabian."

The words caught in Rachel's throat, emerging as a strained grunting sound. Carlos flashed her a reassuring grin, sealing his support with a tender kiss on her cheek.

16

Brandi Chang's frayed nerves threatened to unravel. Her slim figure trembled as she stood in front of the small, worn mirror on the wall of her cramped cabin. Gratitude for the solitude afforded by the lack of a roommate was fleeting. The earlier confrontation with her ex-boyfriend overshadowed everything. It left her feeling emotionally drained. Now she was like a fragile bird trapped inside a cage, and yearning for freedom.

She had enjoyed spending time with Temsin, having dated for the past few months but his persistent, albeit legitimate, questions about her background and family had become deeply unsettling and often ended in arguments. The last one being decisive.

"Why won't you tell me about your parents? Is it

because they won't think I'm good enough for their precious daughter?"

"Can't you just accept that we are having a good time?"

"A good time! That's all this is to you, isn't it? I'm in it for the long haul."

"Temsin, I'm not ready for anything like that."

"That's ridiculous. You're in love with me. Just accept it."

"You're not listening to me. I said I'm not ready."

Following the barrage of questioning, he had shattered her dream in a couple of sentences. "Why aren't you ready? Because your parents won't think I'm good enough, or because you think you're going to be some big sensation on the world stage? Face it, Brandi. That's never going to happen."

Feeling crushed, she had snapped. "I've been thinking it's time to bring this relationship to an end. We're not right for each other."

After noting a momentary glimpse of disbelief in his eyes which nearly stopped her, Brandi had realised there was no turning back. She hurried away from him and her feelings.

When Temsin had started to get serious, it had terrified her he might propose and force her to make an impossible decision. Either perpetuate the web of lies already woven or expose the dark truths that haunted her. Building a life on a foundation of deception would only lead to their inevitable downfall; the weight of her secrets would slowly corrode any bond they made. Yet revealing the grim realities from which she had fled, the dangers that lurked in the shadows, made marrying him or any man inconceivable. The oppressive dichotomy Brandi lived with threatened to suffocate her at times.

Taking several deep breaths, she tried to calm her frazzled nerves and regain her composure. If he couldn't believe in her dreams, then Temsin wasn't the one for her anyway. Brandi didn't intend to stay on the cruise ship once it reached America. There she would pursue her passion. But the unexpected altercation with Temsin left her shaking, churning up a maelstrom of doubts. Would he have hurt her? Could he be just like her father?

Blinking back the sting of tears, Brandi steadied herself, determined not to cry. The mysterious stranger, Carlos, and his sudden appearance jumping to her aid, only compounded her growing unease. Too many unfamiliar faces infiltrating her carefully constructed existence worried her, and her mother's cautionary words reverberated in her mind. *Trust no-one.* Of course, it was easy for her mother to say such things when she had no desire to remarry. But Brandi yearned for a life free from the constant need to look over her shoulder.

Fabian Bigham's promises to give her the world rang hollow. Her lips tightened as she recalled their last conversation, a stark contrast to their first. When he had talked her into joining Queen Cruises, he pledged to unlock doors for the talent she and Crystal had, promising they would be able to showcase their musical prowess in America. There, Brandi believed she would find safety – just another Brit in America, seamlessly blending in with the crowd.

With the changes made to her appearance, she could remain hidden. Temsin could never offer her the life she yearned for, a life where she would be in full control without the constant fear of being discovered. Besides, his aggressive handling of her put an end to any idea that he might be part of her future.

As she stared at her reflection, Brandi tried to push the unsettling events from her mind, instead focussing on her upcoming rehearsal with Crystal. Bigham had revealed his true colours the night before when she asked him where she and Crystal would play once they docked in New York at the end of her contract.

"I'm sure the cruise line will extend your contract. You don't need to worry about it."

"But that's not what you promised. You said that if I joined for three terms, you would set me up with an agent in New York."

"I don't remember saying anything of the sort. Why would you want to leave a decent gig like this? You're good, Brandi, but not that good."

He might just as well have slapped her in the face. "You gave me your word."

"Look. You did me a favour and filled a gap when Crystal might cause trouble."

Brandi recalled his conditions. She had found Fabian in a compromising position with her friend Crystal when Crystal had stayed overnight with her at a hotel in Barcelona. Brandi was coming to the end of her contract at the hotel, and when Crystal asked Fabian to get Brandi a job, Bigham feared Crystal would report him if he didn't. He promised them both new lives in America.

But last night, something had changed.

"That could still become an issue for you." Brandi hated stooping to such depths as to hint at blackmail, but she had been desperate.

His lips had curled in a snarl when he looked down his nose at her. "Do your worst. It means nothing to me."

The man had betrayed them, and now he was gone. If she'd listened to her heart warning her from the outset he was using them, he wouldn't have been able to hurt her. Her instincts turned out to be correct and Bigham got what he deserved.

She and Crystal would forge ahead with their plans without him. Once the ship docked in the States after this tour, they would slip away and start afresh. She couldn't allow the incident, or her feelings for Temsin, to distract her from her passion for music and the opportunity to showcase her talent without fear. With renewed determination, Brandi straightened her posture and smoothed her hair, determined to wear a brave face and not let the troubling encounter define her evening.

While brushing her long, dark tresses, her thoughts drifted back to the photograph the man named Carlos had showed her – an image of herself as a child. A snapshot from a time before she and her mother fled the tyrannical rule of her father. Thinking about it sent shivers down her spine, resurrecting buried memories and nightmares she had left behind.

Carlos had shown no signs of recognising her as the girl in the photograph, but why was he looking for her? The fear and uncertainty that used to plague her resurfaced. Brandi shook her head again. It was imperative she focus on the present and the solace she found in music, the one constant that allowed her to escape the shadows of her past, even if only for precious moments. She knew that dwelling on the photo and the implications it carried would only distract her from the rehearsal ahead, and she refused to let her father's looming presence rob her of the joy and purpose she found in her music.

She finished her grooming and lifted her head up high before heading toward the door. As she pushed down the handle, the door swung open with a violent force. Brandi froze, her eyes staring, her heart leaping into her throat as a figure lurched towards her. In the dim light of the cabin, she couldn't make out her attacker's face, but the menace in his movements was unmistakable.

Adrenaline kicked in and Brandi stumbled backwards, fight-or-flight taking over. Her hands grasped for anything she could use to defend herself. But the assailant lurched at her, his fingers closing around her throat, squeezing air from her lungs. Panic surged through her as she struggled to break free, clawing at his arms in desperation.

"Who... who are you?" she gasped.

Her attacker loosened his grip enough for her to draw a shallow breath. "Where is she?" he growled, his voice low and menacing.

Confusion clouded Brandi's mind as she struggled against his hold. "I... who?"

His grip tightened once more. "Don't play dumb with me. You know who I mean. Where's your mother? Tell me and this will go much better for you."

"My-my mother is dead," she choked out, desperate to protect her mother.

The attacker's eyes narrowed. "Then you're of no use to me."

As darkness encroached on the edges of her vision, Brandi's thoughts raced. At least they would never find her mother. She would die knowing the woman who had protected her and kept her safe could live in peace. Brandi resigned herself to her fate, always sensing this day would come. Her father never gave up; his relentless pursuit had finally caught up with her. This was it. Her swan song. There would be no grand performances on world-renowned stages, no fulfilling the empty promises Bigham made then broke. Her lifeless body would be discovered in the confines of this tiny cabin. Just another nobody lost at sea.

She wondered if anyone would mourn her passing. Would Temsin grieve, or would he move on, his questions forever unanswered? Would Crystal be stung by her absence? How would her mother take it?

Questions swirled in her mind as she mustered the last ounce of strength trying to fend off her attacker. Brandi dug her nails deep into his hand, hoping it would at least leave a trace of evidence for the authorities to find him.

The man cursed, his grip faltering. Brandi gasped for air, her lungs burning as she tried to fill them. But the reprieve was short-lived. The strength of his hands around her throat choked her with a renewed fury.

"You'll pay for that."

All the fight left and her legs gave way. Her strength waned rapidly, and as she felt her body go limp, she accepted the fact her father's evil presence would finish her.

I'm sorry, Mum. I tried...

17

After saying their goodnights to Susan and Brendan, Carlos moved closer to Rachel. "Would you mind taking a stroll through the atrium before we meet Sarah?"

Rachel stopped in her tracks, fixing her gorgeous but penetrating blue eyes on his. "As long as you tell me why?"

The unbidden stress pulsating through his temple warned Carlos there was something amiss and it couldn't wait. "Remember that photo of Emily Graves?"

"The one of her as a teenager. Yes, I do."

"It's just the more I think about it, the more convinced I am that Brandi Chang recognised her. I need to talk to Brandi again. We've got to find Emily before it's too late."

"But why the urgency? Do you think she's in danger?"

"I do. You know I thought someone's been tailing me? Well, I've had that same feeling all day. I'm sure I saw the guy near the lifts when we came up to dinner, and again when we left the restaurant just now. It's as if he's keeping tabs on me."

"In which case, let's go," said Rachel.

When they arrived in the atrium, they found the pianist warming up, but no Brandi. Carlos started toward the pianist, but Rachel tugged on his arm.

"You keep an eye out for Brandi while I speak to her friend."

Carlos nodded. "Excellent plan. She might be more likely to talk to you."

He surveyed the corridors, shifting his gaze back to Rachel, who was engaging in a semi-intense conversation with the pianist. His heart clenched when she returned, her eyes crinkled in a frown. "Brandi was supposed to be here fifteen minutes ago but her friend – her name's Crystal – won't give me Brandi's room number. I can't blame her; she doesn't know me. It's time to speak to Jason in case that boyfriend of hers is doing something stupid."

At that moment Jason turned a corner, grinning at first, but his grin turned to a frown when he saw their grave expressions.

"No time for explanations, Jason. One of your violinists is in danger," Carlos informed him.

Jason's brow furrowed. "Who?"

"Brandi Chang," said Carlos. "The pianist, Crystal, won't tell Rachel which room she's in."

"Wait here."

Jason crossed the carpet and the wood floor where the white piano gleamed, and spoke briefly to Crystal before giving them the nod. Leading the way, he marched past the shops, now brimming with activity, to the stairs at the stern. Carlos and Rachel kept pace with his brisk footsteps. Jason nodded to a few passengers along the way but didn't stop to talk, even when it looked as though a couple wanted to chat.

"Crystal mentioned Brandi's ex-boyfriend's been causing trouble. How did you know?" Jason quizzed, not missing a step.

Carlos felt even more stressed and regretted not telling Jason earlier. If something happened to Brandi, he would never forgive himself. "I was around when he grabbed hold of her this afternoon. I intervened and told him to back off. He walked away."

Jason descended the passenger staircase, taking two steps at a time until he pushed open a narrow door leading into the crew-only depths of the ship, far removed from the passenger areas. They found themselves in the corridor referred to as the M1 by the British crew. A busy route stretching the length of the ship with junctions heading off to various hubs. The last time Carlos walked this route was after being shot on his honeymoon.

"Why didn't either of you report the incident?" Jason inquired as they hurried through another door, climbing down more steps.

"I suggested she did, but she insisted the guy wouldn't have hurt her. She believed he wouldn't risk losing his job," Carlos explained, kicking himself for not forcing the issue.

Jason spoke into his radio. "I'm on my way to B658, where a member of the crew might be in danger. Have medics and backup on standby. We're almost there."

Carlos felt more guilt pangs over not reporting the earlier incident, not helped by Jason's disappointed look. "How did you find out she didn't turn up to rehearsal?" Jason asked.

"I'm sorry Jason. I wanted to speak to her about another matter," said Carlos. "It's a long story, which I'll tell you all about once we know Brandi's safe."

As they rounded a corner, Carlos recognised Temsin staggering out of a room. His face was bruised and blood poured from his mouth and nose. Temsin's glazed eyes desperately darted around, but it was the item in his hand that made Carlos's heart plummet into his stomach.

"Help! She needs help," he cried.

"Drop the knife, buddy, and step back," Jason commanded.

Carlos felt his heart hammering through his rib cage when the bloodied knife clanged as it hit the floor. Leaving Jason to cuff him, he and Rachel rushed into the tiny room, dreading what they would find.

His jaw dropped.

Brandi was trying to get off the bed, pale and trembling from head to foot. Another man lay groaning on the floor, a pool of blood spreading. Carlos's head hurt. He recognised the man straight away.

"This is the guy who's been following me," he explained to Rachel.

Jason barked a few orders into his radio as shouts echoed through the corridor.

"I didn't start it, man! He attacked me. He was going to kill her!"

Loud footsteps reverberated on the metal floors, coming closer with each step. It left no time for questions. Rachel helped Brandi out of the tiny room while Carlos grabbed a towel and applied pressure to the man's abdomen until the medics arrived. Dr Bentley and Bernard burst through the door. Carlos moved aside to let them in.

"He's been stabbed," he said.

Sarah and the junior doctor, Janet Plover, arrived soon after. Only one of the latter two could get inside because of the lack of space.

"He's just about alive. Hand me the bleed kit," commanded Dr Bentley.

Carlos watched from the doorway while Sarah handed him a bottle of water and a towel.

Answering his quizzical look, she said, "For your hands."

Carlos looked down to see his shaking hands were covered in the man's blood. He stepped away from the door to pour the water over them. He could just make out Bernard swiftly retrieving a package from his emergency bag and Dr Bentley efficiently applying the mesh dressing that would stem the bleeding. Carlos had used similar kits to treat comrades during his army days.

"Right, let's get him on a stretcher. We're going to need a medical evacuation."

"Along with a police escort," Jason added. "According to my prisoner here, this guy tried to strangle Miss Chang."

Sarah made herself busy treating Temsin's facial wounds, while Jason kept a firm grip on him.

"I'll call Gwen on the way to the infirmary," said Janet.

Carlos dried his hands. Most of the blood was gone.

"There's nothing else to do here. We'll leave the rest of this mess to the security team. Bring that man and Miss Chang along to the infirmary," said Dr Bentley.

During the short time it took Bernard and Dr

Bentley to apply the anti-bleed dressing that would most likely save the man's life, Janet had sited a drip.

"I'm coming with you," said Jason, pursuing Dr Bentley along the corridor. "Rachel and Carlos can keep an eye on Yin." He handed the cuffed Temsin over to Carlos.

Janet stayed to attend to Brandi.

"Watch him for a minute, Rachel." Carlos stepped inside Brandi's room, circling the blood patch on the floor, and scrubbed his hands at the sink with soap and hot water. After drying them, he was ready for the journey up to the medical centre.

Satisfied Brandi wasn't critical, Janet turned to them. "I'm going to hurry ahead in case that man needs surgery. Will you manage?"

"You go ahead, I'll come up with them," said Sarah.

They began the climb up a couple of flights of metal stairs in relative silence. The ex-boyfriend trembled, too shocked to be any trouble. The wounds Sarah had patched up would need glue or stitches. Rachel paused for a moment, allowing Brandi to sit down at the top of the stairs and get her breath. "She needs a wheelchair."

At that moment Waverley appeared, about to make his way down to the crime scene. "Do you need help?"

"Would you escort this man to the medical centre and send a wheelchair back for Brandi?" Carlos asked.

"With pleasure. Mr Yin and I have a lot to discuss."

"I'm not leaving her," Yin protested.

"It's okay, Temsin. I'll be all right," Brandi assured him, rubbing her neck.

Temsin looked doubtful, but Waverley was in no mood for delays. "Come on. You can tell me what happened on the way."

Temsin looked over his shoulder at Brandi.

"Thank you," she mouthed.

"I'll go with them and bring the wheelchair back," said Sarah.

Waverley took Temsin's arm and steered him along the M1 corridor with Sarah keeping pace.

Rachel sat next to Brandi, allowing her to rest her head on her shoulder. Carlos resisted asking the countless questions he had, biding his time. Within minutes, Sarah returned, along with Brigitte and an empty wheelchair. They helped settle Brandi into the wheeled transport and headed off. With Brandi in safe hands, Carlos and Rachel followed behind.

"I assume Brandi Chang's your missing person," Rachel whispered.

Carlos rubbed his head, still trying to process everything. "It looks that way. I thought she recognised the image in the photo. I didn't think for a moment she could be Emily Graves. Her features are so different, as well as the name. I assumed she was of oriental descent."

"You were meant to," said Rachel.

"She must have undergone facial reconstruction, and her eyes aren't the same colour as the girl's in the photo. It's looking like Temsin Yin is the hero of the moment. Brandi's pretty shaken up."

"Attempted strangulation tends to have that effect on a person," Rachel nudge him, teasing. "So that was the guy who's been following you?"

Carlos nodded, his shock switching to rage. "So much for Allen Graves wanting to be reconciled with his daughter. It looks more like he hired someone to tail me so he could do away with her. Brandi's lucky. Without Temsin's intervention I don't think we'd have made it in time. How did I not see this coming? I should never have taken this job."

"This is no time for recriminations, Carlos. If you'd refused the assignment, someone else would have taken it, and the outcome would be very different. Brandi survived, that's the crucial thing."

Carlos squeezed Rachel's hand, grateful for her support at that moment. "We've got to stop Allen Graves. If my tail survives we need to get him to spill the beans. Because the one certainty is that my client has no intention of handing over the inheritance to his long-lost daughter." Carlos didn't know the full extent of the story yet, but little by little he would piece it together.

"What I'm confused about," said Rachel, "is how that man found Brandi Chang before you did."

"I guess he worked out I've been showing an interest in musicians. Maybe he even witnessed the scene with Brandi earlier. Not that I saw anyone else around."

Rachel shook her head. "No. That's not it. Did Allen Graves give you anything else besides the photo?"

Carlos slapped his head with the palm of his hand. "The locket!"

Rachel looked puzzled. "What locket?"

"I forgot about it. I've been carrying it in my wallet. Graves said it belonged to Emily's grandmother and that when I found her, I should give it to her as a gesture of goodwill." Carlos reached into his pocket and pulled out the gold locket.

"Have you opened it?"

"Graves did, before he gave it to me. There's a photo of his mother on one side and Emily as a baby on the other."

Rachel's eyes narrowed. "What's the betting there's also a listening device behind one of those photos and that your shadow's been following your progress every step of the way? It's lucky you spotted him at all."

Carlos sighed, a mix of relief and amusement washing over him. "It appears you're not the only one with a sixth sense; maybe it's rubbing off on me."

Rachel looped her arm through his. "It's an important part of a crime fighter's armoury. My guess is, the guy needed to be in near proximity to you to listen in, but not so close as to be obvious."

Relief flooded through Carlos. "As you said, Brandi's alive. Thank God." He longed to speak to Brandi, but right now she needed medical attention.

18

When Rachel and company stepped inside the infirmary, it was a hive of activity. Closed curtains around a bed suggested they were treating Brandi's attacker behind them. Hearing Jason's voice through the curtains confirmed it.

Gwen and Janet were assessing Temsin Yin while Waverley prowled around, pacing the floor. He swung around when he saw them and headed straight for Brandi.

"Not yet," said Sarah, firmly. "We need to examine her first and assess whether she's up to being questioned."

Brandi's eyes widened, staring at the closed curtains. "I can't stay here. Not if that man's in the same place."

"Take Brandi into one of the treatment rooms," Gwen suggested.

Sarah and Brigitte about-turned, wheeling Brandi back out of the infirmary. At least she'd be away from the chaos inside one of the rooms the medics used for their twice daily clinics.

Dr Bentley emerged from behind the curtains, speaking to Waverley.

"He's stable for now. The wound's not as deep as the blood would suggest. I don't believe any major organs have been damaged, but we will proceed with the medical evacuation because he'll need detailed scans and further tests to be certain. I've been informed the helicopter will be a few hours. They've requested we sail closer inland. You can speak to him for a little while, Jack."

"Good," said Waverley.

"Who is he?" Rachel asked.

Waverley answered while Dr Bentley left with Gwen to assess Brandi. "His name is George Crispin. I've got the team going through his room as we speak. Yin told me he heard a commotion and found Crispin attempting to strangle Miss Chang. According to Yin, he got there just in time. He pulled Crispin off the young lady and the men got into a fight. Crispin pulled a knife. If Yin's telling the truth he acted in self-defence, but we'll need to hear Miss Chang's version of events. According to Goodridge, Carlos, you stopped Yin from hurting the young lady earlier."

"That's what it looked like," said Carlos.

Jason popped his head through the curtains. "He's ready, sir."

"Do you mind if we sit in?" Rachel asked.

"Why?"

"Because Carlos is working on a case and he believes your man Crispin is an assassin sent to kill Brandi."

Waverley's brow furrowed as he stroked his chin. "Okay, but stay in the background. I don't want the good doctor accusing us of harassing his patient."

Rachel nodded, taking Carlos's hand as they followed Waverley through the curtains. Janet closed the ones around Temsin's bed at the same time.

Considering how much blood George Crispin had lost inside Brandi's cabin, he looked remarkably well. Bernard checked the monitors and recorded readings in a folder while they waited.

"We've stitched the stab wound. Dr Bentley suggested we give him a few pints of blood while we wait for the evacuation." Bernard quickly checked the rate of the blood flowing through a machine before nodding. "I'll leave you to it. Call me if you need me. And don't be too long. I don't want to get into trouble."

"Thank you." Waverley pulled up a seat next to the bed and sat down, his face giving nothing away. Jason remained standing, as did Rachel and Carlos.

"Welcome back to the land of the living, Mr Crispin. My name is Chief Waverley. I'm the head of security on board the *Coral Queen*. If you don't mind, I'd like to take a statement from you?"

"Do I have a choice?" Crispin said, wincing at the effort of shifting to a more comfortable position. Rachel noted he avoided eye contact with her or Carlos.

"No, you don't. Now, let's begin with you explaining why you attacked Miss Chang."

"Is that what she told you? If she did, she's lying. All I'm guilty of is taking a wrong turn. As a result, I ended up in some random woman's room and before I knew anything about it, the woman and another man attacked me. I expect they were going to rob me. I've a good mind to sue Queen Cruises but as the doctor saved my life I'll let it go."

Waverley fixed his eyes on Crispin. Rachel read the hard, no messing about, look on his face. "My engineer, Temsin Yin, tells a different story. He reports finding you attempting to strangle Miss Chang. I haven't interviewed Miss Chang yet, but I'm sure she'll corroborate what he's said."

"Well, she would, wouldn't she?" Crispin snarled. "They're in it together. Have you checked whether they've got my wallet? You know what these foreigners are like."

"It was on the floor," said Jason.

"See what I mean? You can't trust people like them."

Carlos stepped forward on the other side of the bed, teeth gritted. "You're lying and you know it." Crispin paled at the sight of Carlos bearing down on him. Their faces almost touched as they faced off. "Who hired you to follow me? And why did you try to kill Emily Graves?"

"I didn't. I've just told the officer here; she and her boyfriend attacked me and I acted in self-defence. It's my word against theirs. And as for following you, you must be paranoid. I'm just enjoying a leisurely cruise."

Crispin fell nicely into Carlos's trap, but Waverley looked confused. "Who's Emily Graves?"

The man in the bed cursed before trying to backtrack. "Yeah. What are you talking about? He said her name was Chang."

"Too late, man," said Carlos. Carlos explained his mission to Waverley and Jason along with his suspicions about his client's motives. "Mr Crispin here has confirmed that Brandi Chang is, in fact, Emily Graves. I wasn't one hundred percent certain, but I am now. I think you'll find evidence of bugging equipment in his room." Carlos removed the locket from his wallet and checked behind the photo. "Right as usual, Rachel. He's been listening in to my every move." He showed Waverley the tiny device.

"Would you like to retract your statement, Mr Crispin?" Waverley's jaw tightened.

"Okay, I can explain. My employer—"

"Name?" demanded Waverley.

"Allen Graves. He couldn't be certain he'd find her,"

he motioned his head toward Carlos, "so he sent me along as insurance."

"More like as executioner." Carlos gave the man a hard stare.

"No, that's not it. He didn't know whether he could trust you."

"Why? Because I'm a foreigner?"

"Don't be so touchy. I wasn't referring to you when I said you can't trust foreigners."

"How did you work out Brandi Chang was Emily Graves?"

"When I heard you saying you were looking at musicians, it focussed my attention in that direction. I witnessed you playing the hero earlier and watched the girl. Emily Graves had a tattoo on her neck for her thirteenth birthday, Allen knew she would have had it removed but I figured even a good removal might leave a scar."

"That's why she wears beads and why you went for her neck," said Carlos.

"Bingo! If you get close enough, you can see a tiny scar." Crispin's smirk was becoming ever more annoying.

Carlos lowered his voice. "Look, George. You're going to be charged with attempted murder, and as a helicopter's going to pick you up soon, you're either going to end up in a Thai or a Malaysian jail, whichever's nearest. I doubt you'll find either as hospitable as we are, so I suggest you start telling the truth."

The fear in Crispin's eyes gave Rachel a sense of satisfaction that Carlos had hit the right pain point.

"All right, all right. Allen hired me to do whatever it took to get to Emily and her mother and to dispose of them both. When the girl told me her mother was dead, it was a simple decision." Crispin folded his arms as if they should understand his logic.

"I see," said Waverley. "So you're a gun for hire."

Crispin shrugged. "The girl and her mother have been nothing but trouble to Allen."

"Because they left him, you mean?" Carlos said. His jaw tight and his eyes blazed. Rachel put her arm through his, encouraging him to take a step back.

"Are you prepared to provide a written statement to this effect?" Waverley said.

"Along with evidence," Carlos added.

"If we can cut a deal, I can give you what you need. I make it a habit to tape conversations with employers."

"Don't tell me. Insurance," said Carlos.

"Yeah. You never know when things might go sideways. I'm not taking the rap for this. Killing the two birds is just a small part of what Allen Graves is into. The authorities have been trying to bring him down for decades."

Rachel had remained silent until this point but she'd had enough. "Those women are not *birds*. They are human beings who deserve respect. I don't suppose someone like you would understand the meaning of the word."

"Ooh, sensitive. That's the trouble with women, always so emotional."

Rachel's fists clenched by her sides as she glared at the despicable George Crispin.

Carlos took her hand. "He's not worth it."

Rachel stepped away from the bed and closer to the curtains, taking deep breaths to calm herself.

"Where can we find this recorded evidence?" Waverley barked.

"Do we have a deal?" Crispin was in a commanding position and was growing more confident by the minute. It grated on Rachel, but no doubt the end would justify the means.

"I'll see what I can do," said Waverley.

"Pass me my phone. You can listen to what I've got with me, and as long as you keep your end of the bargain, there's a lot more hidden away. I'll need protection."

With the recorded conversations, Crispin as a witness and the promise of further evidence, Allen Graves was unlikely to wiggle his way out of this one. Rachel was pleased about that, even though she hated the fact Crispin would get a new beginning in witness protection once he met with detectives and the Crown

Prosecution Service back in the UK. She remained concerned for Brandi Chang, AKA Emily Graves.

"Tell us more about Allen Graves," said Carlos.

"What do you want to know?"

"A lot if we're going to keep you out of an Asian prison cell," said Carlos.

"Okay. Okay. As I said, I've got records hidden in a safe deposit box. Extortion, organised crime, assassinations, gunrunning and other stuff besides."

Waverley wrote everything down before turning to Crispin. "I'm sure you'll make a full recovery before the ship sails from Bangkok. As long as the authorities and our captain agree, a member of my security team will bring you back to the ship, where we'll keep you locked up until we dock in Southampton. There, you will be arrested for attempted murder and can take whatever deal the prosecution services offer you. Judging by what you've told us about Mr Graves, I would watch your back until that time. It sounds as though he has a very long reach."

"You just keep me safe and I'll do my part. With what I know about him, I'm sure I'll get witness protection."

"Don't do anything foolish in Malaysia like trying to escape," said Jason.

"I'm not daft. The only way I'm staying alive after this failure is by doing a deal."

"Shall we go?" Rachel nudged Carlos. "I believe the

chief can take it from here." She whispered in his ear, "It's time to check on your misper."

Carlos smiled, saying, "Thanks Chief." He looked at Jason, "Sorry I didn't tell you. I didn't want to put you in a difficult position."

"No problem, mate. Catch you later."

Once they moved out of earshot, Rachel squeezed Carlos's hand. "You did well in there. I don't think Waverley would have got as far without you."

"Thank you. Although I'd have loved to give him a thumping myself. I'm just pleased Temsin got to Emily in time. What do you think will happen to him?"

"I doubt George Crispin will press charges, and the crime took place in international waters and was in self-defence. Waverley won't get rid of a prized engineer for rescuing a damsel in distress. Although I expect he'll get a warning to stay away from her."

"Let's hope he heeds it. He's a decent enough bloke, but if he's rough handled her once, he'll do it again," said Carlos.

"It's a shame, but you're right. Besides, if Graves does find out about his daughter's pseudonym, he'll be out for revenge. She'll need to put some distance between herself and the cruise line before he hears anything about it. I'm keen to ask her about something else if we get the chance."

19

Janet was drinking coffee in Gwen's office, along with Gwen and Brigitte, when Carlos and Rachel arrived.

Carlos looked around. "What happened to Temsin? We saw his bed was empty."

"I stitched his face and discharged him with a follow up for tomorrow. We don't want any fisticuffs in the infirmary with George Crispin still being there."

"Good idea. It'll also keep him away from Brandi."

Janet's lips curled into a wry smile. "I don't know how you two do it. Here we are, cruising through a beautiful part of Asia, and yet we have an attempted murder and an assault on our hands."

"We like to keep the medical team busy," said Rachel, grinning.

"Well, you do a good job," said Gwen. "Can I get you a coffee?"

"Actually, do you mind if we have a chat with Brandi before Waverley does?" Carlos admired the way Rachel wasted little time getting to the point. "He's got enough to keep him busy for now," she added.

Janet raised an eyebrow. "I guess a stabbing and a near strangulation beats his usual day."

Rachel chuckled.

Carlos felt the tension releasing, pleased Rachel didn't refer to the Fabian Bigham issue.

She continued, "Your security team has cracked a case that will bring good headlines for a long time. The *Coral Queen* is soon to bring down a major criminal."

"That's not something you hear every day," said Gwen, grinning. "Although I suspect it's more like we're going to take the credit for something you've done… again."

"Not me this time. My husband." Rachel squeezed his arm.

"Well, congratulations to both of you. Thankfully no-one died today."

Carlos felt admiration for how the medics dealt with any emergency thrown their way. He and Rachel had enormous respect for Dr Bentley and his team.

Gwen got up and strolled toward the door. "I imagine the young lady is up to visitors, but I'll need to check she's happy to speak to you."

"Thank you," Carlos said.

Moments later, Carlos and Rachel got the all-clear. They left the team to debrief while they headed into the clinical room where Sarah was explaining something on the monitor to Brandi.

Pleased to see the colour returned to Brandi's cheeks, Carlos moved next to the examination table where the younger woman sat cradling a mug of hot cocoa in both hands. Rachel stood next to him.

"How are you?" she asked.

"Better. Although I'm going to be hoarse for a few days." She rubbed her neck with one hand. Her voice sounded fairly confident, but her eyes remained wary. "No singing for a while thanks to that horrible man. But I'll still be able to play the violin."

"I didn't realise you sang," said Rachel.

Brandi relaxed. "Sometimes we combine singing and playing."

"She's hugely talented," said Sarah.

"If your singing's anything like your violin playing, I have no doubt," said Carlos. "Do you mind if we ask you some questions?"

"As long as you explain who you are and why you're looking for me?" Brandi's otherwise beautiful eyes seemed tainted by years of having to show caution. He couldn't blame her after the events of this evening.

"Fair enough." He spun a stool around on its pedestal until it reached the right height for him to take a seat. "Before I do. Can we confirm that your real name is Emily Graves?"

Her eyes hardened. "My name is Brandi Chang."

Carlos accepted the need to proceed with caution in order to gain her trust. "Okay, Brandi. As you already know, my name is Carlos, and this is my wife, Rachel. We are taking a cruise to celebrate Rachel's parents' wedding anniversary, but I'm also a private investigator. Before we left England, a man named Allen Graves hired me to do a job." He noticed the wince but continued, "My mission was to find his daughter." Trying to ignore the pained expression mingled with fear, Carlos persisted. "I say was, because now I realise his true motives, I will no longer work for him. That said, it remains in your... erm, Emily's interests that he doesn't get to hear that just yet."

Brandi still looked uncertain. "Go on," she said. "What did he tell you?"

"He commissioned me to find his daughter and to inform her that her grandmother has passed away and—"

Brandi's eyes moistened. "Granny's dead?"

"Yes," said Carlos. "I'm sorry."

Brandi looked down at her hands. "I wondered why she hadn't been in touch." Brandi looked at Sarah.

"You can trust them, Brandi. I've been friends with Rachel all my life. Neither she nor Carlos will do anything to put you in danger."

Deciding, Brandi's eyes fixed on Carlos's. "You're right. My birth name is Emily Graves, but I never want to bear that man's name again. As far as I'm concerned he's not my father."

"I respect that," said Carlos. "Can you tell us why he's going to such lengths to hurt you?"

Shaking her head, Brandi ignored the question. "Now Granny's dead, we'll never be safe. She kept checks on him and warned us if he was getting too close, then we moved on."

"The man who attacked you said your mother died." Rachel said gently.

"I told him that to protect my mother. If he killed me, they wouldn't guess my mother was still alive. I won't tell you where she is."

"And we won't ask," said Carlos. "Your fa... my client wanted me to tell you about an inheritance. Is the money the reason he wants you and your mother dead?"

"There is no inheritance," Brandi's voice had risen by a few octaves. "Granny transferred enough money into safe deposit boxes to set me and my mother up for life. We already have more money than we'll ever be able to spend. He didn't hire you to tell me about any inheritance. He's deceived you. All that man wants is me and my mother dead."

"But why, if it's not about the money?" said Carlos.

"My mother hurt Allen Graves's pride, and that man doesn't forgive... or forget such things."

"I'm so sorry," said Carlos, feeling pain for putting her in danger. "I never would have taken the assignment if I'd known any of this."

"How did you find out I worked on board the *Coral Queen*? Granny would never have told him. She was always so careful."

"As she became ill, she might have let it slip by mistake," said Rachel. "Apparently a nurse told her son how proud of you your grandmother was. I expect the nurse inadvertently passed it on thinking it would help ease his grief. I doubt they would realise they were putting you in danger."

"The nurse showed him a postcard sent from the *Coral Queen*. After that, he did his homework and confirmed it came from a destination where this ship docked at the time of sending," Carlos added.

"Poor granny. She loved us all. It was hard for her, but she understood my mother's reasons for leaving him. In fact, without her help, my mother might never have plucked up enough courage. Mum tried once, before I was born, but he sent the police after her and she was prosecuted for drunk-driving.

"Despite everything, he was still her son. Granny helped us escape and kept our whereabouts secret, but she would never turn on him."

"A mother's love," said Carlos.

"I take it he hired that man to kill me?"

Carlos nodded. "Yes. In cases like this, I don't make any promises. I told Graves that if I found you, I would let you know about the inheritance but if you wanted your whereabouts and identity to remain secret, I would respect that and so should he."

"And he agreed to your terms?"

"On the face of it."

"Then sent someone else to do the deed. That's how he works."

"I realise that now," said Carlos. "The man who attacked you has been following me and your father bugged this locket." Carlos took the locket from his wallet and held it out to her. "He said it belonged to your grandmother."

She hesitated.

"Don't worry, the chief of security removed the listening device."

Brandi took the locket and opened it, her eyes moistened again. "She always wore this. Can I keep it?"

Carlos nodded. "Of course. The good news is that Crispin – the man who attacked you – has agreed to do a deal to save his own neck. He's given the security chief enough evidence to have Allen Graves arrested."

Brandi's breath became ragged. "Are you sure?"

"Positive, and he's got a lot more evidence to make sure it will be a life sentence," said Carlos. He didn't add, *as long as the police can keep him alive.*

"He'll still have contacts."

"Maybe, but Crispin believes your mother is dead and so will Allen Graves. Your mother's safe, and we believe you will be too once Graves is locked away."

"Can you trust this man?"

"Not at all, but he understands it's either witness protection or failure. He believes the latter will sign his death warrant."

"It would. Allen Graves doesn't tolerate failure or betrayal," said Brandi. "Crystal and I will be leaving the ship when it gets to America. Do you think we'll be safe until then?"

"With a little misdirection from me and the security team, yes," said Carlos.

The relief on Brandi's face was all Carlos needed.

20

With Carlos happy about the conclusion of his case, Rachel hadn't found the time to quiz Brandi about Fabian Bigham's death, but she was determined to do so today. When Rachel and Carlos met Jason and Sarah in the Jazz Bar the night before, Sarah told them Brandi had discharged herself. Rachel couldn't blame her for not wanting to stay anywhere near George Crispin.

Rachel was biding her time and soon got her opportunity. Carlos and Brendan excused themselves on the pretext of going for a walk, their real purpose being to have another meeting with Simon Peterson.

Rachel and her mother were inside the indoor pool conservatory.

"You don't need to keep me company, Rachel. I've got an enthralling book to finish."

Knowing what her mother was like once she stuck her nose in a book, Rachel had no qualms about taking her chance. "If you're sure, I'll go for a stroll."

"You do that. You still look a little pasty despite all the running you do."

Rachel leaned down to kiss her mother's forehead. "It's called factor 50 sun cream, but thanks for the confidence boost, Mum."

"Would you mind bringing me a sudoku puzzle from the atrium on your way back? I forgot to pick one up this morning."

"No problem. Will you be staying here?"

Susan found a pleasant spot on the edge of the huge conservatory. Seating was available on the peripheries of the pool and air-conditioning made it a comfortable place to sit and have refreshing drinks without having to worry about applying sun cream with tedious regularity.

"Yes. Your father said he'll find me when he and Carlos have done with their man time. He knows what I'm like when I get a good book in my hands. There's never enough time to read at home and I've been itching to read the latest LJ Ross offering."

"Enjoy your reading time. I'll be back in an hour."

"No need to rush. I'll be fine here." Susan waved her away with a flick of the wrist.

Still smiling, Rachel tailgated a trio of laughing crewman into the crew-only part of the ship, pleased they didn't notice her slipping in behind them. Most of the crew were busy working and those she passed hurried on, concentrating on their next destination. Rachel's casual clothes and loose hair covered by a baseball cap gave the impression of someone enjoying being off duty. With so many employees, it wasn't difficult to pretend to be one, as long as she remained calm. When people looked her way, she gave them a nod as if she knew them and they returned the greeting.

Once she left the M1 and descended the stairs, she pulled the cap down to hide her face until she arrived outside Brandi's cabin. She knocked, calling. "Brandi? It's Rachel. Is it all right to come in?"

She heard movement, followed by the door unlocking. Brandi's eyes were brighter and her whole demeanour appeared happier than when they spoke the night before. And, apart from some bruising around the neck, she looked no worse for wear despite her ordeal. *This woman is strong,* thought Rachel.

"Come in," Brandi said. "It's kind of you to look in on me."

Rachel felt immediately guilty for her ulterior motive.

"How are you?"

"Not too bad. They wanted to cancel our shows today but I refused."

"That's brave of you."

"Not really. I just want to forget about everything and music helps me do that. Is that man off the ship?"

"For now. Sarah told us this morning he's been transferred to a hospital in Bangkok. He went by ambulance boat in the end as Dr Bentley deemed the expense of an air ambulance unnecessary."

"What happens next?" Brandi asked.

"He'll have some tests and be treated under police guard before being returned to the ship under supervision when we dock tomorrow. Sarah's husband, Jason, will take over from the Bangkok police on the port side. Don't worry, he'll be safely locked in the brig for the rest of the cruise. The chief of security is liaising with British and Singaporean authorities to have him flown back under police escort to the UK at the end of the cruise." Rachel was pleased to pass on the information, even though she wanted to talk to Brandi about Bigham.

"Do you have any idea when Allen Graves will be arrested?"

"No. I think Waverley wants to avoid him being given too much information until they have a convincing story about what happened to you. Crispin will be encouraged to send him a text tomorrow informing him that your mother is dead and that he's pursuing you, giving a different name to the one you're using. He'll say you're on a trip to Bangkok. Waverley will later arrange for the British police to arrest Graves on conspiracy to commit murder. He's hoping your father will believe Crispin tried to kill you in Bangkok. That's the story they're going to spin. If Allen Graves ever finds out you weren't attacked in Bangkok, you'll already be settled in the United States. Will you keep the same name?"

"I think so, for the foreseeable future. It's got an American work visa attached to it. If I need to change it further down the line, I know how to do it." Brandi shrugged.

"What will you do in America?"

"The same as I've been doing. Crystal and I want to make a go of our talents and play the bigger stages if we can."

"I hope you get what you're dreaming of. You have real talent. Do you mind if I ask you something else?"

"What?"

"Someone mentioned that a man named Fabian Bigham annoyed you." Rachel tried to sound casual, especially as she was only surmising Manfred had been referring to Brandi when he told her Bigham had upset one of his friends.

Rachel watched Brandi closely, noting the flicker of emotion crossing her face at the mention of Fabian Bigham. The violinist's shoulders tensed, and she looked away briefly before her brown eyes met Rachel's gaze again.

"Yeah, he did." Brandi's voice was tinged with

bitterness and regret. "He promised us big things, but it was all a lie. That man never intended to help me or Crystal. He just wanted to use us for his own gain. Crystal stupidly got involved with him and he feared word about it would get out. That's how he recruited me and why he promised us the earth. We agreed to work for peanuts on the understanding he would make introductions. He reneged on that deal."

Rachel nodded, her suspicions more than confirmed. "I'm sorry. It must have been difficult when you've already been through so much."

Brandi let out a humourless laugh. "We imagined he'd be our ticket to success, but he was just another manipulative, power-hungry narcissist." She shook her head, as if trying to clear it.

"Did he ever threaten you?" Rachel asked gently.

Brandi hesitated, her fingers fidgeting with the hem of her shirt. "Not directly," she said slowly, "but he made it clear that if we didn't do what he wanted, he could make things very difficult. But he was also scared I'd report him after I caught him with Crystal in my hotel room when I was working in Barcelona."

Rachel's heart went out to Brandi. Bigham had taken advantage of the two women's dreams and used it against them. "What made him go back on the deal?"

"I'm not sure. Maybe he realised we wouldn't ever tell anyone in authority. Who would believe us anyway?"

"When did he tell you he wasn't going to do what he'd promised?"

"The night of the cocktail party."

"I take it you're aware he died that night?"

Brandi gave a wry smile. "No more relying on false promises from men like Bigham. His death brought us freedom. We'll make our own way."

"I'm sure you and Crystal will achieve great things," Rachel said, returning Brandi's smile. "But do you know of anyone who might have wanted to kill Fabian Bigham?"

Realising what Rachel might be getting at, Brandi stiffened. "Not me, if that's what you're implying."

The sudden stiffness in posture was concerning. Rachel hoped the young violinist wasn't the killer, but she was certain Brandi knew something.

"I'm not accusing you of anything," Rachel said softly, trying to put the woman at ease. "But if you know something that could help me find out who killed Fabian Bigham, it's important you tell me."

Brandi hesitated, her eyes darting around the room as if searching for an escape. "Is this another case your husband is interested in? Did he lie when he said you were on a cruise with your parents?"

"It's true we're on a holiday cruise, but on land I'm a police officer. I found Bigham dead, and for that reason it's me who's interested."

"I don't think I can help you much," Brandi said, her

voice barely above a whisper. "But on cruise ships we hear a lot of rumours. The word's out that Fabian Bigham had a lot of enemies. He'd wronged a lot more people than me and Crystal over the years."

Rachel nodded, encouraging Brandi to continue. "Can you tell me who he wronged?"

"There was talk of someone from his past, a woman he intended to hurt. I don't know her name although I noticed a woman heading towards him on the night of the cocktail party and then turning back again." Brandi's fingers twisted nervously in her lap. "Crystal mentioned business deals where he had cheated people out of money. I know nothing about who might have killed him though. The official line is that he died of a heart attack but we're not stupid. They locked a friend of mine in the brig but released him again."

Rachel's mind pieced together the information. It was as she suspected, Fabian Bigham had left a trail of destruction in his wake, but who hated him enough to want him dead?

"How did Crystal hear about the people he had wronged?"

Brandi chortled. "These people say many things in front of stateroom attendants, waiters, bar staff. Some of the crew like to gossip, especially when the person is as horrid as Fabian."

"I hate to mention this, but as you received

devastating news from him and you were at the party the night he died, it doesn't look good."

"Rachel! I've spent my whole life in hiding. If you think for one second I would put all that at risk by killing someone like Fabian Bigham, you're so wrong. I was angry with him, but I long suspected he would let us down, so it came as no surprise."

"Okay, I believe you. But, other than the woman you mentioned, did you notice anything odd that night?"

"Apart from a dozen or more people getting sick, you mean? The woman was one of them by the way."

Rachel had already surmised that woman was Evie. "Yes."

"Manfred was on a downer. He's my friend, the mixologist who was put in the brig, but there's no way he would have done anything like that. He's harmless. As I said, they've let him go now, so the security people must believe they made a mistake."

"I've spoken to Manfred Heinrich and I agree with your assessment. Did you notice anything else?"

"Nat – she's the assistant cruise director – a lovely woman, but she doesn't get on with her boss."

"Slick?"

"You heard his nickname? Yeah, but she usually hides it. That night she was different."

"In what way?"

"She was on edge. I've never seen her like that before."

"Did she say what was on her mind?"

"No. I don't ask. When you're hiding from your past, you keep a low profile, if you know what I mean?"

"I meant to ask you about that," said Rachel. "It bothers me how you put yourself out there. Aren't you frightened that someday you'll be recognised?"

"I've had plastic surgery to make me look in keeping with the name I've chosen to go by, contact lenses disguise my eye colour, and I look nothing like the gawky teenager in your husband's photo. If Granny hadn't been dying, she would never have made the mistake she did. In America, I'll be just another musician; even if I find fame I'll be hard to recognise as long as that man Crispin keeps his mouth shut. And even if he doesn't, make him believe I left the ship in Bangkok."

"We will. You must really love music if you're willing to risk everything."

"It's all I have in life. I doubt I'll ever marry because I couldn't be sure they wouldn't find out who I really was."

"Is that why you broke up with Temsin?"

"Partly. But also because he became too possessive. When he grabbed me yesterday, I knew I'd made the right choice. Although I'm very grateful to him for saving my life."

"I really do hope things work out for you. If you

remember anything else about the VIP cocktail party night, please contact me or one of the security team."

"There was something else." Brandi screwed up her eyes as if trying to remember.

"What?"

"I saw Fabian arguing with someone. A tall guy with long blond hair. He has something to do with the cruise line because I've seen him with Temsin and others from engineering."

"Orlando Kearney?"

"I don't know his name."

"That's really helpful. Thank you, Brandi. And take care."

"I will. Thank Carlos again for me, won't you?"

"Of course," said Rachel.

As Rachel left Brandi's cabin, her mind whirred, considering her next step. The deeper she dug into Fabian's past, the worse it became. Which secret led to his untimely demise? At least she had a few more pieces of the puzzle to work with.

21

Rachel had been looking forward to the tour of Bangkok for months. Carlos, Susan and Brendan shared her excitement, made even better by Sarah being with them for their tour. The large tour party stepped off the bus onto a bustling main road in the city centre. Vibrant colours, pungent smells, mixed with exhaust fumes, and the cacophony of a busy Asian city assaulted Rachel's senses. As the capital of Thailand, Bangkok turned out to be just as expected.

Carlos stood next to her while they waited for everyone to gather, his hand resting gently on the small of her back. The assistant cruise director, Nat, was leading the tour. During the journey from the port, Rachel had already witnessed how efficient and knowledgeable she was.

"Welcome to Bangkok," Nat said, her voice just

about audible over the din of the city. "Our first stop today is the King Power Mahanakhon, Thailand's tallest building. From the roof, you'll enjoy breathtaking views of the city from the SkyWalk, which I'm sure you'll find incredible. Once you've looked around and taken photographs, you can enjoy a drink from Bangkok's highest rooftop bar. One soft drink is included with your ticket. Now, please stay close and follow me."

The party followed Nat, who held up a sign with the number eleven clearly etched on its surface and visible from thirty yards. Rachel's parents stayed with a group at the front, their eyes wide with wonder as they took in the unfamiliar sights and sounds.

Sarah, a keen amateur photographer, clutched the SLR camera which always accompanied her on such occasions, stopping every so often to take photos of anything that grabbed her interest.

"I can't wait to view the city from the rooftop. Last time we stopped here, Bernard and Brigitte had shore leave, so I only managed a short walk around the terminal. I'm told the views from the SkyWalk are incredible."

They trailed after Nat along a broad pavement, through crowds, dodging tuk-tuks and cars when they crossed a busy road. Street vendors hawked their wares, thrusting them in their faces. Carlos paused to buy a piece of lacquerware, most likely at three times the price he should have paid, but he didn't mind. Rachel was happy, but uneasy. Despite the beauty of Bangkok, her mind kept drifting back to Fabian Bigham's death and Brandi's revelation about Nat being on edge the night he died. She chastised herself inwardly and told herself to focus on enjoying the day with her family and friend. *If only I could learn to switch off.*

"Are you okay?" Carlos asked, while Sarah took a photo of some of the street vendors who seemed more than happy to pose.

Rachel nodded, forcing a smile. "Just taking it all in."

"What an incredible city," said Brendan, swerving to avoid crashing into an over-determined young man waving an armful of silk scarves under their noses.

"And very busy," said Susan, putting a finger in the ear closest to the road. Cars, buses and tuk-tuks drove at speed, honking their horns at any vehicle daring to slow down. A domed temple was just visible in the distance.

"I'm looking forward to the visit to the Buddhist temple after this," said Brendan.

"Me too," said Susan. "At least it'll be quieter." Despite complaining about the noise, Rachel could tell her mother was enjoying the experience. Susan's glowing eyes spoke volumes.

After a short walk, they arrived at the base of the King Power Mahanakhon, its gleaming glass exterior reflecting the bright sunlight. Rachel had donned a light summer dress for the outing. Her mother wore a floral, sleeved, cotton dress selected from her new wardrobe. They both wore sun hats and sunglasses. Carlos's bronze legs were visible beneath his knee-length khaki cargo shorts, while her father wore light cotton trousers and a polo shirt. *It must be nice for him not to have to wear the Roman collar in this heat,* she mused. Some vicars always wore the collar, but Brendan had chosen not to for the cruise, although he had one with him should it be necessary. Like being a nurse or a police officer, vicars could sometimes attract unwanted attention.

Nat led them inside the vast building and the tour party split into four to take the high-speed lifts to the observation deck. The glass lift shot up the seventy-eight floors, affording them spectacular views of the city. Brendan and Carlos discussed the ingenuity of the mechanics, Sarah shot a video and Susan stared through the glass in awe. In no time at all, the lift door pinged, and they moved outside to join a queue of people waiting to step onto the SkyWalk. Rachel felt her breath catch in her throat as she took in the panoramic view of Bangkok.

"It's marvellous," Susan said, her hand clutching Brendan's arm.

"I've never seen anything like it," Brendan agreed, his eyes scanning the horizon, taking everything in.

They waited their turn to step onto one of the glass trays and look below from the 310-metre height.

"It wouldn't be much fun for anyone suffering from vertigo," said Sarah.

"I doubt anyone with vertigo would choose this excursion," said Rachel.

Her friend put on her *what do you know* face, saying. "You'd be surprised."

Sarah snapped as many photos of the views as she could in the time allotted and took one or two of each of them, taking up various poses for her. Once they had spent enough time enjoying the views from the glass tray and surrounding area, they climbed the steps to the highest point of the observatory where they could see the whole of the Bangkok skyline with three-hundred-and-sixty-degree views. It was as breathtaking as Nat had promised. Rachel put aside her troubled thoughts to stay in the moment and enjoy the experience. She took great pleasure in her parents' delight and borrowed Sarah's camera to take a few snaps of her friend with the views behind her, and then Carlos took a couple of her and Sarah.

Their time came to an end all too quickly, and they reluctantly moved, as per Nat's instructions, to the rooftop bar, where they sipped refreshing ice-cool drinks. Rachel was proud of herself for succeeding in pushing thoughts of a suspicious death from her mind. She found herself at ease sharing this time with her loved ones, savouring the beauty and wonder of her surroundings.

Rachel stayed put when Carlos and her parents went for one last gaze at the views. From the bar, she could watch the bustling city below through the glass balustrade. A welcome breeze wafted through her hair as though caressing her neck. Sarah stopped taking photos and returned her camera to its case, joining Rachel at the table.

"I'm glad you got the day off. It's a shame Jason couldn't make it. What happened?" Jason had been due to join them for the Bangkok outing and Carlos had been looking forward to one of their ex-army heart-to-hearts. But Jason's leave had been cancelled at the last minute.

"I didn't want to mention it before, especially in front of Susan and Brendan, but we transferred Fabian Bigham's body to the mortuary this morning. A Thai pathologist requested it to carry out a postmortem. When the ambulance boat collected George Crispin yesterday, we sent blood and urine samples for tests. Something showed up, hence the body request."

Rachel sat bolt upright, suddenly alert. "What?"

"I knew if I told you you'd react like this."

"Like what?"

Sarah chuckled. "You know what. Anyway, I know little more than what I've told you, other than it looks like you're right as usual. Fabian Bigham was poisoned. And not by any emetic." A troubled expression appeared on Sarah's face despite the attempt at humour.

Rachel felt her shoulders slump. "I was sort of hoping I'd be wrong. Whatever you do, don't tell Dad. He was really upset about his old friend's death."

"I'm not stupid, Rachel. Of course I won't. Why do you think I've been avoiding the topic?"

"Sorry. There's something else I want to talk to you about while I've got you alone. I had a chat with Brandi Chang yesterday."

Sarah gawped at her. "You really are too much sometimes, you know that?"

Rachel grinned. "But you love me anyway."

"That goes without saying. Okay, Maestro, what did you find out?"

"Quite a lot about Brandi. Poor girl, she's had such a hard time. You know I don't thank God anywhere near often enough that I've got such wonderful parents."

"Hmm. I suppose that applies to me as well, even though I wish mum wouldn't drop hints the size of boulders about me and Jason settling down to a..." Sarah used her fingers to make air quotes, "...normal life."

Rachel laughed. "She misses you, that's all."

"I know." Sarah chewed her bottom lip, a sure sign of stress. "What else did Brandi tell you?"

"That Bigham promised her the earth and delivered nothing. Apparently he told her and her friend he would open doors in America if they worked on the cruise ship for a pittance." Rachel didn't mention the affair with Crystal because it wasn't her secret to tell. "Needless to say, he reneged on his end of the bargain."

"Please don't tell me Brandi had anything to do with his death?"

Rachel shook her head. "I don't think so. She assured me she wouldn't do anything to draw attention to herself and I believe her. But she saw him arguing with a man on the night of the VIP cocktail party. A man she described in detail."

"Are you going to say who?"

"I'm almost positive the man she described is Orlando Kearney."

"The green-waste guy?"

"Yes. Carlos told me he might be a fraud. Dad cornered him the day before yesterday and quizzed him about his work. Kearney wouldn't, or couldn't, answer his questions and clammed up. Carlos believes he's hiding something, and bearing in mind the argument, I'm inclined to agree."

"Wow!"

"Another thing Brandi said, apart from how she didn't believe Manfred Heinrich would spike anyone's drinks despite him being low that night—"

"Graham was so pleased when Waverley released Manfred, even though he's still being watched and isn't allowed to go back to his old job."

"I know. We saw him serving drinks from the pool bar. That's when he mentioned the ipecac theory."

"Okay, so Brandi believes Manfred's innocent. You said there was something else?"

"Brandi said Nat seemed on edge that evening. Unusual, she said, and from what I've seen of Nat today and how controlled she is, I can see what she meant."

"I noticed it too. Nat's always so focussed on her work and a consummate professional, but she was off that night. In fact, now you mention it, there's something I forgot to tell you," Sarah said, lowering her voice. "It might not be relevant, but after Nat was admitted to the infirmary that night, she said some things that didn't sit right with me."

Rachel turned to face her friend, her brow furrowed. "What sort of things?"

Sarah hesitated, glancing around to make sure they were still alone. "She rambled on about how useless Simon was. She said she was tired of being overlooked and unappreciated and that she'd warned him about Manfred's erratic behaviour. Basically she felt Simon should have reported her concerns to Manfred's boss."

Rachel's heart quickened. "So Nat believes Manfred spiked the drinks."

"She certainly made it sound that way."

"I wonder?" Rachel moved her eyes back to the skyline before returning to face Sarah. "Do you think Nat herself might have laced the cocktails?"

Sarah's brow creased; her green eyes filled with

uncertainty. "I doubt it. She was ill enough to be admitted."

"Maybe that makes it more likely."

"Are you suggesting she would have made herself ill?"

"Was she vomiting?"

"No, but she suffered severe pain and felt nauseous, like many people that night."

"Yes, but as the perpetrator, she could have been putting it on to throw people off the scent."

"But why would someone as dedicated as her want to frame Manfred, or harm passengers, for that matter?"

"Pointing the finger at Manfred could have been mere convenience. Maybe she did it to make her boss look incompetent, or even get him sacked."

"She hinted at something along those lines when she suggested he should have reported it."

Rachel nodded, her mind processing the information.

"Come on, you two. Time's up. Nat says the bus has just pulled up outside and it's only allowed to park there while we board."

Rachel jumped up, taking Carlos's hand. "Let's go."

She needed to speak to Nat.

22

The sheer size and beauty of the Golden Buddha was enough to make Rachel marvel. Their tour group entered Wat Traimit, where the statue sat cross-legged, resplendent in all its golden glory. It towered over them at three metres tall.

"Nobody visiting here and looking at this statue inside the temple can help but be in awe of the craftsmanship that went into crafting such a masterpiece almost nine centuries ago," said Nat, sounding like she was speaking straight from a guidebook. She continued giving them a potted history.

Carlos was as transfixed as Rachel as they stood gazing upwards.

Brendan was in his element. "It's amazing to think that weighs over five tonnes. The people who put it together must have been so skilled to cast something so large and intricate out of gold."

"According to Nat, it comes apart and there's even a key," said Sarah, who had clearly been listening to the assistant cruise director's spiel.

Rachel's eyes traced the delicate patterns of the Buddha's headdress. Brendan and Susan worked their way to the front of the group, listening intently to Nat's exposition of the statue's history.

"The Golden Buddha was discovered by accident in 1955," Nat continued, her voice carrying over the hushed whispers. "It had been covered in plaster and coloured glass for hundreds of years; historians presume this was to conceal its true nature from potential invaders. It remained insignificant throughout the centuries, with no-one knowing its true value lay beneath. During relocation, some of the plaster chipped off, revealing the solid gold beneath."

Susan's jaw dropped open. "It's amazing that something so valuable could have been hidden for so long," she said, her eyes wide with wonder.

Brendan smiled. "Sometimes the greatest treasures are right under our noses, waiting to be discovered."

"On today's market, it's estimated to be worth around 250 million dollars," said Nat.

A few of those present whistled.

"But it will never be melted down, so it's priceless to the Thai people," said Brendan.

After the talk concluded, they separated. Wandering around the temple, Rachel inhaled the sweet scent of incense. A sense of peace washed over her as she returned to the statue. The serene expression on the Buddha's face and pose seemed to radiate a calming energy that soothed her thoughts.

Sarah appeared at her side, a small smile playing on her lips, the camera hanging around her neck once more. "It's amazing," she said, her eyes fixed on the gleaming statue.

"It really is," Rachel agreed, returning her friend's smile. "There's something about being in the presence of something so ancient and sacred that puts everything in perspective. It's the same when I'm inside old cathedrals and churches."

"Sometimes I go to the ship's chapel and feel the same way," said Sarah.

"You never mentioned that," said Rachel, pleased to hear it. As children and teenagers, they had both been committed Christians, but Sarah hardly mentioned God these days. Somehow, Sarah's faith had been challenged by the suffering she had witnessed through her chosen career in a way Rachel's hadn't. As long as there was good and evil in the world, Rachel accepted the fact that suffering was a part of life. She may not like it, but it helped her come to terms with the evil people did to each other.

"Have you seen Carlos?"

"He's with Susan and Brendan. They're wandering around the temple somewhere."

Rachel and Sarah headed outside into the sunlight. She squeezed her friend's arm.

"It's good to spend some time with you."

"Likewise," said Sarah, taking a few more shots of the Wat from outside. Her friend moved around, searching for the best angle before releasing the shutter.

Rachel grinned. "Some might say you prefer your camera to me." Her attention was drawn toward Nat when she spotted her sitting at a small table, one hand scrawling in a notebook, the other wrapped around a glass of iced Thai tea. "Over there," she said, inclining her head.

"And some might say you're fickle."

"Touché."

With a smirk and as if reading her mind, Sarah ambled across to where Nat sat.

"Hello Nat. Great tour so far. Do you mind if we join you?"

Nat looked up, putting her pen down. "Of course not! Please do." She gestured to the empty chairs. "I was just letting people have a little free time."

As they settled in, Sarah ordered two more glasses of the fragrant tea Nat was drinking. The three women fell into calm conversation, discussing the sights they'd seen on the tour and Rachel's plans for the rest of the cruise.

"This is tasty," said Rachel, sipping her tea. "Sweeter than I'm used to, but I like the spicy flavour."

"It tastes more floral to me," said Sarah. "Is it orange blossom?"

"You're right. I've just got that taste coming through now."

Nat looked at Rachel, "It's your dad and husband arranging the anniversary surprise for your mum, isn't it?"

"Yes, it is. Thanks for not giving anything away. It's hard to keep secrets from my mum, but she'll appreciate it on the night."

"No problem. I've organised everything. There won't be any hitches."

Rachel took the opportunity to probe. "Oh? I thought Carlos told me it was Simon Peterson, who was organising it."

Nat's fingers tightened around her glass, her smile faltering for a moment. "Simon delegates. I do."

"I see," said Rachel. "Well, thank you. And you've been brilliant today. Your knowledge is amazing."

Nat smiled, "Thanks. I do a lot of studying and put a lot of work in."

"That's obvious," said Rachel. "You seem to work all hours. I saw you nudging your boss along on the night of the VIP cocktail party. That turned out to be quite an evening, didn't it?"

"It certainly did," Nat agreed, her voice carefully

neutral, but Rachel detected an edge. "No-one expected things to take such a dramatic turn. Did you get ill?"

"No. None of us did. Sarah was rushed off her feet, of course."

"Did you know each other before today?"

"Best friends since school days," said Sarah. "Brendan's the vicar at the village church where we went to Sunday school. We also went to the same university, but Rachel took history and I studied nursing."

"I grew up in Madrid, but most of the friends I had are married now with kids. We don't keep in touch. I studied English in Barcelona and got a job working for a smaller cruise line before joining Queen Cruises. I've worked my way up from scratch."

"And done well," said Rachel, taking a sip of her tea before continuing. "With your hard work, I expect you'll soon be a cruise director."

"That's the dream."

"I hope you don't mind me saying, but I noticed some tension between you and Simon at the cocktail party," Rachel said. "It must be annoying, you doing all the work and Simon taking the credit."

Nat hesitated, her eyes darting away from Rachel's probing gaze. "It can be, and we've had our differences," she admitted, her voice barely above a whisper. "Simon can be... difficult to work with at times, but mostly I ignore it."

"That must be hard to do when it's obvious he isn't as dedicated as you are. I get the impression he likes a good time," said Rachel.

Nat's lips tightened into a straight line.

Sarah took the cue. "About the cocktail party," she began, "you mentioned the mixologist had been behaving strangely, and you thought Simon should have done something about it? Do you still feel that way?"

Rachel leaned back, pretending to be relaxed as she waited for Nat to reply. She could sense the woman's hesitation, the way her fingers trembled around the delicate glass.

"I shouldn't have mentioned it."

Sarah patted her forearm. "Did you see anything else?"

"I did something terrible."

"What?" asked Rachel.

"I should have reported it to security, but I was too engrossed in my anger with Simon for not listening to me. When the people got sick, I thought it served him right."

"What do you mean?" Sarah asked.

"As I told you, Manfred had been off that evening. When I went to get a cold drink, I saw him stuff a sachet of powder inside his trouser pocket. At first, I assumed it was his cocktail's secret ingredient, but when people got sick, I was angry Simon hadn't taken the man off duty.

After I was admitted to the infirmary, I heard Jason say the chief of security had Manfred in the brig, so I didn't mention it and assumed they'd find the stuff."

Rachel exchanged a confused glance with Sarah before challenging Nat. "It still seems odd you haven't mentioned any of this to anyone before. Are you sure you didn't lace the drinks to get at your boss?" Her voice was firm.

Nat's shoulders tensed; her almond-brown eyes burned almost red. "Don't be ridiculous! I would never do anything to harm passengers. I'm telling the truth. If I'd realised what Manfred was doing, I would have stopped him. There was no point – as you English say – shutting the door after the horse had bolted. The only thing I did wrong was not tell the security team what I'd seen. I was tired of Simon taking credit for all my hard work but not enough to do anything dangerous. Besides, if I wanted to get him fired there are other ways of doing it, but I'm not that malicious."

Sarah reached out, placing a comforting hand on Nat's shoulder. "Oh, Nat," she murmured, her voice filled with sympathy. "I'm sorry you're taken for granted. You will make an amazing cruise director one day."

"What I don't understand is how Manfred was released the next day. It's like they don't care about what he did."

"Perhaps they don't believe he did anything wrong," said Rachel, her brow furrowed.

"I don't like what you're implying."

"Did Fabian Bigham drink one of the laced cocktails?" Rachel asked, leaning forward.

Nat shook her head vehemently. "How would I know? I was too busy making sure everything ran smoothly."

"Until people started taking ill," Sarah said, reaching out to take the woman's hand in her own.

"Yes. I realise I should have said something, but as I've already made clear, I got sick myself, and I heard Manfred was in the brig. It didn't seem important anymore."

At that moment, a group of passengers interrupted their conversation, joining them to ask Nat a question. As if by magic, she pasted on her professional smile and continued as if they hadn't just had an intense conversation.

Rachel watched her resume her role and admired her for it.

"How could I have got it so wrong? I'm usually an excellent judge of character. Manfred Heinrich's taken me for a fool," said Rachel, anger surging through her body.

"You've changed your mind about it being her then?"

"Yes. She's either an exceptionally good liar or she's telling the truth. Having seen how much she loves her job today, I can't imagine her risking it all by lacing cocktails, can you?"

"Not at all. In fact, I feel sorry for her," said Sarah. "Simon's a charismatic character, but I wouldn't want to work for him."

"That's what I love about you, Sarah. Always ready to see the best in people. And Nat's right, I'm sure she's got several indiscretions totted up that could get him the sack if she really went for it. The question now is did Manfred poison Fabian Bigham for reasons unknown? And is the ipecac thing a red herring he's thrown into the mix to lead us all down a stupid rabbit hole?"

Sarah put an arm around Rachel while they finished their drinks. "Come on, Sherlock, let's find the others."

"Okay. You realise we'll need to speak to Waverley when we get back. He won't like this, having already been forced to release Manfred."

23

Thankful when Brendan and Susan opted to return to their room for a rest after the tour, Rachel could tell Carlos about the conversation with Nat.

"But I was with you when you spoke to Manfred Heinrich. Neither of us got the sense he was lying about lacing the drinks that night. What do you plan to do?"

"Tell Waverley. Sarah's arranging a confab through Jason." The phone buzzed in her shoulder bag. After a quick glance, she said. "Which is now."

Carlos looked at his watch. "Do you want me to come with you?"

"No need. Have you got something planned?"

"I've got another last-minute meeting with Simon about the anniversary night. Brendan's passed the baton on to me because Susan's getting suspicious. I need to request a change to the chocolate brand for the gift box in the theatre booth. Apparently she's gone off the original ones, preferring dark chocolate these days."

Rachel chuckled. "One of her diet fads, no doubt."

"Although from what you've just told me, it should be Nat I speak to."

"No doubt she'll be there, and if not, he'll hand over the last-minute details to her. I'd better go. Waverley's going to be in a mood."

Carlos kissed her. "Nothing you can't handle."

"See you later," she said, darting toward the stairs and deck three.

Waverley's office door was ajar when she arrived. Sarah and Jason were sitting on the couch chatting while Waverley barked instructions down the telephone. He looked up from his desk, beckoning her inside. She closed the door behind her, giving Jason an embarrassed smile.

"Can I get you something to drink?" Jason asked.

"Ice-cold water, please." Rachel sat on one of the easy chairs.

"Are you happy with ours? Or would you prefer it brought down from one of the bars?"

"Yours is fine. Thank you."

Jason moved towards the water dispenser and filled a glass. Returning, he handed it to her. He and Sarah had a pot of tea in front of them. Waverley put the phone down and moved away from his desk to take another chair. "Ravanos will bring Heinrich down in about twenty minutes, after he's dealt with another issue."

Poor Waverley. Rachel wondered if the stress of being head of security was becoming too much for him. Sarah had mentioned in one of their video conversations that his wife, Brenda, was worried about his blood pressure.

"We've had a pathology report back from Bangkok." He got straight to the point. "It appears you were right," he sighed, "Fabian Bigham was poisoned and they've traced the substance. Something called..." Waverley looked at his smart tablet, "...tetrodotoxin. Fatal at the right dose and seemingly difficult to detect because of its rapid metabolism."

"So how can the pathologist be certain?" Rachel asked.

"She's carried out microscopic examination of the nerve and muscle tissues now and the toxicology she already had confirmed it. It revealed characteristic changes associated with TTX – that's what they call it – poisoning. These include degeneration and necrosis of nerve fibres. She postulates from her tests that the poison was administered within a four-hour window prior to death. He would have had symptoms within minutes or hours depending on the dose."

"What are the symptoms?" Rachel asked.

"Confusion, numbness, tingling, and nausea; that

sort of thing. He died of respiratory failure as a result of the poisoning."

"What is TTX?" Jason asked.

"It commonly comes from pufferfish," said Sarah. "We had a crewman last year who had been eating raw pufferfish. Graham said it was rare, but I remember it because he was really ill. He survived when we realised what was causing his symptoms. Once he stopped eating pufferfish, he improved. There's no antidote and it wouldn't have been a pleasant death if he'd had very much more."

Rachel wondered if any kind of death was nice but acknowledged that some were definitely better than others.

"Good thing our doctor is so knowledgeable," said Waverley.

"It was actually Bernard who recognised the symptoms and alerted us. Once we could quiz the man along the right lines, it was easier."

"I've always said we have the best medical team on the high seas," said Jason, putting his arm around his wife.

"Enough of that. Let's get back to the topic at hand. Sarah says you have some new information." Waverley's tired eyes fixed on Rachel's.

"You won't like it."

"Do I ever?" He ran a hand through his thinning hair and slumped back in his chair. "Just tell me."

Rachel repeated the conversation she and Sarah had had with Nat that afternoon about what she'd seen on the night of the party. Sarah chipped in occasionally to add details. Waverley's face darkened. "Is that what we're speaking to Manfred Heinrich about? I thought you might have discovered something to exonerate him, not make him chief suspect again. Watching him is taking up a lot of security time."

"The thing is, his parents are influential," said Waverley. "And I don't understand why he would poison Fabian Bigham, or the other passengers. Is he some kind of psychopath?"

"And how he would have got hold of this TTX stuff in the first place?" asked Jason.

"That one's easy. With a bit of knowhow, it can be extracted from the fish directly," said Sarah.

"Or purchased on the black market, I presume," Waverley added.

"But if he didn't mean to kill anyone, and Fabian Bigham's death was an accident, what has he got against passengers?" Sarah said.

Waverley rubbed his temples. "Like I said. He must be crazy. He could have been facing multiple murder charges rather than just one... What's the matter, Rachel?"

Rachel was still struggling to believe Manfred Heinrich would have done such a thing. "I get Manfred had means and opportunity, but I still don't get his motive? He's not crazy, he's just depressed."

There was a knock at the door, and Waverley scowled. "Let's ask him."

Shock was plastered on Manfred's face and when he saw Rachel, confusion. "What's this all about?"

"Thank you, Ravanos. You can go," said Waverley.

Once the Italian security guard Rachel had met on previous cruises left the room, Waverley glared at Manfred.

"Take a seat," Jason commanded.

Manfred sat in the one remaining chair. "Why are you all looking at me like I did something wrong? We've been through all this. I'm innocent."

"Not so fast with your denials," barked Waverley. "Fresh evidence has come to light. Our head of operations, Fabian Bigham, died from TTX poisoning, and you're right back in the frame, only this time it's for murder."

Colour drained from Manfred's face. "What is TTX?"

"Don't play the fool with me, Heinrich. You were seen."

Manfred shook his head. "I don't know what you're talking about. I've never heard of this thing, whatever it is."

Waverley sighed an impatient sigh before indicating Jason should take over.

Jason obliged. "Someone saw you stuffing the poison back in your pocket."

Manfred's eyes widened. "Oh. I can explain about that."

"Please do," said Waverley. "Your stories are so entertaining."

"Look. I'll tell you everything I know, but I'm not lying when I say I've never heard of this thing you mentioned."

Waverley wafted a dismissive hand. Rachel could see he was no longer listening.

"Just tell us what happened," she said.

"Okay. I'd had a bad day." He glanced at Waverley, whose face was puce. "Sometimes my depression gets the better of me, and turnaround days put me under extra pressure."

"Oh, so it's our fault, is it?" Waverley snapped.

"Chief. Please let him continue," Rachel implored with her eyes as well as her words.

"Some days I feel everyone's against me. Crazy thoughts fill my head."

Another impatient breath from Waverley. "Are we going to get to the point any time this century?"

Manfred cowed, putting his head in his hands. "I found a sachet of ipecac – all right? I told Rachel and Carlos I thought someone was playing a practical joke on passengers, but it was more than this. Whoever did it had put the sachet inside the pocket of my bar jacket. At first, I thought they were playing a trick on me, but when people started to get sick, I panicked. I took them out and stuffed them in my trouser pocket."

"Ipecac? What's ipecac got to do with anything?"

Ignoring Waverley, Rachel asked, "Because you were depressed, you thought you were being set up?"

"Well, I was, wasn't I? Who was the first person *they* put on a charge?" He glared at Waverley and Jason.

"Hang on a minute," said Waverley. "You now claim you found an emetic in your bar jacket and after all these lies, we're just meant to believe you? Of course. You're free to go, Mr Heinrich."

Manfred made to move, but realised Waverley's voice was dripping in sarcasm, so he remained. "What I'm telling you is the truth." His eyes pleaded with Rachel. "I gave you as much information as I could when I said it could have been ipecac, but I didn't mention finding the powders because it would have made me look guilty. I didn't lace the drinks with ipecac, but I'd rather be accused of that than murder!"

"How did you know it was ipecac?" Rachel asked.

"It said so on the labels."

"Were the labels branded?"

Confusion crossed Manfred's face. "I see what you mean. No, they were handwritten."

"Where is this powder now?" Waverley demanded. "And why am I only hearing about ipecac powder now?" He glared at Rachel, who didn't respond.

"I flushed it down the toilet. After I saw people becoming ill, I took a toilet break."

"So, Mr Heinrich, all we have to go on is your word?"

"It's the truth."

"And I'm the fairy queen. Once more, Mr Heinrich, you are going to the brig. And I suspect this time it might be a little harder for your mother to wiggle you out of it. Take him away, Goodridge."

"Please?" Manfred looked at Rachel. "I didn't kill anyone. Why would I?"

As soon as Jason left the room with a protesting Manfred Heinrich, Waverley stood up. "That wraps that one up. Thank you, ladies."

Rachel opened her mouth to protest, but she caught Sarah's warning shake of the head.

Once they were in the corridor, Sarah spoke. "You can't reason with him when he's in that sort of mood."

Rachel puffed out her cheeks. "What if whoever killed Fabian Bigham poisoned him a few hours before the party like the pathologist suggested and later laced Manfred's signature cocktail with tiny amounts – just enough to cause symptoms before planting the mislabelled TTX in his pocket?"

"He looked crestfallen, and it's the same as for Nat. Either you've got a pair of good liars on your hands or one of them is the killer. But I got the impression he'd never heard of TTX. What do we do now?"

"We investigate. There's no way I'm letting whoever

did this take advantage of Manfred's illness to frame him."

"Do you think it's Nat then, or another member of the crew?"

"I'm not so sure. Perhaps the person who poisoned Bigham knew nothing about Manfred but had heard someone mention his signature cocktail. When he told me about the ipecac, he said Slick had been recommending his Poisoned Paradise. Maybe the killer's opportunity to cover their tracks was too good to miss."

"So they laced the cocktails and then planted the poison in the mixologist's bar jacket before he put it on. It's all very circumstantial, isn't it?"

"No less circumstantial than the evidence Waverley has. We need to pull the pieces together, because now I'm determined to trap a killer."

"But where do we begin?"

"If the pathologist believes Bigham ingested the poison earlier in the day, we need to trace his contacts from when he boarded. We can start by excluding Manfred. Do you think Jason would trawl CCTV footage to track Fabian's movements on boarding day?"

"He will, but I expect he'll want to run it past Waverley."

"It makes sense to do it even if Manfred is guilty because they don't have enough to go on at the minute."

"You're right. I'll speak to him, and we can meet up

in the Jazz Bar later. What are you going to do in the meantime?"

"I'm going to have a chat with the man Bigham was seen arguing with at the party."

"Orlando Kearney?"

"Precisely. But first I'd better get ready for dinner before anyone suspects I'm up to something."

"I bet Brendan's sussed that one out already."

"You're probably right. He can read me almost as well as you and Carlos can."

"Just when we thought everything was going smoothly. I'll help in whatever way I can, Rachel, but I'm on call from eleven."

24

Frustration was boiling up as Rachel had found no time since re-boarding the ship in Bangkok, nor during the subsequent sea day, to pursue the investigation she was desperate to continue. The only good news was that she'd discovered Waverley had no intention of handing Manfred Heinrich over to law enforcement until they arrived back in Singapore at the end of the cruise. She hated the thought of a man she believed was innocent languishing in the brig, but it was better than the alternative.

Carlos pulled her into his arms just before they left their room. "Today's the day. I'm sure of it. Your opportunity will come."

"While you and Jason are on your scuba diving adventure, you can pick his brains. Ask him if he's found anything on CCTV, will you?"

"Mission accepted, ma'am. Straight to the top of my list." Carlos tipped a mock cap.

Rachel huffed. "Come on, we'd better get going."

"Try to look forward to the day, darling. We're visiting the beautiful and exotic island of Koh Kood, which has the most extraordinary beaches, please give yourself some time off."

"You're right. I'll make sure I enjoy myself just as long as you grill Jason. It's a shame he's been so busy; I'd almost say he's been avoiding me."

"Both Sarah and Jason have been busy since Bangkok. You know how it is for them and you have to remember they're not on holiday. And Rachel, I'll ask Jason if he's had the time to look at CCTV, and if so, whether he's managed to trace Fabian Bigham's movements on boarding day. If you don't mind too much, we'll also enjoy our diving?"

Rachel thumped him playfully on the arm, grinning. "Just don't let your male bonding get in the way of my investigation."

"I wouldn't dare," he replied, giggling.

Rachel's mood improved dramatically when she spied Evie and Linda boarding the same tender as she was taking to shore. Evie waved. "Good morning, Rachel. Are you enjoying your holiday?"

"Very much so," said Rachel. Rachel was pleased to join Brendan and Susan when they took the bench behind the two women.

"Where's your handsome husband?" Evie asked, winking.

"He's going scuba diving with a friend."

"Oh, lucky him, Linda and I are visiting a waterfall."

"So are we," said Susan. "Are you taking a tour?"

"Yes, we are."

Rachel detected a not-so-pleased reaction from Linda, who ignored them and stared ahead.

"Here's my young friend." Evie nudged Linda. "I persuaded him to join our trip."

If Linda had seemed irritated that Rachel and her parents would be on the same excursion, she was downright furious to hear that Danny Martinez, the young gamer, was coming along too.

Danny lowered his head to avoid hitting the roof of the tender and took the high-five from Evie before making his way to the back. He didn't acknowledge Rachel, although a slight flush of the cheeks suggested he had noticed her. She got the impression again that he wasn't the social type and the outing was more because of duress than preference. She imagined Evie could be very persuasive when she put her mind to it.

Rachel's day got even better when the next person to board was Orlando Kearney. "Carlos was right."

"Right about what?" Brendan asked.

"That we're going to have a wonderful day." The sticky label on Kearney's vest was the same as theirs, meaning he was also joining their excursion. Her life had just been made a lot easier. All she needed was for her parents to be distracted enough by the outing to give her the opportunity to speak to Kearney. She was also determined to speak to the less than friendly blogger to ask if she had noticed anything unusual about Fabian Bigham's behaviour on the night of the cocktail party. Rachel hadn't excluded her as a suspect yet. Perhaps she could do that today.

After the bus dropped them off on a main road, their local guide, who had explained on the journey that her name Pimchanok meant chin up in English, led them along a trail.

"It's not too far to the waterfalls from here but please be aware the ground is uneven. Those of you wearing heels should be extra careful." Pimchanok's gaze stopped at Linda Parker, who must have been the only person not to have read the brief about wearing sensible footwear for this excursion.

As they started the walk, Orlando made a point of ignoring people, straggling behind at the rear. Rachel wondered if he was avoiding her father, which annoyed her slightly. With Brendan and Susan on the heels of the front group determined to take in what Pimchanok was saying, Rachel slowed her pace until Orlando couldn't avoid catching up.

"Hello again," she said innocently. "We met at Raffles, didn't we?"

"Oh yes, so we did. Do you share your father's enthusiasm for ecology?"

"In theory, but I don't have time to get into the bones of things like that. He was sorry to have asked so many questions the other day. Carlos, my husband, told me he felt he might have come across as over-interested." Although it had grated with her to play the part of the appeaser, Kearney appeared to relax, which had been her intention.

"So what are you interested in? Sorry, I don't remember your name?"

"It's Rachel. I'm interested in people, but more specifically, catching criminals. I'm a detective in serious crime back home." Linda, who was just ahead, turned her head, frowning, but Evie and Danny ushered her forward.

Kearney's jaw tensed. "I see."

"I don't know whether you heard, but a man you were seen arguing with at the VIP cocktail party died shortly afterwards?"

"I knew Fabian had a heart attack. I was supposed to meet him on the day I met Carlos and Brendan, but I wasn't sorry our rendezvous was cancelled. Why would you be interested in that?"

"You weren't sorry he was dead, then?" said Rachel, ignoring his question and keeping the group ahead in sight in case this conversation turned nasty.

"What are you implying?"

"I'm interested, that's all. What were you arguing about?"

"That's none of your business. You might be a detective on land, Rachel, but you have no right to question me, especially about someone who died of natural causes."

"That's just it, you see. He didn't die of natural causes. But you're quite right. I can ask the chief of security to speak to you instead. Nice chatting." Rachel picked up her pace and marched forward.

"Wait!"

Rachel slowed down, but still kept the stragglers in sight.

"Look. There's no need to involve the security team in anything. If I'm honest, Fabian was drunk and confused when I spoke to him that night."

"And yet the conversation was heated?"

"Who said so?"

"Someone who was there. Are you going to tell me or not?"

"Okay, but I'd rather this didn't get out. Fabian was trying to blackmail me."

Rachel wasn't surprised, having listened to a similar story from Evie. "What about?"

"If you must know, one of my directors had been illegally disposing of waste until a few months back. As soon as I found out, the board sacked him. Somehow Fabian found out and threatened to expose it to the world."

"I assume that would negate any contract you have with the cruise line?"

"Exactly."

"But wasn't it his duty to report it? I thought he was some bigwig for Queen Cruises."

"Yes, he was the director of operations, but with Fabian it was always him and money first. Work second. Wife third."

"Hmm."

"Look. After Fabian's threat, when Brendan started quizzing me the other day, I thought he might work for the press. That's why I shut him down."

"You can rest assured my dad's interest is genuine."

"I realise that now, but Fabian spooked me. Trusting strangers who came across as interested in the mechanics of my business wasn't on my radar."

"What were you going to do about the blackmail?"

"Pay him. It would cost less than losing a business I've worked my whole life to build up."

"So you'd rather cover up for a criminal than let the truth come out?"

Kearney shook his head. "You make it sound simple. Just hand the guy in, invite the press and put greener waste disposal back decades. These things aren't always clear cut."

"As an upholder of the law, they are to me."

"Come on, Rachel. I bet you've had to make some

borderline decisions in your work." Orlando had a point. Sometimes Rachel had to allow people to get away with crime in order to go after the bigger fish. Philosophers would call it the greater good. Indeed, wasn't that what they had done with George Crispin?

"If it makes you feel better, we reported the incident to the relevant authorities, but no-one wants another ecological scandal. If they decide to prosecute, he'll pay a high price for what he did, but it won't be in the public eye. We, as a company, are paying for the cleanup operation. I'm committed to protecting the planet, even if I have to blur the boundaries now and then."

"But you have to admit it was a bit of a coincidence, Fabian dying not long after the two of you argued about him potentially ruining your business?"

"Until a few moments ago, I believed the man had a heart attack. He wasn't making much sense that night; even his threats weren't clear. Now I think back, he seemed breathless, but he told me to shove off after I agreed to pay him. I made it clear there would be a limit to how much I was prepared to pay."

Rachel thought back to the symptoms of TTX poisoning, which she'd looked up since hearing about it. If Kearney had noticed Fabian behaving oddly, other people might have done so too. "Did you see anyone else with Fabian Bigham that night?"

"That blogger woman who writes negative articles about the cruise line had a brief chat with him. I'd avoid her if I were you. She's poison. Please don't mention any of this conversation to her. If I'd realised she'd be on this tour, I wouldn't have come."

"It will remain our secret unless I find anything to suggest you poisoned the man."

"Poison? Is that how he died? And are you investigating his murder?"

"I am."

"Then maybe you should speak to the blogger after all. She was videoing him and a lot of other people from the bar. If you're looking for a motive, she had every reason to kill him. He was suing her for defamation. You can only imagine what big-time lawyers would do to a small-time blogger like her."

"I thought she was retired?"

"People like her don't retire. Worse than the paparazzi. In fact, it wouldn't surprise me if she was behind the story that Bigham had multiple affairs."

"Where did you read that?"

"It was one of the stories Queen Cruise lawyers got a gag order for. Remember, I work with these people. They tell me things."

"Thanks for the tip. I'll bear it in mind when I speak to her."

"I can't really see her killing him," Orlando said. "But after he shoved me away, I heard him threatening someone else. Before you ask... I didn't see who it was.

The garden was packed by that time and I had a meeting with the chief engineer, so I left."

The group ahead had come to a halt and the sound of the water and excited voices filled the air.

"Would you do me a favour?" Rachel asked.

"Sure."

"Please apologise to my father. I'm not asking you to give away any trade secrets regarding your work. He believes he offended you."

"Sure I will. I love talking about my work. I'll give him a tour of what we're piloting on this ship, without giving away the secrets of course."

"Thank you."

Orlando strolled over to Brendan and said something before they shook hands and started chatting. If he was telling the truth, she could be right about Manfred being innocent. But who poisoned Fabian Bigham? Surely not Linda or Evie?

Rachel put her thoughts aside as the group made their way up a rugged trail to get a view from above the large waterfall. Some of the more adventurous people took hold of a swing rope and swung over the pool, then dropped into the water below.

"Go on, Rachel. Have a go. I know you're itching to." Her mother nudged her.

What she was itching to do was to speak to Linda Parker but as she, Evie and Danny were congregated above the waterfall engrossed in conversation, now wasn't the time for interviews. Rachel wanted to give Brendan more time with Orlando, so she stepped toward the queue for the rope.

"Why not? Here, keep this." She handed her phone over to her mother, who placed it in her handbag. "See you at the bottom."

Rachel waited in the queue for the rope and eventually it came her way. Wrapping her hands and legs around it, she lifted off. A rush of adrenaline swept through her veins as she swung over the water and let go! Dropping underwater and resurfacing, the deep water was cool and refreshing. She was soaked through, but certain her clothes would dry quickly in the heat. She turned onto her back and waved to her mother before backstroking away to allow the next person to drop.

She had just closed her eyes when a terrified scream pierced through the air.

25

Rachel opened her eyes and saw a person plummeting like a rag doll, bouncing off the ledge before landing with a loud splash. A few people still in the water swam towards the splash. She hurriedly swam towards them. A couple of men had waded in from the side.

The woman lay face down in the water. Rachel pushed herself forward and turned her over. Linda Parker's eyes stared into nothingness. Blood stained her clothes, presumably from the bashing her body had taken against the shelf on the way down.

A young girl gasped.

"Come away." A man led her from the scene.

Rachel and the guys got the body to shore where Pimchanok was waiting, breathless and wide-eyed. The poor woman must have run down the hill. A man declared himself to be a nurse and attempted resuscitation, but Rachel knew it was no use. Linda had died of her injuries on the way down, not in the water. Pimchanok phoned for the emergency services, speaking Thai in short, shocked gasps. Afterwards, she gathered herself together and corralled everyone away from the scene except for the nurse and another person who was a first aider.

"Please move back. An ambulance is on its way. I think it would be best if you head back to the bus."

"Aw. Come on *Chin Up*. I'm sorry the old lady slipped and all that, but we've not long got here. Can't we enjoy the views for a bit?"

The view of a woman being resuscitated was hardly a tourist attraction. Rachel stared at the middle-aged woman who came across so insensitive. "Please do as the guide suggests," she said.

The woman was about to argue, but a man took her arm. "Come along, Bessie. We'll make sure we get a refund later."

"Some people are so selfish," Rachel muttered under her breath. When she caught sight of Brendan and Susan arriving at the bottom of the trail having come down the hill, she took a long look at the dead blogger before going to meet them.

"What a thing to happen," said Susan. "Will she be okay?"

"I don't think so, Mum."

The nurse stopped resuscitating and said something to the guide. "Maybe you should do your thing, Dad?"

Brendan approached the guide, speaking briefly to her, before he bent down to place a hand on Linda Parker's forehead.

His lips moved to utter a prayer.

When Brendan returned, Orlando joined them. Rachel noticed Evie sitting on a tree stump, eyes popping with horror. "I'll check Evie's all right," she said.

"Of course. It must have been a terrible sight from where they were," said Susan.

Evie looked up when Rachel sat next to her. "I warned her not to wear those stupid heels, but she wouldn't listen."

"Did you see what happened?"

"Not really, just that she slipped. We were standing at the top, enjoying the view and watching people swinging from the rope. We saw you go down. I waved, but you didn't see me. Anyway, one minute she was there, the next I heard her scream. She might have survived if she hadn't bounced off that shelf. Why did she have to wear those silly heels?"

Danny appeared, looking pale. He sat on the other side of Evie. "Were you there when she fell?" Rachel asked.

"We all were, but I was focussing on the people swinging from the rope. Did Evie tell you we saw you?

She was joking about some of the less adept swingers looking more like gorillas than monkeys. Then Linda screamed."

Rachel looked up to see her parents still chatting to Orlando. She exchanged a look with him. *Where were you when this went down? Had Linda uncovered your secret?* The questions went through her mind. Her suspicion radar was on high alert. If it hadn't been for the events at the cocktail party, she would have chalked this tragedy down to an unfortunate accident because Evie was right about the high-heeled shoes being inappropriate for the terrain. Rachel wondered if the guide would get into trouble for allowing Linda to join the trip.

While she and Danny waited for Evie to recover from her shock, the last groups of people left the scene when the ambulance crew arrived. Rachel watched the paramedics speak briefly to Pimchanok and the nurse. They examined Linda, shook their heads, and loaded her onto a stretcher before moving swiftly to take her away.

Susan signalled she and Brendan were leaving with Orlando. Rachel waved them away, gesturing she would wait with Evie and Danny. The gawky man seemed impatient to get moving, but Evie was stuck in a repetitive cycle of head shaking and muttering about the shoes repeatedly.

"We should leave," said Rachel finally, dragging Evie from her trance.

"I agree. Come on Evie, lean on me," Danny said.

After she stood up, Rachel remembered something Orlando had told her. "I think I might have left my phone at the top when I went for a dip. You two go ahead, I'll catch up." Before they had time to answer, Rachel turned, jogging up the rocky terrain leading to the summit of the waterfall.

Her phone was in her mother's handbag, but she wasn't looking for that. At any other time, Rachel would have marvelled at the view like she'd done when she'd been there earlier. Instead, she peered over the edge, looking down at the ridged shelf, hoping she was right.

Water cascaded downwards in a torrent. The guide had told them there had been an unusual amount of rain in recent weeks. Her eyes focussed until she saw what she was looking for. If she was careful, she should be able to scramble down the rocks to get behind the waterfall and climb down to the ledge. She and Carlos had been rock climbing many times in Derbyshire, but this was something else. It wouldn't be easy, and even if Linda's phone was in her handbag it might be beyond repair. Was it worth the risk? She had to try.

After scrambling onto all fours and getting herself into position on what seemed the most secure part of the roof, Rachel lowered herself, swinging a leg to reach rocks that looked like they would provide a firm foothold. Once her right foot was in place, she gripped a steady rock with her hands and brought her left foot down over the edge. The speed of the water bellowed in her ears and would drown out any sound if she were to slip behind the waterfall. Still, she persevered, uttering a silent prayer before starting her descent.

Rachel took deep breaths with each precarious step towards the ledge where Linda's handbag had landed. The roar of the waterfall was even louder now, thundering in her ears as she tentatively navigated the slippery rocks. Her fingers gripped tightly to maintain balance while her feet sought the next foothold. She had to be cautious. One missed step could send her plummeting the same way Linda had gone into the churning waters below.

Inch by inch, Rachel lowered herself, testing each foothold before shifting her weight downwards. Realising there was no turning back, this equated to one of the dumbest things she had ever done. The spray from the cascading water showered her clothes, which had only just dried out. Moss and lichen made the rocks even more treacherous than the water. She paused for a moment, pressing her body against the cool, wet surface to take a breath and check her balance.

As she reached for the next handhold, the rock below Rachel's right foot slipped, causing her heart to lurch into her throat. She held on tight, scrambling to regain her footing. Thankfully she had a good grip where her fingers dug into the crevices of the rock face. With a determined heave, she managed to stabilise herself, breathless from the exertion.

Steadying her nerves, Rachel continued her descent, the ledge now tantalisingly close. She could see the bright yellow handbag, its vibrant colour a stark contrast against the shaded, glistening rocks. Just a few more steps down and she would be able to reach it.

Another rock gave way, this time just as she had released one of her hands from its grip, causing Rachel to slide down the rock face until she landed with a thump on the ledge. Her palms stung and her right leg screamed out in pain, but she pushed the pain aside.

Rachel reached for the handbag, which had nearly gone through a hole at the back of the ledge. She clutched it to her, breathing a sigh of relief. Rachel edged along the narrow platform, the waterfall's spray now drenching her. Putting the handbag to one side while checking her leg for damage, she was dismayed to see a deep cut. The water made it difficult to see how much blood there was, but she knew the gash would need stitches. Rachel grasped the strap of Linda's handbag, inspecting its contents. Everything was wet but not soaked. Rachel was thrilled to find a headscarf, which she took out and applied to her leg, pulling it tight to stem the bleeding. With her temporary dressing in place, she left everything else in the handbag as it was, closing the clasp.

"Now, for the next tricky part. How to get off this ledge without damaging the bag or your leg any further," she muttered.

There was no choice but to jump into the pool below, hoping she could leap far enough away from the ledge to avoid banging her head and that the water's depth would cushion her fall. Rachel forced herself to stand, hugging the handbag to her chest. She was determined to keep what she had risked her life for as dry as possible.

Taking a deep breath, Rachel hobbled to the edge and summoned all the strength in her legs from her years of running. She leapt into the air. Her body struggled to pass to the other side of the plummeting waterfall, which pushed her down faster than she would have liked. Rachel hit the water with a resounding splash. Her body went under, but she reached up with her hands to keep the prized possession from dropping too far below the waterline.

When she surfaced, she was able to move into the calmer waters away from the waterfall, treating the handbag like someone whose life she was saving. The shock from the exertion temporarily stunned her. Rachel gasped for air but could feel the ground beneath her. She held the handbag aloft, relieved to see it had survived the jump relatively unscathed, and made her way to the shore once more.

She heard concerned voices close by. Rachel turned around to see her parents and Pimchanok running in her direction.

How was she going to explain this one?

26

"What happened?" Pimchanok asked, stress etched on her face. Rachel assumed this had been an outing the guide wouldn't forget in a hurry.

"I saw the handbag had fallen onto the ledge when I was at the top of the hill and thought it might be important for the dead woman's relatives to have it."

"That was thoughtful of you, but you could have been killed. Let me patch that up before we head back to the bus."

Trying to ignore the sceptical look on her father's face, Rachel sat on a rock and allowed the guide to examine her injured leg. "Thanks."

Rachel winced when Pimchanok removed the soaked scarf and seemed to have anticipated further injury. Opening a first aid kit, she began tending to

Rachel's leg. "This is going to need stitches. I think we should take you to the hospital."

"No need," said Rachel. "The medical team on board the *Coral Queen* will do that. Just do your best for now."

Was that relief on Pimchanok's face? Rachel suspected she would have enough to do reporting what had happened to Linda without having another tourist transferred to the hospital. She was adept with a first aid kit and patched Rachel's leg up well. The worst pain was when Pimchanok had to pull the wound together before fixing it with adhesive strips, which would hold it together temporarily. Once her leg was bandaged, they began the walk back along the trail.

"Will you manage?" Pimchanok asked.

"Yes. I'll take it slow," said Rachel. "You go on, we'll follow."

Pimchanok seemed happy to be released. There would be disgruntled tourists waiting for her back at the bus. Once she was out of hearing distance, Rachel prepared herself for the grilling.

"What were you thinking, Rachel?" Her mother had remained quiet while the guide saw to Rachel's leg, but now her tone was angry but tinged with concern.

"Sorry," Rachel's eyes implored her father to intervene.

He got the message. "I'm sure Rachel had her reasons."

"Such as?"

Rachel swallowed the lump in her throat, "I thought I saw the handbag from where I was in the water when Linda fell, which is why I checked from the top."

"I'd rather you didn't lie to me, Rachel. You know better than that. If you don't want to say... fine."

"Okay."

Brendan looked from his wife to Rachel. Realising they were at a standoff, he smiled.

"We can discuss this once Rachel has had her leg stitched. Is it sore?"

Rachel had been trying her best not to hobble, lest her mother be even more concerned. In truth, every movement gave her more pain. "It's not too bad. Although I'll be happy to rest it. Sorry if I've ruined your tour."

"That poor woman's death was shocking enough," said Susan. "But I don't understand why you felt the need to risk life and limb to retrieve a dead woman's handbag... or why you told Evie you had left your phone at the top of the waterfall when you had given it to me for safekeeping."

This grilling was going to continue until Rachel offered a plausible explanation. "In the aftermath of what happened back there, I forgot I'd given it to you and thought I'd take a quick jog up the hill to see. Did you mention to Evie that you had my phone?"

"Of course I did. She looked as bemused as I feel.

You could have been killed, Rachel. As it is, that's a nasty gash you've got to your leg."

Brendan put an arm around his wife. "But she wasn't killed, darling. Let's give her some space. I'm sure Rachel had her reasons." It was clear her father wasn't buying her memory lapse explanation, but at least he was being supportive.

"Let's hope they're good ones," said Susan. "Because I don't like our daughter telling fibs."

As if to make a point, a familiar ringtone sounded from Susan's handbag. She reached inside and held it out to Rachel.

"Oh look, here's your phone!"

Rachel took the phone, a sheepish grin on her face.

"Hi Carlos. How's your day?"

Brendan gave a placatory shrug as he chivvied his wife toward the group boarding the bus. Pimchanok was ushering people aboard, trying to placate the less patient members of the group. Once most were aboard, she and the driver spoke in Thai.

A few people gave Rachel an odd look, none more so than Evie who stared, wide-eyed at the soaked handbag Rachel wasn't able to conceal. Danny was sitting in an aisle seat next to Evie, his face fixed on his handheld, engaged in what Rachel assumed was another video game. He snapped the device closed, giving her a brief nod when Evie nudged him.

Rachel sighed. If Evie was a murderer, she now

knew Rachel had lied about leaving her phone at the summit and that she was investigating Linda's death.

"It's been a lot better than yours, by the sound of it. Can you talk?"

"Not really," she said.

"Then just listen. Jason heard that the blogger you met fell to her death. He wants me to ask you if there was anything suspicious about it?"

"Nothing obvious."

"But from the tone in your voice, you don't believe it was an accident."

"Something like that." Rachel was aware of people looking at her while she was climbing the steps and made her way back to her seat.

Jason's voice could be heard speaking in the background. "He's asking if he should contact the local police?"

"I wouldn't have thought that would be helpful at this stage."

"Understood. You don't sound quite yourself. Is everything okay?"

"I had a bit of an accident. Could you tell Jason I'm going to need first aid when I get back to the ship?"

"How bad?"

"It's just a gash in my leg, but bad enough to warrant stitches."

"Rachel? I can't—"

"Sorry, the line's bad—" The call ended.

The bus had started its journey back to the ship, and they'd obviously hit a blind spot for mobile phone signals. Rachel stared at the phone.

"Is everything all right?"

"Fine. They enjoyed their dive. I expect they'll be waiting for us when we get back to the ship."

Rachel closed her eyes, not wanting to be subjected to any further interrogation from her mother. She felt unusually weak. After what seemed like a much longer journey than it had on the way to the waterfall, she felt the bus draw to a halt. Looking down at her leg, she saw a huge red patch seeping through the bandage. *That explains the tiredness. Just how much blood have I lost?*

Her father leaned over to say something but stopped, frowning when he saw the bloodstained bandage.

Rachel shook her head in warning, and they waited for everyone to disembark.

"Take my arm," Brendan said. Rachel was grateful to do so, and this time couldn't avoid hobbling. Once they were in the bright sunlight, Susan turned around, about to speak, but her jaw dropped. "Rachel, you've gone awfully pale."

Before they could say any more, Carlos arrived and swept her into his arms. Jason took charge, leading them through the ship's own security entrance. "I've radioed ahead."

"Thank you," said Rachel.

Carlos carried her all the way to the medical centre without saying a word.

Janet Plover was waiting with Sarah, whose eyes betrayed her concern when she saw the blood.

"Put her in there," said Janet.

Carlos hurried into the infirmary and placed her on the first bed. Rachel was pleased to see Gwen intercepting her parents, particularly her mother, who was shaking.

Mum never shakes.

"Let's get you a refreshing drink while you wait," she heard Gwen say. Brendan nodded, leading her mum to a small sofa while Sarah closed the curtains around the bed.

"What happened?" Janet asked while Sarah busied herself loading a trolley with an assortment of dressing packs and solutions.

"I had a fight with a rocky ledge and it won." Rachel's head was swimming. "Carlos. Please take this." Rachel handed over the bright yellow handbag to her husband while Sarah donned gloves and started unravelling the blood-soaked bandage.

"It's not really my shade. I prefer lemon," said Carlos, grinning.

Their laughter broke through the tension.

Jason slapped him on the back. "Nice one, mate."

"See. She's going to be fine," Brendan's concerned voice reached her ears.

Rachel was grateful to her husband for de-stressing them all. Her eyelids felt heavy.

Right now, all she wanted to do was sleep.

She was jolted back to life when Sarah applied pressure to the wound. Rachel grimaced in pain as she then cleaned it with saline. Janet gave her a smile. "This might hurt."

"It already does."

"Yes, but this might hurt more."

She wasn't kidding! Janet frowned as she inspected the wound, but by the time she reached for the local anaesthetic, she looked assured. "Time to numb this for you," she said.

"I'd be grateful," said Rachel. She felt some stinging as the local anaesthetic was injected, but soon she was relieved to be pain free.

"It's too deep to glue, so I'm going to have to stitch it. Is that okay?"

"Go ahead," said Rachel. "I can't feel a thing."

While Janet and Sarah stitched the wound together, Rachel motioned to Carlos to come close. Lowering her voice, she said, "See if someone can salvage the contents of the phone inside that handbag. It might contain evidence from the night of the cocktail party."

"I'll do it. You stay there," said Jason. "I've always had an affinity for yellow."

Sarah chuckled as her husband left with the bag

attached to his shoulder, but the look Rachel got from her made her realise she was in for another grilling.

"How is she?" her father asked Jason.

"You know what they say. You can't keep a good woman down!"

"I wish someone would tell me why that handbag is so important," Susan said.

"Rachel said the lady might have personal effects inside that might help her family grieve."

"If you say so. At least Rachel is going to be all right. Why she does these things, I'll never understand."

"I hate to inform you, Mum," Rachel called. "I can hear every word. These curtains aren't soundproof."

27

For the first time in years, Rachel wished she was anything other than a police officer. At times she wondered whether she was suffering posttraumatic stress disorder, but she hastily shook such thoughts from her mind whenever they cropped up.

"Shaking your head doesn't make the stress go away, you know. Somewhere down the line, you're going to suffer when these suppressed emotions surface for all to see," an inner voice warned.

"I'm fine! This is just about yesterday's fall," she muttered. "It's taken a greater toll on my body than I realised. And now I'm talking to myself."

Getting up was an uphill battle. Rachel grabbed her clothes for the day and limped into the shower. She had just finished dressing when Carlos arrived back from breakfast, which she had opted to skip. Her parents had popped in to see her before they went on a trip, but she had been in no mood to discuss her injuries.

When she was ready, Carlos stood in front of her, looking at her with his penetrating brown eyes. "Are you sure you're up to this?"

"You've asked the same question three times, Carlos. My answer hasn't changed."

He looked doubtful, his eyebrows rising toward his hairline as he watched her limping toward the door. She wished he would go first and then he wouldn't see how much pain she was in. But he knew anyway. Every time she'd moved during the night, she couldn't stifle her groans, waking him repeatedly.

"Sarah and Jason will understand if you want to cancel."

With her hand grasping the door handle, she almost gave in, but her stubborn streak wouldn't stand for it. Instead, she huffed an exasperated sigh. "Are you coming or not?"

She heard him mutter something in Italian under his breath. From her small grasp of the language, she got the gist: *pig-headed and idiotic.*

They rarely argued, which was surprising considering how much stress they lived under, but this could turn out to be one of those times. Rachel shuffled as fast as she could along the corridor. She had donned mid-calf cropped trousers to hide the large plaster dressing covering the wound on her right lower leg. It might be childish, but if she made it to the lift first, she was going down without him.

She did just that. Usually Rachel used the stairs, but even she couldn't do that today, not with the tour that lay ahead of them.

When she arrived at the guest services, Sarah and Jason were waiting.

"Good morning," Rachel said.

"I wasn't sure we'd see you today," said Sarah, unable to disguise the concerned frown.

"Don't you start! I'm not a child."

Sarah's face flushed while the corner of Jason's eyes crinkled, but he held back on laughing. Instead, asking, "Where's Carlos?"

"Still fussing about somewhere upstairs. How should I know?"

"He's worried about you," said Sarah.

"Right. That's it. I'll see you outside. I need some air." Rachel attempted to stomp away, but pain in her leg and the aches everywhere else made it a clumsy effort.

"Hang on. I'll come with you."

Rachel glared at her best friend, harrumphing. "Fine."

Once they were on the port side, Rachel appreciated the refreshing breeze on her face. She continued hobbling quickly until Sarah grabbed her arm.

"Rachel?"

"What?"

"Slow down, please. Okay. I recognise the determined look and accept you won't be dissuaded, but let's just take a breath, shall we?"

Rachel opened her mouth but closed it again, muttering. "Fine."

"Extensive vocabulary, by the way." Sarah nudged her and they both burst out laughing.

They were still laughing when Jason and Carlos arrived. Her husband had a sheepish look on his face. "Sorry," he said.

It should be her apologising, not him. "Me too."

"Right. That's settled then," said Jason, rubbing his hands together. "Harley-Davidson here I come."

"Yeah right." Sarah gave him an eye roll.

Once they were through the customs building, they found a woman holding a sign for their excursion.

"Imagine it's a Harley," said Carlos, nudging Jason as he took a helmet from a woman examining tickets. He strolled towards a row of well-worn scooters where guides were waiting.

"No need. I'm happy with a faithful workhorse any day. After all, I am one." The men continued bantering while Sarah and Rachel listened.

Following a brief safety lecture, they each climbed onto a seat behind a motorcyclist to ride pillion and set off for their first destination. The quartet zipped through the bustling streets of the city, taking in the sights, sounds and scents of the vibrant metropolis. Rachel marvelled at the stunning architecture, with ancient temples juxtaposed against modern skyscrapers. The air was heavy with the aroma of sizzling street food and fragrant flowers.

As the expert guides navigated the winding roads of Ho Chi Minh City, Rachel found herself momentarily lost in the thrill of the ride. The pain in her leg was temporarily forgotten. A warm breeze caressed her face, and the laughter of her companions when they lined up at junctions, mixed with the hum of the scooters' engines, was therapeutic.

Their guides took them to see hidden gems throughout the city, sharing the history and culture at each stop. They paused outside a park where locals were practicing tai chi. Rachel preferred karate, but she appreciated the fluid movements of the ancient art and how it created a dance of tranquillity amidst the urban chaos. Next, they explored a bustling street market, its stalls overflowing with colourful textiles, aromatic spices, and exquisite crafts.

As lunchtime approached, their guides brought them to a Vietnamese restaurant tucked away in a quiet alley. The interior was adorned with traditional decor, and the mouthwatering scent of what their guide told them was pho and banh mi filled the air. They were shown to a table where a selection of delicious-looking food was placed in front of them along with iced drinks.

"Part of the tour," said Ming, Rachel's guide.

One of the guides pointed to each dish and named them, but Rachel lost her after noodle soup and banh mi street food.

After the soup course, Rachel began sampling food from other bowls before turning to Jason, her voice muted. "Did you have any success rescuing Linda's phone data?"

Jason shook his head, a slight frown creasing his brow. "Not yet. The water damage was pretty extensive, but our tech team is working on it. I have to admit it's not the boss's top priority."

Rachel exhaled, disappointed. She had hoped, after risking her life to acquire it, that the phone might hold clues to Fabian's death and what occurred on the night of the fateful cocktail party.

"But," Jason continued, leaning in closer, "it might interest you to know we're expecting a background report and further details about Fabian Bigham later on today. When we got the official foul play conclusion, we were able to request a background investigation and employment details. It might come to nothing, but then again, it could shed some light on the situation."

Rachel's interest piqued; a glimmer of hope sparked within her. "Will you let me take a look?" she asked.

"I'll have to ask the boss. He still believes we've got the right man."

"And that Linda Parker's demise was accidental, I suppose?"

Jason nodded.

Returning to the delicious Vietnamese feast, the conversation flowed easily. Carlos and Jason continued their light-hearted banter while Sarah chatted about how Bernard thought wedding bells were on the horizon for Gwen and Dr Bentley. Rachel found herself relaxing, the warmth of the food and the conversation soothing her mind and body. Although she'd enjoyed the motorcycle tour, her muscles ached from the effort of keeping herself from jolting anything that already hurt.

"Do you think Bernard's right?"

"They are practically living together on board, but I'll wait for the official announcement rather than Bernard's suppositions. That said, he's usually right about these things."

"If they get married, will they leave?"

"I hope not. If they do, it might be time to consider doing the same thing. We're such a close-knit team."

"Your mum would be happy if you settled in England." She would too, if she was honest. Spending more time with her best friend would be wonderful. A familiar voice interrupted her thoughts.

"Hello Rachel? I'm pleased to see you here! And with your husband this time."

Rachel turned to see Evie standing beside their table, a bright smile on her face.

"Evie! How are you?"

"As you see."

Considering how awful she'd looked yesterday, Evie seemed remarkably well.

"Please join us," said Carlos, standing to pull in a chair.

"Thank you. I decided to explore the city on my own today... well, not quite alone. I have a guide."

"Surely not a scooter?"

"No dear. A driver."

Evie took the chair offered. "I've been here before. The food's amazing, isn't it?"

"Delicious," said Sarah. "Rachel told me you were with Mrs Parker when she had her accident yesterday. How are you holding up?"

Evie sighed, her smile fading. "It was a dreadful shock, but I didn't know her that well, apart from joining her when we were on the same cruise for mutually convenient trips. I still can't stop thinking about how suddenly it all happened. If only she hadn't worn those heels."

Rachel leaned forward. "I didn't get the chance to ask yesterday, but did you detect anything unusual in Linda's behaviour before the accident?"

Evie hesitated, glancing around the restaurant as if to ensure no-one was eavesdropping. "I heard you telling that man you're a detective back home. It made me realise why you ask so many questions and why you went back for her handbag."

Evie was as sharp as Rachel gave her credit for.

"Sorry about the subterfuge."

"What? Oh, about leaving your phone behind. I quite understand, because there is something Linda said that's been bothering me."

The group fell silent, their attention focussed solely on Evie.

"Please tell us," said Rachel.

"It was odd, really. Out of the blue, during the trip, Linda told me she knew who had killed Fabian Bigham," Evie whispered. "I didn't believe her... she was always making things up... or exaggerating for that blog of hers. She got quite annoyed with me and told me she had proof."

"What kind of proof?" Rachel was even more determined to retrieve the data from the dead woman's phone.

"She didn't get the chance to tell me more before..." Her words trailed off.

Rachel exchanged a glance with Carlos.

Jason's brow furrowed, concentrating. "Did Ms Parker give you any indication of who it was she suspected?"

Evie shook her head. "None. I think she may have been about to, but then we got distracted by more people gathering at the top of the waterfall, and then people started jumping from that rope. I keep wondering. If only I had pressed her for more information, but I thought she was making it up. That's why I was so upset."

Rachel reached out, placing a comforting hand on Evie's arm. "It's not your fault. You couldn't have foreseen what was going to happen."

Evie offered a weak smile, her eyes glistening. "I just wish I could have done more. Danny was such a comfort. You know, for a computer nerd, he's quite good company. He took me to play bridge last night to cheer me up."

"You didn't persuade him to join you today?"

"I tried, but he'd already booked something." She put a finger to her head, eyes scrunched in concentration. "Something to do with practicing for a virtual first-person shooting competition? I think it's one of the video games he enjoys. He could do with spending more time in the real world, away from all that fantasy stuff. Still, he's been an absolute rock."

There was a lull in conversation while each person processed what she'd told them. Rachel cogitated over what Linda might have known and wondered whether someone could have silenced her. Orlando?

One of the guides came inside and ushered them out. "Apologies, Evie. We've been summoned," said Rachel.

"No problem. I'll enjoy my brief interlude. I love Saigon – I still call it that – but the air quality's terrible." As if to prove a point, she coughed.

They bid her farewell and returned to the street.

Carlos held Rachel's eyes, his expression grave. "Are you thinking what I'm thinking?"

She nodded. "That someone pushed Linda over that ledge? Yes."

"Who?" Sarah asked.

"Another option could be that Evie is trying to misdirect us, especially now she knows you're a cop back home," said Jason.

Rachel mulled it over. "It's possible. But if she's not, she might be in danger herself. I might need another chat with Orlando Kearney. He had good reason to want to silence Fabian, and he has access to the kitchens."

"What reason?" Jason asked.

"Just something he told me yesterday, which I can't divulge for now. But I think you should check if any supplies have gone missing. In particular, pufferfish."

"I'll get on it as soon as we get back."

Rachel puffed out her cheeks, exasperated. "And we can't rule Danny Martinez out at this point, either. Why is he hanging around Evie?"

"Because she's a forceful character, from what you've said." Sarah frowned. "And, for what it's worth, I don't believe Evie's trying to mislead us. You said she seemed upset about Fabian and Linda's deaths."

"You like to believe the best in everyone, darling, but appearances can deceive," Jason reminded her.

"If Evie's involved, we'll find out. I'd like to know if we met by coincidence just now, or whether she was on a fishing trip. She noticed the handbag when I got back to the bus and Mum basically told her I lied to her, so maybe she felt it necessary to find out what I know. We really need to get inside that phone. I'm sure it holds the key." Rachel climbed back aboard her scooter, leaning into the backrest for comfort.

"I'll see what I can do," said Jason.

As the others mounted their scooters to continue the tour, Rachel's mind was whirring. At least it distracted her from the pain.

28

Waverley didn't look pleased to see her waiting outside his door, but Rachel didn't care. Her body ached and her leg was sore, so his sensitivities were the least of her concerns. She was sure he had once again jumped to conclusions in his haste to solve a case.

"What can I do for you, Rachel?" Waverley unlocked his office and motioned for her to go inside.

Now she was here, she didn't know what to say, or more importantly, how to put it into words.

"Drink?" He marched over to his fridge.

"No thanks. I'm on my way to dinner."

"Then I'm sure you'll want to tell me what's on your mind."

"Well... I..."

"Let me help you. Jason has already informed me

that you met Evelyn Mitchell while you were out today and what she had to say. He's also made it clear that neither of you believe Manfred Heinrich is guilty because you believe Linda Parker was pushed from the ledge. How am I doing so far?"

No wonder he was in such a mood. Her, he might choose to ignore, but not his loyal security officer, Jason. "I believe Manfred was in the wrong place at the wrong time, that's all. Somebody spiked his cocktails, I'm not sure how, and then covered their tracks by planting the powder in his bar jacket pocket. I doubt they cared who the jacket belonged to. And I might as well say, I agree with Jason that someone pushed Linda Parker from the top of the waterfall."

"I don't suppose you can tell me who?"

"Not yet, but if it's the same killer, and I believe it is, the suspect list is narrower. As far as I can tell, there were only three, more likely two, people present who might have done it. Two with motive and one uncertain. I'm sure the evidence is on Linda's phone, or in her notes. I expect you've already searched her room?"

Waverley cleared his throat. A sure sign bad news was about to follow. "Erm. I'm afraid the stateroom's been ransacked."

"Which proves it is the same killer and Manfred's innocent."

"We can't jump to conclusions. Robberies take place on board this ship more often than I would like. Anyone on that outing might have seized the opportunity to look for valuables. Her safe was empty."

"So the killer made it look like a robbery. This person's clever. Is there any CCTV footage?"

"Yes, we have someone dressed in dark clothing with their head down, well aware of where the cameras are, entering Ms Parker's room using her keycard at two o'clock in the morning. They left with a bulging rucksack."

"The killer stole her key?"

"Or she gave it to someone."

"That's unlikely. What about the contents of her handbag and the phone?"

Waverley shook his head. "Nothing else so far."

"It's time for some background checks on our prime suspects and a look at their whereabouts in the early hours, wouldn't you say?"

"I assume you mean Evelyn Mitchell and Orlando Kearney? Already happening."

"You should also include Danny Martinez. He's an unlikely candidate, but I'm sure he had come across Fabian Bigham before. And once met, never forgotten."

"Gut feeling I suppose?"

"It was the way he reacted when Linda announced Fabian's death on boarding night. But he's an odd character, socially inept, I'd say. He probably sits somewhere on the spectrum, although Evie's managed to get through to him, so it might be nothing."

"No harm in looking. So that's two American residents and one British. If the police authorities will play ball, I'll get onto it. While you're here, you should know we've had some interesting information back from head office. It transpires that Fabian Bigham handed in his notice shortly after boarding."

"Now that is interesting. Do you know why?"

"They didn't mention whether he gave a reason. Do you think it's important?"

Rachel thought for a moment. "Yes, I do. In fact, I'd say it might give us the answers we're looking for."

"Okay, I'll make a call after dinner." He looked at his watch.

"Hot date?"

Another throat clearing. "Brenda wants me to eat regular meals. I don't have time to explain, but I'd like to talk to you at a later date."

"Of course." Rachel was flummoxed. One minute he wasn't happy to see her and the next he wanted a heart-to-heart. "I'd better get going. Can we meet later?"

"I'll be working into the night. Stop by when you're ready."

Rachel hurried to the Coral Restaurant, where her parents and Carlos were already seated. "You look stunning," said Susan.

"Thanks Mum, you don't look so bad yourself." Susan Prince had kept her looks and, on this cruise, she was taking advantage of wearing flattering colours that suited her complexion. This evening, a teal evening dress hugged her figure.

"I was just saying the same thing to your mother," said Carlos.

"Sorry I'm late."

"We've only just sat down. Are you okay with red wine?" Brendan asked.

Rachel nodded. "Did you enjoy your trip?"

"We were just telling Carlos about it. I think we saw just about every tourist attraction Ho Chi Minh City had to offer. The guide was extremely knowledgeable and her English was superb," Susan continued, describing the places they had visited, with Brendan chipping in to add facts of historic interest.

Before long, Rachel had forgotten about Linda and what Evie had told them and was relaxing in the company of the people she loved.

After dinner, Susan wanted to peruse the shops. Rachel suggested they take a shortcut through the casino.

"Why?" Susan asked.

"I just want to check on Evie."

Nobody objected to her mission, so they took the route through the casino. Evie was playing bridge. Her partner this evening was a man nearer her own age. Danny wasn't there.

"Hello again," Carlos said.

"Good evening," Evie called back.

Susan waved and carried on through, seemingly in a hurry to vacate the busy casino.

"No Danny tonight?" Rachel said.

"Not a chance. There's a gaming competition on deck sixteen."

Rachel grinned. "That sounds more his thing. Enjoy your evening," she said.

"You too."

Rachel would have liked to quiz Evie further, but Carlos took her elbow. "Your parents are waiting."

On the very night Rachel was in a hurry to meet Waverley, her parents didn't seem in any rush to go to bed.

"Orlando's giving me a behind-the-scenes tour tomorrow," said Brendan while Susan looked at clothes she would never buy, judging by the price tags.

"That's interesting," said Rachel, still not sure where Orlando fitted in with the sudden deaths. The frustrating thing was that he and Evie both had motive and opportunity for the time of the deaths, but each had plausible explanations as to why they didn't do it and only one had the means, and that was her father's new best friend. If Manfred wasn't the killer... and he certainly didn't kill Linda... if indeed she was killed... then it had to be someone who would kill again to cover their tracks. From her research, it wouldn't be too difficult for anyone who travelled a lot or with a bit of scientific knowhow – such as Orlando – to buy or extract the pufferfish poison. If it was Orlando, his next target might be Evie. She would have to ask Waverley to put a tail on Evie.

Suddenly. Rachel stopped in her tracks. "What is it?" Brendan asked.

"I just remembered something important. Sorry, Dad."

"If you need to be somewhere, your mother and I will manage without babysitters. And if it's anything to do with Fabian's death, you have my full support."

Rachel kissed her father's cheek. "I love you. Give mum my excuses and tell Carlos I'll be in the internet café."

By the time Carlos joined her, Rachel had most of what she needed.

"From that smug look on your face, I'd say you've cracked it."

Rachel took his hand. "Almost. There are still a few gaps, but I'm hoping Waverley can help with those. If I'm right, we need to act soon before other lives are put at risk. Including mine."

"Let's get on with it, then."

29

Rachel rapped on Waverley's door before entering with Carlos. Jason was with the security chief, tapping notes on a tablet while Waverley looked up from his desk.

"Good evening. Your timing's perfect. We've just had news back from head office confirming Fabian Bigham's resignation. Further details have come via his PA. Apparently he was about to come into an enormous sum of money."

"Which he got word of the night before boarding," said Rachel.

"What makes you say that?"

"Admittedly, we still need the last link in the chain, and I'm sure we'll get it. In the meantime lives are at risk."

"Including Rachel's," said Carlos.

With this revelation, Waverley motioned for them to sit. They all moved to the comfortable seating. "Tell me everything," Waverley said.

"Earlier this evening, while chatting to my father, I had a flashback. We stayed at Raffles Hotel for an overnight before boarding. While I was checking into the hotel, Fabian Bigham created a huge scene in the lobby. It was difficult to ignore because he was loud and rude. I think I mentioned our paths had crossed?"

Waverley nodded. "You did. Go on."

"Bigham was fuming about something. He was waiting for word about whatever it was, and once he received it, he calmed down. After talking to Evie and finding out they had had an affair a long time ago, I thought it was all about their past and that what he had received was a message saying she had agreed to meet him on the cruise."

"It would have been nice to have known about that affair before now. Goodridge says she could be deceiving you."

Jason gave her a sheepish grin.

Rachel shook her head. "No. It's not her. She did get in touch with Fabian, agreeing to meet him on the cruise, but it wasn't her who sent the email he received that night. It came from a different source. The email contained an offer he'd been waiting for. It was all about money. That's why he could hand in his notice."

"Even if what you're saying is true, how can we be sure it led to his death?" Waverley asked.

"I called the hotel and spoke to the manager via a video link. I showed him my erm... detective ID."

Waverley frowned but didn't comment.

"Not only did the manager remember Fabian, but he'd also kept a copy of the email, not daring to delete it in case Bigham returned. I have a copy which he forwarded to me."

"Not very professional," said Waverley.

"It's okay. I implied I was looking into a man's death and gave him my work email so he believed I was on official business. It pays to be a cop sometimes."

"There's no point in my mentioning your lack of jurisdiction, I suppose?"

"I didn't exactly say I was on official business."

"Moot point. May I see this email?"

Rachel handed Waverley her phone and carried on with her story. "Later that evening my father introduced us to Fabian – they were at university together."

"Something else you didn't mention," said Waverley, looking up from his reading.

"They knew each other in their late teens, so it wasn't relevant to his death and I wanted to tell Dad about Fabian's death myself but changed my mind. He found out anyway and was upset about it. But back to the night at Raffles. Something struck me as odd at the time, but I was so glad to see the back of Fabian, I thought no more about it."

"You mean how he entered the Long Bar as if he was going for a drink and then left suddenly?" Carlos said.

"Precisely. What I remembered tonight, was how when he stopped short because someone smashed a glass, he scowled in the direction of the bar before hotfooting it out of there. There were three significant people sitting at the bar."

"I know Simon Peterson and Orlando Kearney were there…" Carlos said, scratching his head.

Without going into detail, Rachel told them who she thought was responsible and what they must do next. Waverley remained unconvinced.

"We have no evidence."

"The evidence is implied in the email. I'm right, I know I am. It makes sense now."

"Not to me, I'm afraid. What I see is that Bigham had come into money and was about to vacate his job as a result. This email just confirms that fact." Waverley handed her phone to Jason who read the contents of the email. "What makes you think this person's our killer?" Waverley continued.

Rachel couldn't give him a rock-solid reason, just what she had.

"I'd like to speak to the man, please?"

"There isn't enough to go on," Waverley protested.

"I'm assuming you don't think our cruise director is involved."

"No." Rachel could have said that Simon was guilty of being unprofessional but that had nothing to do with the investigation.

"What about Orlando Kearney?"

"It could still be him. He has a motive and he was there when Linda went over the waterfall yesterday. If she knew about his secret, he could well be the person we're looking for, but it's definitely not Evie."

"You're going to have to tell me about Kearney's secret if it pertains to my investigation," said Waverley.

Rachel debated within herself and came to a decision. "Fabian was blackmailing Orlando over something that he wanted kept quiet. The issue has been dealt with but Orlando doesn't want it out in the open."

"What is this thing that he wants kept quiet?" Waverley was losing his patience.

"One of his directors was illegally dumping waste. The director's been sacked and Orlando's company is paying for the cleanup but if word gets out, it will cause irreparable damage to the company."

"I'd say that's a strong motive, wouldn't you? And we can be sure that if Linda Parker knew about it she would have made it public. Sadly, that lady would have enjoyed exposing any scandal, particularly one relating to a company working with Queen Cruises. Do you think she knew?"

"Well, she was seen videoing throughout the evening of the cocktail party. She would have seen and possibly heard, Orlando arguing with Fabian. Now I think of it, Orlando told me Bigham appeared drunk. That could have been confusion from the TTX poisoning. I fear, if we don't act soon, Evie could be the next victim. I'm certain Linda was pushed, and the killer heard Linda telling Evie she knew who poisoned Fabian."

"It's still a bit of a stretch with a lot of supposition. Nevertheless, I'll pay Kearney a visit and interview him. He won't be going anywhere near Evelyn Mitchell. Meanwhile, I'll ask Rosemary Inglis to keep a watch over her."

"Good idea," said Rachel. Rosemary Inglis was a capable member of the security team and, unlike her boss, didn't jump to conclusions.

"In the meantime you should enjoy the rest of your evening. We can't go accusing any other passengers of poisoning people without evidence. Please leave it to us now, Rachel."

Rachel huffed, exasperated. "Whatever you say, Chief."

"Rachel's usually got an instinct for these things, Chief. I don't think we should ignore her." Carlos had remained quiet up to that point, but now he was willing to fight her cause.

"It's not that I don't appreciate your trying to help, but we have enough information to question Orlando Kearney and nowhere near enough to quiz anyone else. Evelyn Mitchell could still be lying to you, and Linda might well have fallen to her death."

Rachel rose from her seat, furious. "She's not lying! We'd know a lot more if *someone* could prioritise getting Linda's phone to work."

Waverley sighed, looking at Jason and Carlos for support but got none. "Okay. Please sit down, Rachel. Let me make a call."

30

"Goodridge will go with you while I interview Kearney, but proceed with caution. I don't want us being sued for harassment."

Shame you don't think that way when it comes to your employees, thought Rachel, but she kept her thoughts to herself.

"Thank you."

With the information she was about to use clear in her head, Rachel, Carlos, and Jason hovered outside the room, waiting for people to leave for a break.

The man they were waiting for came out last, looking happier than he had done all cruise. Until his eyes met Rachel's.

"Might we have a word?"

"Sorry, I'm busy. I've only got fifteen minutes before the next half."

"I'm afraid I must insist," said Rachel.

"You can't do that."

"No, but I can," Jason said firmly.

"Fine, but whatever this is about, we need to hurry."

The four of them took seats around a table, Danny Martinez looking more and more uncomfortable, like a caged bird.

"Could you start by telling me how you knew Fabian Bigham?"

"Who? Oh, the man they say was poisoned. I didn't know him at all."

"This will take a lot longer if you lie," said Rachel.

"I don't know what you mean."

"How about we start with how just seeing you in the Long Bar at Raffles made him turn around and scurry away like a frightened rat. Why do you think that was?"

Danny didn't answer, his eyes darted from her to Carlos, then to Jason and back to her.

"Was it about a video game, by any chance?"

Fear turned to rage in the young man's eyes. "How do you know about that?"

"Bigham didn't strike me as intelligent enough to design a video game and yet he appeared to have sold one for a vast sum of money. What happened?"

Danny avoided eye contact but answered. "He wasn't intelligent at all. He was a fraud. The man stole my work and sold it as his. That's what happened."

"How could he do that?" asked Rachel.

"When I heard Queen Cruises was developing a whole new gaming department and were looking for original works, I approached them. Somehow my message ended up on Fabian's desk, and he arranged a meeting. He told me the cruise line was interested in my game, and even if it didn't go anywhere with them, that he could find a buyer. He told me he would do the deal on my behalf. When he mentioned the figures, I was staggered. Fabian emphasised any deal was time-dependent and rushed me into signing the paperwork." Danny looked down at his hands. "Turns out what I signed was what's called an assignment of copyright form. When I realised I'd been duped, I saw a lawyer, but he told me the agreement was watertight. It would cost a fortune to take Fabian to court and I'd lose anyway, because it would just give the impression I changed my mind. I later discovered Fabian had sold my game in principle to another cruise line for millions of dollars. The final offer was imminent."

"Which is why you booked a last-minute cruise, having discovered he'd be out of the country. And why he was shocked to see you that night. What did you hope to achieve?"

"I thought if we talked, he'd be reasonable. I even offered him a fifty percent share. He laughed in my face. Do you know what he said to me...? 'Why have fifty when I can have it all. Go home, boy.' That's what he said."

Danny's shoulders sagged as he crumpled.

"So you poisoned him," said Rachel.

"No, I didn't." Danny was blubbering, choking out words through ragged breaths. "I wouldn't know how."

"We have video evidence of you sprinkling powder into a jug of cranberry juice… one that would later be used by Manfred, the mixologist," said Rachel, pleased to be able to play her trump card. It turned out Linda's phone had contained information useful enough to warrant her injury after all.

Danny's eyes widened. "I was adding sugar. The cocktail was too sour."

"So why do it while the mixologist's back was turned? And why place a sachet into his pocket? The video evidence we have is quite revealing," said Jason.

"Do you have this powder?"

Clever, thought Rachel, saying, "I understand you enjoy fishing, Danny. There are lots of photos on your social media account with you holding up your catches. Pufferfish appears to be a favourite," said Rachel.

"So what?"

"Your internet searches are also quite revealing," said Jason, taking the baton. Waverley had managed to get access to Danny's laptop and the tech team who had got Linda's phone working, had managed to access his search history. "You spent weeks studying how to extract TTX from pufferfish and once you succeeded, you used it to poison Fabian Bigham."

Rachel took over. "I could understand it if you lost your temper and hit Bigham with something, but what you did, counts as premeditated murder. You came on this cruise knowing full well that if you didn't get what you wanted, you would exact your revenge."

Danny's face contorted, the blazing eyes admitting to his guilt. "He didn't deserve the money. He stole my work. Don't you understand? And you have no right going through my things." He glared at Jason.

"What we see, Danny, is that you enjoy playing video games in which people die. Anyone who stands in the hero's way is eliminated. You're not much of a hero in real life, are you? But when you play games, you are. Alas, this isn't a game. You killed a man, and then yesterday you pushed a woman to her death," said Rachel.

"I thought she saw me putting the sachet in the cocktail guy's jacket. I assume the video evidence you have, came from her phone?"

"Why didn't you get rid of the poison yourself?"

"I held onto it in case the first dose didn't work; I wasn't sure I'd given him enough. Okay, I admit I spiked the cranberry juice that would be used to make up the Poisoned Paradise, but with a low dose. Nobody who drank one that night would be harmed."

"Interesting you think making people feel terrible is not harmful," said Carlos.

Danny glared at Carlos before turning back to Rachel. "But then you started asking questions."

"I do have one more question. The pathologist thinks the poison was administered before the party, so when and how did you poison Fabian Bigham?"

"I'd been following him after he dismissed me like I was some sort of bug to be trampled underfoot," Danny said, his jaw tensing. "About an hour before the party, he bought a cocktail and left it on a table while he went to guest services to ask about something. It was too good an opportunity to miss.

"Afterwards, I continued following him in case the dose wasn't enough. He was a big guy. When he went to the cocktail party, I kept tabs on him. I wasn't invited but it was easy enough to sneak in. Fabian was starting to show symptoms that the poison was taking effect, and I didn't want anyone to notice. That's when I got the idea to create a diversion."

"So you spiked the jug Manfred would use to mix the Poisoned Paradise," Rachel said.

"I figured that with other people getting ill, they would be less likely to notice how ill Fabian was. If I could make it look like some sick joke, no-one would be any the wiser."

"And the crew would think Fabian Bigham had a heart attack or a reaction to something he ate?" Rachel realised how close Danny had come to succeeding in getting away with murder.

"It would have worked too if it wasn't for Linda, and you." Danny looked at Rachel and then away again, unable to hold her gaze.

"I'm surprised I'm still alive," said Rachel.

"I couldn't kill you. You're too beautiful."

"In your games, the hero gets the girl, no doubt," said Carlos, empathy in his voice.

"Something like that," said Danny.

"Was Evie next on your list?"

"No. She admitted last night Linda hadn't told her anything."

"That's why you pretended to be making sure she was okay. She told us today how thoughtful you've been. It's a shame she doesn't know the real you."

"I'm not great with people, but Evie's been cool to hang with. She's bright."

"Lucky for her, Linda didn't tell her what you'd done."

"How did you work out it was me? Was it the phone?"

"Getting the phone working, and the ship's tech guys accessing your search history provided the final pieces in the puzzle. It was then a matter of putting the pieces together. When I first met you on boarding night, I thought you looked familiar. It was only tonight I realised I'd seen you in The Long Bar before and after Fabian made his hasty exit. That, and the fact you hung about with Evie because the blogger clung to her and you wanted to hear all the gossip. There's no excusing the manner in which you ended that poor woman's life."

Danny put his face in his hands. "It's much easier on screen. You don't have to look at the body. If Linda hadn't told Evie she knew who the killer was, I wouldn't have done it. It was the way she looked at me when I got on the tender that told me she knew. Then, when I heard her tell Evie she knew who poisoned Fabian, she left me with no choice."

"You always have a choice," said Rachel. "And to be honest with you, I don't think she noticed you doing anything with the sachet. The video she shot didn't linger over it. We'll never know for certain, but I believe she thought the killer was Orlando Kearney."

"Who's he?"

"Another person who was on the excursion yesterday and who had motive enough to want to silence Fabian Bigham. He made a lot of enemies."

"What have I done?" Tears streamed down Danny's cheeks.

"You'd better come with me, Mr Martinez." Jason's terse voice ended the interview.

Danny watched his fellow gamers returning to the competition with longing eyes.

"I almost feel sorry for him," said Carlos.

"If I hadn't witnessed both deaths and helped pull Linda's broken body out of the water, I might feel the same, but I don't."

Carlos kissed her forehead. "How's the leg?"

"Improving," she replied, grinning.

"Now. If it's all right with madam, may we enjoy the rest of our cruise? Remember, it's your parents' anniversary tomorrow."

Rachel slapped her head with her palm. "Do we need to do anything else?"

"Nope. It's all prepared."

"I just need to have another word with Waverley. I'll see you in a bit."

"Don't be long or I'll be asleep."

"I'll be as quick as I can."

Carlos held her hand. "Did I ever tell you how clever you are and how very much in love with you I am?"

Rachel kissed him tenderly. "You may have, once or twice, but I'm happy to hear it again. See you soon."

31

Waverley was at his desk when Rachel walked in.

"I didn't expect to see you again tonight, Rachel. You'll be pleased to hear Manfred Heinrich's been released and your man is in the brig. Having spoken to Mr Kearney, I don't feel there's any need to disclose what happened in his company. It's not our concern. Queen Cruise's waste wasn't involved in the issue. I should have listened to you."

"We got there in the end. You wanted to talk to me? I thought now might be a good time as it's my parents' wedding anniversary tomorrow."

Waverley sighed. The bags under his eyes suggested he hadn't been sleeping well. He looked exhausted.

"Let's sit there. Will you join me in a glass of Scotch?"

"I'll have a brandy if you've got one." Something told her she was going to need it.

Waverley handed her a glass, and he sat in one of the comfortable chairs. She followed suit.

"I'm retiring."

Rachel wasn't sure what she'd been expecting him to say, but that wasn't it. She didn't know what to say. They'd had their differences, but in terms of cruising, he had become a familiar figure and one who, despite his stubbornness, listened to her in the end and whom she had become fond of.

"You'll be missed."

"I'm getting too long in the tooth for this job and my blood pressure's a problem. Brenda wants us to settle down in a proper home. She wants a garden and has ambitions to open up a small bakery in an English village, preferably by the sea."

Waverley had met his wife, a senior baker, on board the *Coral Queen,* and was much happier since they'd wed, but Rachel knew the job was taking its toll on him. It appeared they had similar struggles coping with work tension. At least for the most part, being a chief security officer on board an enormous cruise ship didn't involve internal corruption and politics. And he didn't encounter ruthless killers and victims of vicious crime every working day. "What about you? What do you want?" she asked.

"I want to put my head down on a pillow every night

knowing I won't be woken up in the small hours to deal with drunken yobs, violent crew members and whatever else is the latest crisis."

Rachel nodded, tears stinging the back of her eyes. "When will you go?"

"I've got three months to serve."

Rachel wondered whether Jason was aware of this. He hadn't said anything, and neither had Sarah.

His voice broke into her thoughts. "The thing is, Rachel, I'd like you to take my place for a while."

Her mouth dropped open as their eyes met. The earnestness in his, suggested he meant it. "What about Jason?"

"He doesn't want the responsibility and no-one else is qualified. Inglis has potential but is still getting used to the role of security guard."

"What's your definition of a while?"

"It won't be forever. We have a replacement, but she's got nine months left to serve in the navy and then she wants to take three months holiday before starting. You know how we operate, Rachel, and you're more than qualified to take over from me. I'll put a word in with recruitment. Captain Jenson already agreed for me to ask. Say the word, and the job will be yours."

"But Chief... Jack. I've got a job," *albeit one I'm falling out of love with,* she didn't say, "and I'm married. Carlos has a thriving private investigation business."

"I realise I'm asking a lot of you, but if you don't start

until after I've served my notice, nine months will go by in a flash. You could request a sabbatical. I believe that's possible. Carlos could join you anytime he has a holiday. All I ask is that you think about it."

Rachel should have dismissed the idea immediately, but she didn't. Why was that? Could it work? She would most likely gain approval for a sabbatical and she could do with the break. The biggest challenge was that of being away from Carlos. Her head ached already. Her inner self warned her that running away wasn't the answer to her problems.

Rachel drained the brandy glass and stood. "I will think about it, but I'm making no promises."

"Thank you. That's all I ask."

"Goodnight, Chief."

"Goodnight, Rachel."

What would Carlos say about this one?

32

Having pushed the conversation with Waverley to the back of her mind, Rachel had nothing else to think about but her parents' special day. She threw herself into the celebrations.

During dinner, Chef Mason appeared at their table.

"Good evening, ladies and gentlemen. I hope the food is to your satisfaction. Particularly the lobster." He winked at Susan.

"This is the best lobster dish I've ever tasted," said Susan. "I adore your signature dish."

"Thank you. I'll have the recipe sent to your room. May I take this opportunity of wishing you a very happy anniversary." He leaned down and kissed Susan's hand.

"What a nice man," said Susan after he moved on to the next table.

Sarah chuckled. "He's a charmer and so genuine.

The kitchen staff love him because he doesn't get flustered."

"Is it true that some chefs are volatile?" Brendan asked.

"Not on this ship. They are told that if they want to get the best out of their workers, they have to treat them with respect."

"Although there have been one or two incidents," said Jason. "Remember Basil?"

Sarah's face flushed as she explained. "He chased one of his juniors around the kitchen, threatening to gut him because he wasn't doing a good job gutting a fish. Needless to say, he didn't last long."

"The chef or the junior?" Brendan asked.

"The chef."

"Oh my," said Susan. "That must have been awful."

They continued their ship antics conversation during dinner and ended with coffee.

After dinner, they headed to the theatre. Brendan steered his wife away from the usual entrance. "Not tonight, Susan. We're sitting elsewhere."

"But I like—" Susan stopped arguing when Rachel put a finger to her lips.

The booth was decorated with coral coloured decorations, symbolising the beauty of a long-lasting marriage. Two bottles of champagne and six glasses were on the table alongside Susan's new favourite chocolates, which took pride of place in the centre. Susan's mouth dropped open.

"Happy anniversary, darling." Brendan handed her an enormous bouquet of exotic flowers, specially brought aboard from Ho Chi Minh City.

"This is what all those secret meetings were about. I was beginning to think Rachel was embroiled in another murder investigation the way you were all behaving."

Rachel laughed nervously. "Don't be silly, Mum. Cruises are safe and secure. Your last experience was a one-off." She winked at Jason, who smirked.

"But if ever there was a murder, we could always rely on your daughter to catch the culprit." He winked back.

"Enough of that talk. Pop the cork on that champagne," said Sarah. "I've got the night off and I want to enjoy it."

"What about Jason?" Rachel asked. "He doesn't drink."

"Don't worry, I've got something for him," said Carlos, stepping toward a shelf.

"There you go, mate." He handed him a bottle of zero alcohol lager.

Rachel sidled alongside Jason while he opened his bottle.

"Why didn't you mention Waverley was leaving?" she whispered.

"He's asked you then?"

"I suspect you know he has."

Jason smirked. "What does Carlos think?"

"Shush, you two," said Sarah. "It's happening."

Rachel rejoined the others, leaving Jason to sit with his wife.

Apart from the confusion raging within her, she was happy. By the time Nat took to the stage, Susan was relaxed and enjoying the show. Her eyes lit up when Nat mentioned her name.

"We have a special anniversary tonight. If anyone has a glass in their hand, please raise it to wish the Reverend and Mrs Brendan Prince a happy Coral Wedding Anniversary."

As their booth lit up, Susan looked as though she might cry, but the best was yet to come.

"And our resident band is going to perform a special song. I hope you enjoy it."

Susan Prince's eyes could no longer hold back the happy tears when the band struck up and sang: *The Air That I Breathe*, by the Hollies.

"This was our first dance wedding song, Brendan. You remembered."

"The words are as real to me today as they were on that day, darling. Happy anniversary." Brendan leaned over to kiss his wife, leaving Rachel choking back tears.

"I'll never forget this holiday. Thank you," said Susan. "And the years have made you far more eloquent than when you asked me out on a first date."

"I won't forget this holiday either," said Carlos, leaning in and whispering in Rachel's ear. "Now I know what it's like to cruise with Rachel."

"Be quiet," said Sarah, whose eyes were also misting over at the words of the song.

Rachel considered the coral coloured decorations surrounding them; symbolic of longevity and success in relation to marriage. Watching her parents' happiness after thirty-five years together gave Rachel hope that she and Carlos might be the same when they reached that milestone. But first, they needed to have a serious conversation.

THE END

Cruise into Darkness (book 14) now available to preorder.

AUTHOR'S NOTE

Thank you for reading *Toxic Cruise Cocktail* the thirteenth book in the Rachel Prince Mystery series. If you have enjoyed it, please leave an honest review on Amazon and/or any other platform you may use. I love receiving feedback from readers.

Book fourteen in the series: *Cruise into Darkness* is available to preorder.

Keep in touch:

Signup for my no-spam newsletter and receive a FREE novella. You will also receive news of new releases and special offers and have the opportunity to enter competitions.
https://www.dawnbrookespublishing.com/subscribe

Check out my store for savings and offers:
https://www.dawnbrookesbooks.com
Follow me on Facebook:
https://www.facebook.com/dawnbrookespublishing/
Follow me on YouTube:
https://www.youtube.com/DawnBrookesPublishing

CHEF MASON'S LOBSTER SYMPHONY

"My signature dish is called "Lobster Symphony," a harmonious blend of succulent lobster meat, vibrant seasonal vegetables, and a symphony of herbs and spices, all brought together in a rich and velvety lobster bisque sauce." Chef Mason Carpenter.

Here's the recipe for creating this exquisite culinary masterpiece:

Ingredients:

2 lobsters (about 1 ½ to 2 pounds each), cooked and meat removed
    4 tablespoons unsalted butter
    1 onion, finely chopped
    2 cloves garlic, minced

2 carrots, diced
2 celery stalks, diced
2 tablespoons all-purpose flour
4 cups seafood stock
1 cup heavy cream
1 teaspoon paprika
½ teaspoon dried thyme
Salt and pepper to taste
Chopped fresh parsley for garnish

Instructions:

1. Begin by preparing the lobster bisque sauce. In a large pot, melt the butter over medium heat. Add the chopped onion, garlic, carrots, and celery. Sauté until the vegetables are softened and aromatic, about 5-7 minutes.

2. Sprinkle the flour over the vegetables and stir to combine, cooking for an additional 2-3 minutes to create a roux.

3. Gradually pour in the seafood stock, stirring constantly to prevent lumps from forming. Bring the mixture to a simmer and cook for 10-15 minutes, allowing the flavours to join together and the sauce to thicken.

Chef Mason's Lobster Symphony

4. Once the sauce has thickened slightly, stir in the heavy cream, paprika, dried thyme, salt, and pepper. Continue to simmer for an additional 5 minutes, stirring occasionally.

5. While the sauce simmers, chop the cooked lobster meat into bite-sized pieces.

6. Add the chopped lobster meat to the sauce, stirring gently to combine. Allow the lobster to heat through in the sauce for 2-3 minutes.

7. Once the lobster is heated through and the flavours have mixed, remove the pot from the heat. Taste and adjust seasoning if necessary.

8. To serve, ladle the Lobster Symphony into bowls, ensuring each serving contains a generous portion of lobster meat and vegetables. Garnish with chopped fresh parsley for a burst of colour and freshness.

9. Serve hot and enjoy the symphony of flavours and textures in this luxurious lobster dish!

Bon appétit!

BOOKS BY DAWN BROOKES

Rachel Prince Mysteries

A Cruise to Murder #1

Deadly Cruise #2

Killer Cruise #3

Dying to Cruise #4

A Christmas Cruise Murder #5

Murderous Cruise Habit #6

Honeymoon Cruise Murder #7

A Murder Mystery Cruise #8

Hazardous Cruise #9

Captain's Dinner Cruise Murder #10

Corporate Cruise Murder #11

Treacherous Cruise Flirtation #12

Toxic Cruise Cocktail #13

Cruise into Darkness #14

Lady Marjorie Snellthorpe Mysteries

Death of a Blogger (Prequel Novella)

Murder at the Opera House #1

Murder in the Highlands #2

Murder at the Christmas Market #3

Murder at a Wimbledon Mansion #4

Murder in a Care Home #5

Murder at the Regatta #6

Murder on a Bus Tour #7

Carlos Jacobi PI

Body in the Woods #1

The Bradgate Park Murders #2

The Museum Murders #3

Memoirs

Hurry up Nurse: memoirs of nurse training in the 1970s

Hurry up Nurse 2: London calling

Hurry up Nurse 3: More adventures in the life of a student nurse

PICTURE BOOKS FOR CHILDREN

Ava & Oliver's Bonfire Night Adventure
Ava & Oliver's Christmas Nativity Adventure
Danny the Caterpillar
Gerry the One-Eared Cat
Suki Seal and the Plastic Ring

ACKNOWLEDGMENTS

Thanks to my beta readers for comments and suggestions, and for their time given to reading the early drafts, and to my ARC team – I couldn't do without you. And a big thank you to Alex Davis for the final proofread picking up those punctuation errors and annoying typos!

I'm hugely grateful to my immediate circle of family and friends, who remain patient while I'm absorbed in my fictional world. Thanks for your continued support in all my endeavours.

I have to say thank you to my cruise-loving friends for joining me on some of the most precious experiences of my life, and to all the cruise lines for making every holiday a special one.

ABOUT THE AUTHOR

Dawn Brookes holds an MA in creative writing with distinction and is an award winning, bestselling author of cosy mysteries and crime fiction. The *Rachel Prince Mystery* series combines a unique blend of murder, cruising and medicine with a touch of romance. The Lady Marjorie Snellthorpe mysteries sees four octogenarian friends solving murder and is packed with humour. Carlos Jacobi PI is a little grittier but Dawn remains true to her view that good fiction can still be written without cursing, graphic violence and explicit sexual content.

Dawn has a 39-year nursing pedigree and takes regular cruise holidays, which she says are for research purposes! She brings these passions together with a Christian background and a love of clean crime to her writing.

The surname of her protagonist is in honour of her childhood dog, Prince, who used to put his head on her knee while she lost herself in books.

Dawn's memoirs have been bestsellers since publishing. *Hurry up Nurse: memoirs of nurse training in the 1970s, Hurry up Nurse 2: London calling,* and *Hurry up Nurse 3: More adventures in the life of a student nurse* cover her days working as a student in Leicester, London and Berkshire. Dawn worked as a hospital nurse, midwife, district nurse and community matron across her career. Before turning her hand to writing for a living, she had multiple articles published in professional journals and co-edited a nursing textbook.

She grew up in Leicester, later moved to London and Berkshire, but now lives in Derbyshire. Dawn holds a Bachelor's degree with Honours and a Master's degree in education. Writing across genres, she also writes for children. Dawn has a passion for nature and loves animals, especially dogs. Animals will continue to feature in her children's books as she believes caring for animals and nature helps children to become kinder human beings.